The Citizen of Eastport

V B Ruth

Book 1 of The Eastport Ledgers

Copyright 2025 © by V. B. Ruth
All Rights Reserved

No part of this book may be reproduced in any form or by an electronic or mechanical means, including information storage and retrieval systems, without permission in writing from the author, except by a reviewer who may quote brief passages in a review.

Cover art by Eva I.

for Claire

Wish you were here

Table of Contents

Chapter One..1
Chapter Two..21
Chapter Three...37
Chapter Four...53
Chapter Five..73
Chapter Six..91
Chapter Seven...107
Chapter Eight...123
Chapter Nine...141
Chapter Ten...157
Chapter Eleven..175
Chapter Twelve...195
Chapter Thirteen...211
Chapter Fourteen..225
Chapter Fifteen...241
Chapter Sixteen..259

Chapter One

Vi's bar was packed. A solar liner had docked this morning, and while few of its sapphire-banded passengers would make their way as far down as Vi's for a first terrestrial drink, plenty of Eastport citizens had opted to drink in the lower sectors instead of bumping refined elbows in the High Street bars. There were newcomers at Vi's too, as always, but they were the type that came to town by train. Vi had her eye on a knot of them clustered around the lefthand corner of the bar, where Luce was slinging beers out as fast as she could pour. Their glazed eyes said they'd come straight off the train, and the natural cloth on their backs said Midwest. They had the look of men eager to measure themselves against big bad Eastport and find out that they were bigger and badder.

Luce caught Vi's wary look and rolled her eyes pointedly. Vi got it; Luce could handle herself. Better than Arthur, whose tray of empty glasses jangled dangerously as he set it by the sink.

"Watch it," Vi snapped before catching the next two customers and getting their orders. Arthur hovered while she started mixing cocktails.

"Um, boss."

It was Thursday, so Vi was waiting for the 'Um, boss' that preceded asking for a wage advance. "Spit it out," she said, rattling the shaker.

"The corner table wants John J. Martin, neat."

"I told you we're out. Give them the Jack if you think they won't know the difference."

"They want to see the bottle."

"Then we're out. You think I got a secret stash just for customers that are extra annoying? We're out and we'll be out until the ninth."

"They said they came here special for it."

"I can't fix that for them. Dusty's called order up three times, why're you still standing here?"

Arthur scurried through the kitchen door just in time for Vi to catch the commotion on the left side. One of the Midwest imports, six feet and change of surly muscle, was gripping the bar and leaning in toward Luce.

Luce only *looked* delicate, as plenty of Eastport citizens had learned the hard way, but a busy night was no time for a demonstration. Vi, who hadn't looked delicate since birth, moved to put herself directly in front of him.

"Problem?" she said curtly.

"That little girl said I'm cut off."

"Then you're cut off."

"I came here to DRINK."

He swayed dramatically with the shout. He was less drunk than he was acting. He was playing it up, maybe to himself, so whatever happened next he could say it was the booze made him do it.

"My bar's not for fighting. You wanna take a swing at someone, Mikey on Orange runs fight nights every day but Sunday."

"Who said I wanted a fight? I just want another drink."

Vi pulled a chip out from under the bar—right next to her club, which she might need, and her stunner, which she wouldn't—and tapped Mikey's location into it.

"Here you go." She slid the chip to him. "He serves drinks too. Isn't as particular about cutoffs."

It was about 60-40, Vi thought, whether the man would leave with the chip or decide to start something here. She stood still and held his gaze. If he started something, it was going to be with her. He looked for a minute like he would; then he abruptly let go of the bar and picked up the chip.

"Shitty bar anyway," he said, and stalked away.

"Fight night at Mikey's!" Vi shouted after him for the benefit of the others. "That man knows where he's going!"

Most of the Midwest contingent followed him out, so that'd be a nice boost for Mikey. With the crowd a little thinner, she noticed for the first time that Officer Daniel was here. He was sitting at the back of a booth with his usual order of a beer and Dusty's corn cakes and honey, and raised his eyebrow wryly when she looked his way. Vi grimaced, but he just gave a little *I'm off duty* shrug and went back to his drink. Mikey had his own arrangements with the cops and would be fine, but it was a lapse. Vi tried to know exactly who was in her bar at any given moment.

As soon as the rush died down a little, Arthur came at her with another 'Um, boss,' and this time it was the one she was expecting. She tapped the amount into her wristband while he was stammering out his reasons for needing the advance this week. It didn't really matter. She knew his situation—kid with a lung condition and a gang debt he'd be paying off until he died— so whatever was making him short this week, it all came out the same. As soon as she'd transferred the money, she sent him back to help Dusty, the fastest way to cut off the flood of thanks and promises they both knew he couldn't keep.

An hour before close, a cop puppet walked in the door. You could always tell who was new to the Northeast by the way they looked at the shining, seven-foot figure—especially by the way they stared and whispered behind its back. Nothing ever happened behind a cop puppet's back, they had vision all the way around, but newcomers had a hard time getting used to that even if they'd been told.

Vi sent a quick look around the floor but didn't see anyone she knew worked on the underside of the law. She did a second look just for Kilo, who had a way of going overlooked if ze wanted. Kilo hadn't been around in months, and it would serve zem right if ze got arrested the first night back, but Vi still didn't want to be caught by surprise. There was no one who could plausibly be Kilo, though, and instead of aiming for any customer, the cop came right up to the bar and demanded to know if she was the proprietor.

Not one of the regular beat cops, then. Official press had it that cop puppets were a way to ensure the face of the law was uniform and impartial, but anyone buying that needed some street lessons and fast. Behind each silver figure was a person, safe back in their station, and inside each person was the same snarl of habits and impulses anyone had. Vi could recognize some of her beat cops just by the way they turned a corner.

This one was new though, so there was no knowing what to expect. She tried to radiate calm for her customers and staff as she answered yes, she was the proprietor.

"We'll need to see the provenance of goods sold here."

"No problem. Which goods?" The last provenance check had only been two weeks ago. In theory they were random, but a good business owner—under the cops' particular and sometimes fluid definition of good—could generally rely on a consistent six-week schedule. Maybe Vi had pissed someone off, or maybe it was a new officer being overzealous.

The cop flashed the list onto the bar tablet. It was mostly various liquors, beef and cream, soy sauce—the usual list, the goods Vi didn't take risks with. Down near the end though, she saw pickles, limes, and pecans, which were very much not on the usual list. Pecans were fine, she went through them slowly and her last crate had come through legal routes, but pickles and limes would be a problem.

There was nothing to do but throw a quick scrubber onto the

files as she loaded them onto a chip for the officer. She corrupted the vodka too, for appearances' sake, and then handed the chip over.

There were no eyes in the smooth silver face, but she knew the cop would be watching her expression. She wasn't good at this part. Guilt wanted to climb onto her face no matter what she did. She tried letting irritation get there first. "Seems like just last week you were in here."

"Every business owner is subject to random checks."

"Sure. Just the more random checks there are, the harder it is to run my business."

"Complaints can be directed to the office of the sheriff."

There was nothing on the featureless metal to read as the cop scanned the files, no clues in the sensor band running around the forehead. Nothing to indicate when it got to the corrupted records. It read all the way to the end, then said, "Pickles, limes, and vodka. Unreadable."

Vi allowed herself to slam the bartop. "Luce, how many times have I told you? Keep your fucking gaming gloves away from the record files!"

Luce, as always, was quick on the uptake. "Sorry, boss. It was only for a second."

"A second is plenty of time for damage!" She turned back to the cop with a grimace. "Apologies. I can get those reverified, it will just take a trip to the depot. If you come back tomorrow..."

"How long have you owned this bar?"

"Four years."

"And in four years you haven't seen fit to get a shielded box for your import records? I think I'd like to see where they're kept."

A flush of real fear washed through Vi. This wasn't how it was supposed to go. The cop was supposed to accept her lie with a fine—how much was up to the individual cop, likewise how much passed from the cop's hand to the city coffers—and follow up in another couple of weeks, by which time Vi's records would be clean and orderly. They only investigated if they wanted to make an arrest, and they only arrested for underside buying if they wanted to make a point. Vi had worked very hard to avoid being the kind of person the cops would want to make a point about.

"Trouble, officer?" came Officer Daniel's agreeable voice from behind the cop. The silver figure was so tall Vi hadn't seen him walk up.

The cop straightened up at once. Bad form: cops in uniform weren't supposed to give away their off-duty fellows. Another sign that this one was new. "No trouble. Just checking into some discrepancies." The *sir* that wanted to punctuate the sentence was loud in its silence.

"I've been coming to this bar a long time. I'm sure Citizen Ferreira's papers are all in order."

"Three of the records are unreadable."

Daniel stepped out from behind the cop and leaned easily against the bar. "I'll have another of the same. What's the trouble, Ferreira, records get scratched?"

"Afraid my employee must have been gaming too close to the file boxes." Vi hoped what was on her face would pass for a casual smile.

He shook his head. "And now you have to go and get the

provenances recertified."

This was the dance Vi knew. "Afraid so. Unless the officer wants to inspect my back office?"

"That won't be necessary," said the cop shortly. He knew the steps as well as Vi did and clearly liked it as little. Daniel stayed at the bar until the cop had exacted a moderate fine and said he would return in two days to see the clean files. Vi's heart sank. Two days would mean a rush job she couldn't afford. Daniel's eyebrows flickered up at the timeline, but he didn't intervene any further. Vi didn't meet his gaze. Hard to say what she resented more: needing his help in the first place, or it not being enough. She knew Daniel ranked high, and the new cop was probably out of line, but whatever consequences landed on him afterward wouldn't pay Vi's bills.

About half the customers had quietly left while the cop was there. The few that remained weren't demanding enough to keep Vi from ruminating on her pending cashflow problems. Next week would be a bad week to be short, with the summer's whiskey shipment coming in on top of the quarterly rent due. It would all come down to how much the Fontaines wanted for the forged provenances. She was so preoccupied with running up the sums every which way—if they charged high, if they charged low, if the next couple nights were as busy as this or if they ran light—that she didn't even see the night's last customer until she was standing at the bar.

Then she couldn't see anything else. The numbers in her head evaporated, and the rest of the room faded to grey mist. All that was left was one face, oval and pale, and a pair of wide-set grey eyes.

"Vi. When I heard the bar's name, I thought it was irony. I didn't think it would be fate."

The voice was exactly the same. The face had changed, of course, become a grown woman's and not a teen girl's. The filled-out cheeks balanced the great grey eyes better now, made them look less like they were about to burn their way out of her face. But the voice was the same, and however long Vi looked, she couldn't make it so the face could be anyone else.

"Oh," she said at last. "You're here."

Tempe smiled. That was the same too, slow and small and private. "You don't seem surprised to see me."

"I see you all the time."

Tempe's head tilted a fraction, and it occurred to Vi that she was not being cool. She had no idea how to be cool. She hadn't vaulted over the bar and grabbed Tempe with both hands, so she was doing about as well as anyone could ask. "I mean I think I see you. Far away, usually. If I get close enough to look it always turns out it was someone else. I don't know if it ever really was you."

"It wasn't. I only arrived in Eastport today."

"On a train or on the sunliner?"

"The liner."

So they hadn't even been under the same sky. Vi nodded like this wasn't inexplicably devastating. "How long you been offworld?" That wasn't any of the things she wanted to ask, but it seemed safe.

"The whole time. You seem to be well established here. How long has this been Vi's Bar?"

That was a clear redirection, and Vi accepted it. If Tempe didn't want to say more about how she'd lived the last fifteen years, Vi had no right to ask. "Four years. It was called Daly's before. I'd have just kept that name if I'd liked Daly better."

"Do you make drinks or just run the place?"

"Of course I make drinks." It took her a minute, and a little quirk at the corner of Tempe's mouth, to pick up the hint. It wasn't fair; most of her brain hadn't even caught up to the idea that Tempe was here, let alone a customer. She cleared her throat. "What'll you have?"

"Gin with lime."

That told Vi a couple of things at least. Offworld, even bad gin was a luxury import; Tempe must have been living comfortably for a little while if she'd been drinking it straight. And she hadn't learned to like sweet things. Vi selected the most medicinal and complex of her top-shelf gins.

"I think you'll like this one. Tell me if I'm wrong."

Tempe tasted it. "You're not." She held out her wristband to pay. It was a custom band, thinner than standard-issue and edged with the manufacturer's trademark deep blue glow.

Vi shook her head. "On the house." She held her breath, watching Tempe decide whether to argue that. She still couldn't tell what Tempe felt, seeing her now.

After a second Tempe pulled her hand back and shook her sleeve over the wristband. "Thank you."

All of a sudden the air felt clearer, slid easier into her lungs. Tempe wouldn't accept a drink from someone she hated. Vi dug her knuckles into the counter behind the bar, trying keep her hopes from rising too high. "You said it was fate. What kind did you mean?"

Tempe took another sip of her drink. The grey eyes held Vi's, clear and steady. "A recurrence. Perhaps a restart. I heard about this place from a friend of mine, you see. I think she might have left something for me here."

And just like that the air was thick enough to choke on. Vi knew what she meant. All over Eastport, in bars and shops and cafes, friends were leaving things for other friends. The "thing" might be a shipload of goods or a thumbnail chip or just a word, and the "friends" were sometimes very unfriendly. But no one, friendly or not, ever left anything in Vi's bar.

A recurrence was right. If this was fate, it was the cruel kind. Vi looked at Tempe's hands, not her eyes. "I don't hold things for friends. Maybe you got the wrong place."

"She said she came here often. Curly brown hair, barely over five feet."

Of course it was Hannah. Hannah had been a regular; Vi had liked her, flirted with her a little. Never tried to take it further because she'd known Hannah was an idealist. "Okay. I know who you mean. She did ask to leave something here, a few weeks back. I said no."

Hannah had done more than ask. She'd begged, and Vi had believed her desperation, and she'd still refused. When she lay awake at night hearing the pinched *please* and feeling Hannah's grip on her arm, she'd had to remind herself sternly how much worse it could have gotten if she'd said yes.

As if knowing exactly how the scene had gone down, Tempe

said, "Just like that? A flat no? She was in a bad situation."

"I don't know anything about that. I made sure not to." She couldn't look at Tempe's face, but the flexing of her long fingers around the glass was almost as bad.

"She was out of options, and she trusted you."

"She shouldn't have. You of all people should know that."

Tempe's fingers froze. "What happened?" The ice in her voice reminded Vi again that she might have done worse than refuse to help. That Tempe might think she had. She steeled herself to meet Tempe's eyes so that she'd see the truth in Vi's.

"Nothing happened. Not here. She left, and she took whatever it was with her. No one's asked about her until you."

At least there was this between them: Tempe didn't doubt her word. "She didn't leave any kind of message?"

"No. And I wouldn't have let her if she'd tried. I can't give up what I don't know."

Tempe nodded, one slow incline of the head. "All right. I understand. I suppose you haven't seen her since."

"No." She'd offered to help another way. She'd have given Hannah money or bought her a ticket out of town. But all Hannah had wanted from her was the thing she would not give.

"Then I won't keep you." Tempe stood. "Is your Nana still well?"

It might have been a friendly question if it had come at the beginning of the conversation. Now, it scalded. "She is," said Vi, around a mouthful of shame.

"I'm glad to hear it." It didn't sound sarcastic, and neither did her parting "Be well, Vi."

Vi stood at the bar unmoving after she'd gone, looking down into the unfinished drink.

After locking up, Vi left Luce to finish cleanup while she went into the back office to look at the books. One of the smaller gangs might offer a better deal on forged provenances, but she couldn't be sure they'd hold up, especially on a rush job. Vi didn't like to gamble with her bar. She already bought more goods legit than most proprietors, which left her margins razor-thin. She looked through the accounts until her eyes watered and the numbers swam, trying to find a place she could scrape even thinner to pay the Fontaines.

It didn't help, the way Tempe's face kept floating behind her eyes. The whole scene already felt unreal. She'd dreamed their meeting hundreds of times and hundreds of ways. But the way her fingers had flexed when Vi had said she couldn't help her: that felt real. She could still see the way Tempe's hands had moved fifteen years ago, when she'd stepped into the headmaster's office, seen Vi, and realized she'd been betrayed. All this time and nothing had changed. Vi couldn't do anything but fail her, even without knowing it was Tempe she was failing.

They wouldn't see each other again. Eastport was large and they'd hardly be moving in the same circles. That was for the best. She should be thankful for this one brief meeting. At least she knew now that Tempe was alive and well, not wasting away in a prison or rotting under red soil. Everything Vi had bargained for, she'd gotten. Didn't that go to show that she'd made the right choice?

She looked back at her screen, and hatred rushed in like a storm. She hated all of this—the little box of an office, the apartment above pressing down, the bar in front screaming the noises of cleanup. She hated the screen with its merciless numbers and the office chair with its sticky wheel. She hated the punching bag in the corner that was supposed to be for moments just like this. She didn't want a clean, reasonable outlet. She wanted to shatter something. She gripped the edge of her desk and yelled.

A few seconds later the office door opened. Dusty filled the doorway, stocky and solid, mouth pursed above his ginger beard. He folded his arms and cocked an eyebrow. Vi slumped back in the chair. "I'm fine."

"Sure," said Dusty neutrally. He'd seen worse. "Heard about the cop. Anything I need to know?"

"Just cashflow problems." The screen danced in front of her eyes.

"Then you should lay off the books for tonight. They'll still be here in the morning."

"Not if I set the whole place on fire. How much would we get for that?"

Dusty huffed, not quite a laugh. "If you're going to commit arson, talk to Roman first. He'll figure out how to make it look right."

He knew she wasn't going to do anything. Just white-knuckle through this mood and then get up in the morning and keep scraping by, keep being safe, one sickening choice at a time. "I fucking hate this."

"Wanna pour some beers and sit out back?"

"No." What he meant was, *want to talk about it?* and she didn't. There was nothing to say.

"Okay. Bins are in the hall. I'm headed upstairs, if you're sure. Roman'll have heard that yell."

She dug the heels of her hands into her forehead. "Sorry. Check on Nana, too? I'll be up a while. Might go for a walk." She wasn't going to be able to sleep anytime soon.

"Long as you come back." There was a shadow of real worry in his brow. How bad did she look?

"I'll come back. Won't torch the place, either." She'd never yet had a mood so black she could forget how many people were counting on her.

"Okay. Night."

It took a couple of trips to get all the trash down to the alley. This time of night there wasn't much stirring in Vi's neighborhood. The alley light had burned out a year ago, so she worked mostly by feel. She waved her wristband at the dumpster, threw the bags on the compactor side, poured the dry trash into the sorter. She'd been doing it so long she didn't need to look at the balance: the dry trash credit would come out ten or twenty bucks over the bag fee. Big help that was. Keep it up every night for a decade and it might almost cover what she'd have to pay the Fontaines tomorrow.

She slammed the dumpster lid shut, making sure it locked. Then she was out of jobs to do. The idea of a walk had been stupid; the way her muscles were trying to shake off her skin wasn't going to be settled by any brisk stroll. What she really wanted was to go down to Mikey's and get a few rounds in. Then in the morning she could add Nana's worried face to her guilty reel.

"Hello, barkeep," drawled a voice from the shadow behind the dumpster.

Vi's body moved without any say-so from her brain. She dove into the shadow and seized the speaker by the throat. She didn't need to see to know who it was—if the voice hadn't been unmistakable, the breathy little laugh when Vi's hand closed would have been—but she hauled zem out anyway, into the narrow slab of light that cut in from the street. Ze looked just the same as when Vi had last seen zem: mocking eyes under black brows, pointed chin, half-open pink mouth that Vi wanted to crush into paste. She squeezed a little, felt the movement in the slender throat.

"Careful," Kilo whispered. "I'd hate to pass out before we even say hello properly."

"You picked a hell of a night to come back around," said Vi through her teeth. "I was just thinking I wanted to hit someone."

"I thought you might be happy to see me."

"Not after you disappeared for five fucking months."

Kilo smiled, wide and delighted. "You counted. Did you miss me?"

"Fuck you." Vi pushed zem back against the wall of her own building, where it wasn't pitch-black but the light didn't hit quite so warmly on Kilo's lips and chin and cheek.

"That's an idea." Kilo didn't make a sound when zer back hit the concrete wall, just kept looking up at Vi through dark lashes.

She'd never understand how ze did it. Kilo was the one pinned against the wall, but Vi felt like she was the one being cornered. She couldn't do anything but move closer, leaning into the quiver of Kilo's trapped body. Zer thighs slid apart and captured one of Vi's between them. Ze didn't do anything as obvious as grind against her; ze only seemed to melt, syrupy and thick enough to cling to Vi's skin and clothes.

She moved her grip to Kilo's jaw, tilting it up, watching the column of zer throat rise and fall. "You think you can just turn back up and I'll let you in like nothing happened?"

"Or what?" ze purred. "If you're planning to kick me to the curb, your hand's in the wrong place."

"Shut up." She thrust two fingers into Kilo's mouth. Ze grinned around them and bit down.

The pain lanced the knotted black rage in her chest. She stayed still for a minute, letting it sharpen, and then shoved her fingers deeper, forcing Kilo's jaw open and pushing into the back of zer throat. "Right here, like this," she said through her teeth. "Take it or leave it."

Kilo closed zer lips around Vi's fingers, sucking them deeper even as zer eyes started to water. Zer arms wrapped around Vi's back, nails digging into her shoulders. She hoisted zem higher against the wall. Ze was wearing a sheath that barely reached zer thighs, and whatever was underneath tore easily under Vi's fingers.

"My barkeep, so subtle," Kilo murmured.

"Who's yours?" Vi shoved both spit-wet fingers into zem,

sudden and without ceremony. Kilo hissed and clawed at her back.

"I warned you," Vi said. Her black mood was already melting into a hot, blood-red satisfaction. She felt all through her the moment Kilo went soft, let her in. She nipped at the side of zer neck and pushed deeper. Kilo didn't nip: ze bit, hard into Vi's trap, locking zer teeth and grinding.

"Fucking hell!" She pushed away, hand on Kilo's sternum holding zem against the wall. The bitten spot pulsed angry heat.

"Maybe I missed you too."

"I never said I missed you." She spun zem around, pushing zer face into the wall. "If this is what you came for, try and behave."

Zer fingers curled into the wall as she started thrusting again. Zer hisses turned to gasps and then to low, throaty grunts. Vi gave all her rage to zer body, burying it with each thrust of her hand, and Kilo arched back into her, taking it. When ze finally dissolved into shivers, Vi had nothing left but a fiercely tender ache. She leaned close and pressed her mouth to the hot, sticky cheek, let her fingers still in the velvety warmth.

"I thought you weren't coming back," she whispered. Kilo wasn't anything like Tempe, and the five months hadn't been anything like fifteen years. But with zem pressed quivering against her chest, she could admit, at least in her own head, that zer absence had stung.

Ze laughed, low and guttural. "Someday I won't. But I can't quit you just yet."

Vi pulled out and stepped back. She should know better than

to look to Kilo for warmth. "Hope you got what you wanted, then."

Kilo turned at her tone of voice. "Eh? Don't get me wrong, barkeep." Ze smoothed down zer sheath and closed in, draping both arms around Vi's neck. "I'll be coming back around. We'll see how long it takes before you're willing to let me in and fuck me on that horrible couch."

It was always games with Kilo, and Vi was both a bad player and a bad sport. She untwined zer arms and stepped away again. "Maybe next time I'll kick you to the curb after all." If she stayed out here, Kilo would manage to coax and cajole her into a few more moments of tenderness, but it would all end up the same anyway. She went up the steps to the office back door.

"Hey, barkeep," Kilo said, looking up in the thin sliver of light. "I'll tell you this for free: I got off the sunliner this morning."

"So what?"

"Work it out yourself." Ze sauntered away, and Vi watched until the alley shadows swallowed zem. Then it clicked: if Kilo had come in on the liner, ze'd been offworld for at least four of the five months ze'd been missing. And ze'd come to see Vi nearly first thing on getting back.

That threatened to raise a whole horde of feelings she didn't want to be having. "Fuck that," she said into the empty alley, and went upstairs to bed.

Chapter Two

Tempe had two problems that mattered. The first was to gain her employer's confidence as quickly and securely as possible. She was already starting at a disadvantage: the three other consultants in the entourage were born Eudoxians. Tempe's official background had many omissions and fabrications, but it said truthfully that she had been born and raised on Earth. Given Eudoxian insularity, she would be the natural target of any suspicions that might arise concerning the team. It was up to her to change that. In a few months, when Taillefer Quentin began to wonder if someone was deliberately sabotaging his efforts, Tempe needed him to feel certain it couldn't be her.

The second problem was Hannah's missing intel. The message waiting for Tempe on arrival had been brief: `Fire somewhere in the building last night, need to head out until the smoke clears. Planning to meet` a friend at Vi's bar on Teal and then find somewhere to crash. Sorry I can't put you up, will ping again when I can get back into my place.

That meant she was burned and she didn't know by whom, so Tempe couldn't rely on any of the contacts Hannah had sent in preparation for this mission. After being rejected at Vi's, she should have sent a follow-up message. The silence meant that she was either dead or in deep hiding, probably the former. Either way, that was one of the problems that was unsolvable and thus irrelevant at this time. Tempe had neither the resources nor the mandate for a search and rescue operation. She would do what she was expected to do, which was continue the mission.

Hannah had sent regular transmissions over the past year, and Tempe and Rosa had spent hours poring over each one while working out the mission strategy. Now she tore a sheet from her paper notepad and copied them down from memory as precisely as she could.

Much of Hannah's work had been finding weaknesses and leverage points for the various influential persons Quentin planned to work with in Eastport. The last few transmissions had centered on 'Canary,' Hannah's codename for the Eastport businessman who was courting Quentin for a culture and technology sponsorship. The messages had contained no specifics: even a priority intersolar transmission was not secure enough for names and details. Those would have been in the lost intel drop.

What a strange, bitter coincidence that Hannah had turned

to Vi in her moment of desperation. It was easy to understand why. Even as a half-grown child, Vi had been like a tall tree on a barren hill: if you needed shelter, of course you would run there. Fifteen years had only added mass and maturity to that presence. She could not blame Hannah for thinking Vi was the safest bet she could make. If blame was to be assigned, some of it must go to Tempe herself, for leaning on that shelter too hard, too young.

That was another of the irrelevant problems. Tempe turned her attention back to her notes. Hannah had been tracking down a specific potential weakness on Canary, which she'd identified with the phrase 'Promethean trespass.' A few messages after that phrase first appeared, she'd introduced a new contact, codename 'October.' And in the last transmission, sent while Tempe was en route and relayed to the liner, she'd included the phrase 'nail found.' That meant she'd discovered something that would be immediately actionable, if Tempe could only find out what it was.

Hannah liked her classical allusions: what kinds of things could 'Promethean trespass' mean? Theft, maybe embezzlement. Some kind of technological advance. Something literally to do with fire. Tempe would meet 'Canary' soon; he was eager to welcome the Eudoxians and solidify the tentative partnership. She would keep her eyes open for anything along these lines, and for the contact October. Rosa might also have ideas, once she'd received Tempe's status report.

When she'd decided she could get nothing more from the copied messages, she lit the edge of the paper and watched it burn to ash. That was one beauty of material things: there was no possible reconstruction of the words from the little heap of grey dust on the tabletop. People saw her fondness for paper as an affectation, but she found it reassuring to watch a small flame consume her secrets and know for certain they were erased.

Kilo slept soundly zer first night back in Eastport. The noises and smells of the city wrapped around zem, busy and intrusive and familiar. Ze was glad ze'd followed the impulse to go right to Vi's—ze hadn't lacked for company, especially on the voyage home, but the barkeep's blunt, muscular handling scratched an itch that nothing else could.

It had been a long trip, and the job had gotten tedious by the end, but the payout had been more than worth it. Kilo could take a little vacation now, maybe focus on slinking back into Vi's good graces. Maybe coax the lovely sadist ze'd met on the liner into continuing their fling as well. Sift through offered jobs and only take any that looked really interesting.

Ze opened zer message box mostly for the pleasure of looking through offers ze wouldn't take. There were many of these, none unusual enough to be tempting. Annoyingly, there was one message that ze did need to do something about: not a new job, but the completion of an old one.

The contact went by Derby, and they had hired Kilo not only to steal a piece, but to keep it on ice for a year or more. Kilo should never have taken the job—ze wasn't a keeper of things—but the money had been too good and the challenge too irresistible. The piece was a master pass token, the generator of all the keypairs a gang's hands would use to authenticate with its smuggling runners. This one belonged to one of the biggest gangs in Eastport, and had been kept under high security in a top lieutenant's home. Lifting it had required three separate cons and all zer cat burglar skills.

Now Derby wanted the token; they had messaged asking to arrange a handover at Kilo's earliest convenience. Kilo would be more than happy to have it off zer hands, but the timing was worrying. For one thing, it was too soon: several months shy of the year Derby had asked for. A change in Derby's plans didn't necessarily mean trouble, but the message had come in the day before yesterday, just before zer return. Kilo had not told Derby ze was going offworld, much less when ze expected to be back. The timing might only be a coincidence, but Kilo had been in the game long enough to look at a coincidence with both eyes.

Kilo had a few favorite places for handovers. For the meet with Derby ze picked Riverside Park. The park was one of Eastport's most hyped-up tourist destinations, which itself was a prank played by every Eastport citizen on tourists and newcomers. "Park" was a flattering name for the two-mile strip of grass running between the air towers and the docks that spilled into the river from the heart of Eastport. The river was pretty enough on a sunny day, and the path was dotted with plaques and statues commemorating great Eastport citizens of old, but the odor was inescapable. When the wind ran downstream you got the sickly violet whiff of rocket fuel, and when it ran upstream you got the stench of the docks. If a visitor said they'd been there and praised it, they were either lying or they were the kind of person who'd believe the word of a hundred strangers over their own nose.

Its main advantage for this exchange was clear visibility. Ze entered the park on the south end, dressed as a tourist, with a hat bought off a High Street kiosk and a jacket in a style that had been popular in Hong Kong a few years ago. Ze walked slowly, pausing to read every plaque and taking in the full sweep of path in zer peripheral view. Derby was supposed to be carrying a light blue umbrella. The path was busy, and Kilo recognized a few faces from the liner ze'd come in on. It was tempting to play, see how long ze could go in conversation without being recognized, but there was a job to do.

A large cluster of visitors came down the path, obscuring the view ahead. Kilo stepped to the side to peruse a plaque about the Three Rail Barons, waiting until they'd cleared. Zer instincts had been sound: several yards on, at a bench set back and uphill from the path, was trouble. There was the blue umbrella as promised, but the man sitting beside it was Arlo, the Trav lieutenant whose home Kilo had stolen the token from. Three men in tracksuits were doing half-hearted calisthenics near Arlo; they couldn't more obviously be Trav guns.

Kilo hadn't brought the token. Too many question marks on this meet. Ze did have in zer pocket the passkey fob that was supposed to confirm zer identity to Derby and vice versa. Slipping a casual hand into zer windbreaker, ze let it fall to the ground and kicked it down the slope toward the river as ze turned from the plaque. There would be no meeting with Derby today.

To turn around now would only attract attention. Kilo was confident in zer disguise, but most tourists came in pairs or groups; the Travs would be looking closer at anyone walking solo. The best chance was to pass by as naturally as possible. Ze kept walking, coming nearer and nearer to the bench with the Trav contingent. One glance up toward them, such as any traveler would naturally make, confirmed that there was no one besides the three guns and Arlo, all lying in wait. Ze didn't like how obvious they were being. They must be confident of spotting their target, and the Travs weren't green enough to act confident without reason. Kilo ordered zer legs and arms to move easy, steady, told them there was nothing to worry about as ze passed the bench where Arlo sat.

Just a couple yards past the bench was another plaque. Kilo's nerves wanted to get out of sight as fast as possible, but that would be another conspicuous act. When in doubt, stick to your character—that had been one of the earliest lessons drilled into zem. Ze paused at the plaque and made zer eyes focus on the words.

A tiny haptic buzz from zer wristband signaled that it had been scanned. So that was it: a remote scanner hidden near the plaque. Illegal, but that wouldn't worry the Travs. Would ze have gotten away if ze had bypassed the plaque and kept walking? Or would a gun in a tracksuit have jogged up behind zem? Too late to wonder. A gun in a tracksuit was coming down from the bench now. Running would do no good; they were undoubtedly faster.

The gun came around Kilo and stood directly in zer path. Ze looked startled and prepared to take offense, as an unknowing tourist might. "Come have a chat with us," said the gun.

Kilo made zer face a mask of confusion and answered in Cantonese. The gun just grunted, took zer elbow, and marched zem up toward the bench.

Up close, Kilo saw there was something wrong with how Arlo was sitting. Instead of the relaxed alertness of a waiting predator, it was the quivering tension of trapped prey. Ze had assumed Derby was being kept in extreme discomfort somewhere on the Trav compound while these men came to catch the accomplice, but as Arlo raised despairing eyes to Kilo, it hit zem with a certainty: Arlo was Derby.

A few tiny unsolved puzzles about the job suddenly fell into place, including why someone would go to massive trouble and expense to steal the Trav master token only to keep it on ice. If Arlo had wanted to use the token for his own purposes he could have done so any time. He'd wanted it gone, unavailable to the Trav boss, who would need it sooner or later to establish a new smuggling line or to replace a broken one. Whether Arlo was trying to prevent some specific action or undermine the boss, it was an act of treachery, and Kilo had been an accomplice.

Kilo didn't worry overmuch about the occasional job going sideways; wiggling out of trouble in one way or another was part of the game. But involvement in a gang betrayal was the kind of trouble that left very little wiggle room. Arlo was already as good as dead, and the thief who'd been his hands would be crushed as ruthlessly as he was. If Kilo didn't want to be that thief, ze had to become someone else, and quickly.

The gun, still gripping zem implacably by the elbow, was showing his colleague what the scanner had found. It was only a shell identity that Kilo had quickly laid in this morning before heading out. There was a name and a place of birth, enough to get through transit and the park gates, but little more: no travel records, no local residence, and most damningly, no credit link. Anyone with half a brain would be suspicious, and this gun looked like he had most of a whole one.

Kilo kept up zer protests in Cantonese while the guns searched zem. They were as thorough as they could be without stripping zem, and by the time they'd finished ze'd settled on zer new identity. Ze waited until it was clear they weren't going to let zem go just because the search turned up nothing, then turned on Arlo with a snarl.

"What the fuck is this?"

"So you do speak English," said the gun holding zem by the arms. He wasn't the one who'd scanned Kilo; he probably did only have half a brain.

"I'm talking to him," Kilo snapped. Arlo might have plenty of brain on a good day, but from the looks of him he'd already been through some strenuous questioning. He was looking at Kilo with dumb, glazed hope, like Kilo might be able to do something for him. Stupid. If Kilo managed a lifeline at all, it wasn't going to support a second person.

At least his stupor gave Kilo room to run the conversation. "You said the chips were good," ze continued. "What'd you do, lift them off of these goons? If so I don't want 'em."

"Don't want what?" said the gun holding Kilo.

"Chips, the goddamn chips I came to buy! But you can keep 'em and let me out of it."

"What chips? This is—"

The gun with the scanner and the brain cut him off. "No more talking. Wait for the boss."

A few minutes later a man came down the path, flanked by four more Trav guns. Kilo hadn't met him before, but his face was known throughout Eastport's underside: the oldest son and acting boss of the Travs. His name Kilo only knew by inference, since no one ever called him anything but Junior. If that bothered him, he never let it show.

The small-time, less competent criminal Kilo was currently portraying wouldn't know Arlo but would certainly know Junior. Ze let horror spread slowly over zer face, a dawning awareness of being well and truly fucked.

"Shit," ze said as Junior approached and looked down at zem. "Who is he? What is this? Whatever it is, I swear I didn't know, I'm just here to buy some chips, I don't want any trouble." Ze let it escalate to shrill panic, until the gun cuffed zem on the back of the head.

"Chips?" said Junior, looking inquiringly first at Kilo, then at the gun with the scanner.

"Don't know, boss. We had him save it for you."

"What chips?"

Kilo kept zer voice high and panicked. "Just some bus chips this guy said he had. He was selling them cheap, but I swear to god if I knew he'd stolen them from your people I never would have touched them."

Junior gave another questioning look at the gun.

"Nothing on him, boss, unless it's hidden deep."

Junior turned to stand directly in front of Arlo. "What is this about chips?"

Arlo's eyes darted, panicked, from Kilo to his boss and back again. "I. Like he said. I was going to meet him here to sell some bus chips."

You couldn't expect too much of a man whose life was probably measured in a few very unpleasant days or hours. It wouldn't get him off the hook even if he'd been able to sell the lie, which he hadn't.

"You fucker," said Kilo, twisting free and lunging for Arlo. "There aren't any goddamn chips, are there? What did you set me up for?"

Ze managed to grab his collar and yell in his face before the gun recovered from the surprise and hauled zem back several steps. Junior gave a nod to another of the guns, who punched Kilo expertly in the stomach. "Arlo has been a Trav man for nine years, and he'll die a Trav man. No one lays hands on him but us."

Kilo doubled over, wheezing. Word on the street said Junior was no dummy; hopefully that had been enough to turn his mind in the right direction.

"Did he contact anyone else?" Junior snapped.

"Not on a secure channel. Maybe on an open board."

Kilo kept wheezing through zer relief. *Maybe* was all ze needed. It would be impossible to prove Arlo hadn't set up a quick anonymous sale to cover his real contact.

"This one's definitely fishy, boss," said the gun holding Kilo, whose grip suggested that he'd taken zer brief escape personally. "His ID is obviously fake. My ma could've done a better one." Kilo could have kissed him.

"So could the thief we're after," said Junior with a trace of disdain. To the gun with the brain he said, "Watch the path. We'll question this one in private."

Kilo had plenty of time to run the scenario for gaps as they marched zem down the path. Getting hauled away was about the best ze could hope for. There had been enough fuss up by the bench that no one would be certain the real thief hadn't seen it and bolted. They'd find Kilo's discarded passkey if they were any good, but there wouldn't be anything to show it belonged to Kilo rather than the mythical other thief.

The Travs were a secure gang, not as powerful as the Fontaines but established enough to stick to customary and proportionate retaliation. Ze was in for a thorough search and a thorough beating, but as long as ze held to zer story, ze should be released before tomorrow morning. Ze'd be watched after leaving, but dodging eyes was rarely a problem.

Something else was tugging at Kilo's brain, something immediate rather than hypothetical. Ze dropped the situational assessment and focused on zer surroundings and had it quickly: they were being followed. Even the greenest tourist had their animal instincts, which would guide them away from the quartet of large men with Kilo at its center. The people they passed tended to glance at them and then quickly become very interested in something else, usually something which took them enough off the path to give the Trav guns a wide berth. But one set of footfalls had kept steady pace with them for a quarter mile or more. The guns were aware of it too; Kilo caught their glances and faint conversational nods over zer head. The steps continued behind them, unhurried, all the way to the black cube of a private car marked with the Trav insignia, waiting ostentatiously near the park's entrance.

"I must ask you to stop there," said a smooth tenor voice. Kilo knew the voice, but hadn't known until this minute that hearing it would pull a cold sliver of fear into zer gut. That was bad; ze hadn't been afraid of a mere presence for many years. Ze matched zer turn to the Travs, no faster, no slower, and pulled all the impassive boredom ze could muster into zer gaze as ze looked into the eyes of Loren Caine.

"This is Trav business," said Junior.

"Not when you're apprehending someone on an errand for the Pikes," Caine answered. "I held back before out of courtesy, but I can't let you take zem away to Trav quarters."

Caine spoke the pronoun distinctly, pointedly, and a little pop of rage burst against Kilo's ribs. Ze let business associates decide for themselves how to refer to zem; the choice was often informative. Ze still didn't know how Caine had discovered zer personal choice, but its message, to both Kilo and Junior, was clear.

"If you belong to the Pikes, you should have said," Junior said to Kilo.

"I don't." The simple denial was enough for zer character, but Kilo let it fly with a spitting vehemence that came from zer own chest. It didn't darken Caine's smile at all.

"Not as such, but zer errand was for us."

"And what errand was that?" Junior's voice was dangerously cold. Of all the places the token could land, Pike hands would be among the worst for the Travs.

"To make a purchase from your lieutenant. We wanted it handled by a neutral party, to avoid negotiations becoming complicated."

"A purchase of what?"

"I'm not sure why I should tell you that," said Caine affably. "It seems the purchase went awry. Perhaps your agent deceived mine? In any case, I don't feel compelled to give the Travs information on what the Pikes seek to buy."

Kilo didn't need to read Junior's face to map out his current difficulty. If Kilo did have the token, letting zem go to Caine with it would be disastrous. If ze didn't, letting the Pikes know that it had been stolen and was at large might be nearly as bad. And Caine had drawn a territory circle around Kilo: if they took zem away by force, the Pikes would be entitled to retaliate.

Caine was a master player. He paused long enough to let Junior absorb the situation, then drew breath with a catlike narrowed gaze that told Kilo he was about to land a winning strike.

It was time to make some bad decisions. Kilo elbowed the nearest guard in the gut, ducked back between two of them, and started to run. They caught up in three steps. Pavement scored Kilo's cheek as ze was pressed into the ground. A knee on zer spine; a hand on the back of zer neck. Ze kicked up as hard as ze could just to make it good, felt something soft connect and heard a stifled grunt. Two more hands pressing zer legs down. Zer hands were twisted behind zer back, harder than necessary. Must have hurt the guy.

"Enough of this," said Junior sharply. "Put zem in the car." With his voice turned in a different direction, he said, "If this really is your agent, you should teach better manners."

A pair of shining brown shoes stepped into Kilo's view. The pressed trousers slowly bent as Caine crouched by zer head. "I should, at that. You could have walked away today."

Kilo grinned with the side of zer face that wasn't pressed into the pavement. Ze could taste blood in zer teeth. "I don't work for you."

Caine shrugged, stood, and stepped away, watching at a distance as the guns hauled Kilo up and shoved zem into the car.

Chapter Three

Vi slept hard, dreaming a muddy succession of old faces and old shames until her alarm pierced through them. She'd set it early, so she could go down to Orange Street before opening the bar. She was still the last one up; when she trudged out into the big room, Roman was already at the table with his coffee and the extra-wide screen he liked to work on. In a collared shirt, crisply white against his deep brown skin, he could have been preparing to report to some fancy-ass board about how their dollars were moving. In reality, he was probably coming up with new ways to ferret information out of the dark corners of the net or analyzing what he'd already gathered up. Sometimes he sold bits of information, and the less Vi knew about that the better, but he mostly just liked knowing about things. It had come in handy for business once or twice.

He looked up as she came into the kitchen. "Dusty said there was some trouble last night."

Vi poured herself the last of the waiting coffee. "Not trouble as such. Just an unexpected visit from the law. Going out to get it sorted. She up?"

Roman nodded toward the front room. "Already working."

Vi didn't often get up early enough to see Nana painting. She went quietly to the open door and leaned against the doorframe, watching.

Nana sat in the window, her soft grey curls outlined with gold in the morning sunlight. Her small strong hand moved with firm strokes. Her mouth pursed in concentration, cheeks sucked in against her teeth. Her hands had been steady all Vi's life, through safety and danger. Her cheeks had been soft to touch whether they were hollow or full—but they'd been full for several years now, and Vi aimed to keep it that way.

She finished a series of strokes and then turned to Vi, laying her brush down to sign. "Why up so early?" Her gestures were casual, her brows arched: curious rather than worried. Vi tried to keep her tone light.

"I have to go down to Mikey's this morning. Not to fight. I just need a little help from Mikey's Rebecca." Before Nana could ask why, she added, "Can I see the painting?"

Nana's eyes narrowed; she knew who Rebecca worked for. But instead of asking, she beckoned Vi over to the easel. The painting was a fantasia in orange, blue, and green, with giant lush plants hiding a chimerical figure, human-faced. Nana had begun painting a year after they first came to Eastport, and now she sold a few every year. Last year she'd been approached for an exhibition, which she'd declined. Vi had asked why, thinking maybe it was because she was afraid of being asked to speak. She'd been prepared to march up to the fancy Heights gallery and hammer out the strictest terms, including Roman's presence to interpret or hers to knock down anyone who dared ask questions Nana hadn't pre-approved. But Nana had said that wasn't the problem: she just didn't want to paint on someone else's schedule. It was her peace, she'd said, and she didn't want it to become work.

That was all Vi had needed to hear. Nana had already worked enough for several lifetimes. She'd worked herself to the bone for Vi, and the rest of her life was going to be as soft and free of worries as Vi could make it. All the money from the paintings' sales went into a secured account, and Roman, who helped her with the business side, had assured Vi that it was getting to be quite robust. Vi slept a little easier knowing that even if something happened to her, Nana would be taken care of.

Admiring the painting turned out to be only a temporary diversion. As Vi leaned close to look at the hiding figure, Nana scrutinized her face. "What happened at the bar last night?" she signed.

"What didn't happen? It was a busy night."

"What happened to upset you?" The sign she chose suggested she was more focused on Vi's expression right now than anything she'd heard. Vi wasn't going to let her worry about money, but there was something she could offer up.

"Not upsetting really, just surprising. You remember

Tempe?"

Nana's eyebrows climbed her forehead. Of course she did.

"Yeah. Well. She showed up last night, and it threw me a little. She's fine, though. She looks good. She asked about you."

Nana hadn't ever needed to be told what Tempe was to Vi, back when they were children. She'd probably understood it before Vi had. Her brown eyes scanned Vi's face now, as if gathering up all the things Vi wasn't going to say. When she moved her hands, all she said was, "I'm glad she's well."

"Yeah. Me too." Vi started to stand, but Nana caught her arm.

"Why are you going to the Fontaines?"

She was extremely difficult to distract. Vi shook her head. "Just a little business issue. Normal stuff." She straightened up and patted Nana on the shoulder. "Really, there's nothing to worry about."

Nana frowned, but she didn't stop Vi from turning to go.

Mikey's arena was empty at this hour, the bar dark, the previous night's trash swept into piles. As Vi entered, a hulking figure loomed up from the shadows to the right, then relaxed when they registered her.

"Vi."

"Jackie."

"Rematch?"

"Not today."

That had been the exchange for five years running, ever since Vi put Jackie on their back after nine rounds. It had been Vi's last fight in the ring, and it was still being retold in Eastport dives over pitchers of watered beer. Jackie hadn't retired as thoroughly as Vi had, coming out to the ring for special occasions amid their work as bouncer and bodyguard. They offered a rematch every time they saw Vi and took her rejection with the same easygoing grin. It was one of Vi's least complicated relationships.

"Mikey's in the back," Jackie offered.

"And Rebecca?"

"Her too."

"Thanks."

In the back office, Mikey was full-steam on a harangue that had been going on some minutes, judging by the level of Rebecca's eyebrows. They'd go up and up and up, and then when they got to the top she'd slam a surface and take her turn. Mikey and Rebecca never fought *at* each other, but they'd yell so loud in turn about some external grievance that anyone outside would think they were about to start throwing fists.

Mikey saw Vi and cut himself off midsentence. "It's the Iron Fist! Hey, was it you sent those boys my way last night? They were spiked to the sky, every damn one of them. Wanted to climb right into the ring even though I had young Mutt in there and I said plain as day they couldn't fight him. Had to have Jackie sit on one of them to show the rest I meant business. But then Dallas was game for a couple rounds so they got their show, and the guests did too."

"Hope they brought in some bread at the end."

"Enough, and most of them itching to come back for another shot. I told them show up mostly sober and they can fight anyone they want. They'll do well for a couple weeks."

"Glad to hear it." Vi cleared her throat and turned to Rebecca. "I was hoping you could spare a minute."

"Certainly," said Rebecca with a pleasant smile.

"I'll just go clean up out front, shall I?" said Mikey. Vi nodded. Mikey and Rebecca separated their respective businesses neatly: he made it a point not to know what she did for the Fontaines, and she made it a point not to know who was backing bets and fighters. He exited, closing the door carefully behind him.

"Sit down, kiddo, you'll strain my neck," said Rebecca. She was only about ten years older than Vi, but anyone who fought for long in Mikey's ring got mothered by her, however the years stacked up. Vi sat. "What's it about?"

There was a formula to these conversations. Vi put the request together in her head before speaking. "I'm looking for a new source of some goods. Hoping for your advice."

"Happy to help. What goods?"

"Pickles and limes."

Rebecca's eyebrows went up. "Really."

Vi nodded. Rebecca's surprise was a little bit of comfort; at least Vi hadn't been wrong to think those were still some of the safer goods to buy underside.

"Well, if you give me a little while, I'm sure I can find a supplier or two to suggest. When do you need to place an order?"

"Tomorrow afternoon, at the latest."

The dent at the corner of Rebecca's mouth wasn't encouraging. "And when was your last shipment?"

Vi gave her the rough dates and other details the forged provenances would need to carry. Rebecca absorbed it all without taking notes. Vi knew her mind was like an ordered cabinet, with every piece of information she wanted to store kept pristine and accessible. She'd been working for the Fontaines for over a decade, and they didn't tolerate errors.

"Once I've done a little research, I'll let you know the vendors' exact rate. I'll warn you though, goods like these come pricey." She drew a number with her finger on the desk. It was over the highest amount Vi had been running her imaginary sums on. Vi grimaced.

"I wonder if any of them will take payment in installments," she said, not very hopeful.

"The interest rate would be high."

"Yeah." Vi ran her fingers through her hair. She had just about that much in hand, but two of her biggest expenses were coming due next week. What other choices did she have? She could see if the Travs or the Pikes would do it cheaper, but she'd spend all day just finding out who to contact. And she knew for certain the Fontaines were reliable.

Rebecca clearly read her line of thought. "Unusual goods like these, and a rush order, are going to come high wherever you go." Obviously she'd want to keep Vi here rather than going to the competing gangs, but Vi didn't think she'd lie.

"Any suggestions?"

"There's always payment in kind."

Vi frowned. "Meaning?"

Rebecca sighed and leaned forward on the desk, broad

bosom flowing over her freckled arms. She was wearing a light blue dress and a floral-patterned scarf. Her eyes were kind, but her mouth was tight. "You must already know that you're an attractive business partner for many... vendors. If you were willing to cooperate on a project or two, I could negotiate a very favorable rate. Perhaps even a net gain to you." She let it sit for a minute, eyes on Vi's face, then added, "I'm only speaking of a temporary partnership."

"Nothing is temporary," Vi said shortly. "Nothing is just once. I've lived here a long time, Rebecca. I know how it works." You'd do a favor to one of the gangs, and suddenly a supply line run by one of the other gangs would go dry and you'd have to lean harder on the first one. Or something would go wrong and you'd have to use their connections to call off the cops. And suddenly you'd landed yourself on a side in the underground warfare that tore Eastport down as fast as it built it up.

"I'll pay up front," she said, standing. She'd figure out the money somehow. "You'll have something for me by tomorrow?"

Rebecca nodded. Neither she nor Mikey ever wasted time arguing when Vi had made a decision. "I'll walk you out."

She walked with Vi all the way out to the pavement and onto the street. "You'll forgive me for being nosy," she said comfortably when they were several steps away from the building. "Do you know who did it?"

"Did what?"

"Sent shining justice your way."

Vi's stomach dropped at the implication. "Thought it was just my bad luck."

Rebecca shook her head slowly. "Think again. That kind of luck doesn't come up unless someone's stacked the deck."

Vi didn't have serious enemies. She'd carried a lot of cost and compromised several principles just to keep it that way. "Someone you know, maybe? Drove me right here."

"I don't think so. My friends would be happy to have your partnership, but it wouldn't be worth rattling the cans for. Not unless there's something you've got I don't know about."

"If there is, I don't know it either."

"If I were you, I'd give it more thought. You don't want more surprises."

"Fucking right I don't."

"Take care, Vi," said Rebecca, turning back into Mikey's. Vi didn't say anything back.

She tried to keep the worry off her face while she had breakfast with Nana and Roman. She knew she'd failed when Nana opened the second-to-last jar of peach preserves, carefully hoarded since peaches had become hard to get. Vi wasn't in a mood to enjoy it, but she took a generous helping to please Nana.

Before heading downstairs to open the bar, she pulled Roman aside, well out of Nana's earshot. "Can you find out what cop was on a particular beat at a particular time?"

"Might take a couple days. What beat?"

"Ours, last night. Don't take risks for it, it might not even help."

"I might be able to get you more if I know exactly what I'm looking for." He had a level, reasonable way of talking that was hard to argue with. She didn't want to pull anyone else into her problems, but he and Dusty would compare notes anyway.

"Got busted on some goods last night. Rebecca seems to think it was targeted. I don't know who it would be, and I don't know where else to start."

"Understood."

"Really, don't push it too hard. It might not be anything, and I don't even know what I'll do with the information if I get it."

"You okay on the bust?"

"No problems but money."

He flashed a wry grin. "I know that song. Okay, I'll get you what I can."

Kilo had hated Eudoxia. It had reminded zem of the diplomat's house ze'd worked in when ze was nine, all full of cold grand things that mustn't be touched. The pay had been extravagant and ze'd been excited for a chance to visit the luxury satellites, but once there ze'd spent most of zer time wishing for the mess and grime and heat of home.

Well, here ze was, and Eastport had welcomed zem back energetically. Ze'd been in a locked room somewhere in the Trav stronghold for what must be at least a full day now, with mess and grime and heat amply supplied by the guns who had come in to ask questions. In the way of mob guns, they'd been sparing with their words and generous with their boots and fists. Kilo's whole right side was tender, zer head pounded, and zer shoulders throbbed from when one of the guns had tried some fancy arm-twisting maneuvers. They'd taken a break now, to let Kilo think about whether ze had anything more to tell them. Instead ze spent the time pondering what they did on Eudoxia when they had to ask someone questions. Probably something much more refined, something with white tables and electrodes, bloodless and tidy.

They didn't have any new information against Kilo; if they did, the tone of this interrogation would have changed. They probably wouldn't have held zem this long if Caine's interference hadn't heightened their suspicions. And what the hell had he been doing there, anyway? Ze didn't think he'd been working with Arlo. For one thing, the Pikes would have wanted to get their hands on the token right away instead of leaving it with Kilo for months, and for another, he wouldn't have been able to resist gloating afterward that he'd tricked Kilo into working for him after ze'd sworn ze never would again.

The timing of all this happening right as Kilo returned planetside was still an unexplained coincidence. No one in the Travs had the background on Kilo to recognize the name that had been on the liner's manifest. But Loren Caine did. If he'd found out the token had been stolen—never mind how—he would have thought of Kilo immediately. He might even have been the one to tip off the Travs about Arlo. The trail from Kilo to Derby to Arlo would have been hard to trace, but not impossible. And Loren Caine was very good, fuck him. He could have set this whole thing up, expecting Kilo to take his protection at the end. If ze had, he'd have landed both the token and Kilo.

Ze tallied all zer current discomforts and the lost remainder of zer pay from Derby, and added it to the score ze was going to settle against Caine someday. At least he'd gone home empty-handed. Ze hoped he was losing sleep over it.

Ze was still nursing that grudge when the door opened again and reminded zem that there were more immediate enemies to worry about. Two guns came in first, one ze'd seen before and one new, but instead of approaching Kilo, they scanned the room and then stood on either side of the door to let another man in.

It wasn't Junior this time. He'd been here for the first round of interrogations, watching closely and doing the asking so his guns could focus on using their fists and boots. He'd left the later rounds to his staff, which showed good sense. There wasn't much variety to the questions; it was all a matter of whether they'd get tired of asking before Kilo got tired of not answering, and mob guns had more time and patience for that kind of thing.

This man was dressed like Junior—almost comically so. His suit was dark green herringbone instead of Junior's dark grey pinstripes, but it was cut the same and also included a vest but no tie. Clearly one of them was aping the other's look. His hair was a lighter brown than Junior's, face a little younger, and he looked to both of the guns before stepping all the way into the room. Junior hadn't shown the need for that kind of reassurance; he'd looked straight at his target, counting on the guns to tell him if there was something he needed to know. At a guess, this guy was the imitation.

He came right up to Kilo, crouched down, and looked sorrowfully at zem. Although the guns had mostly kept it professional and stayed away from zer face, ze could feel that there was a scrape on zer cheek from the pavement, and a lump rising on zer temple where one hit had sent zem off-balance into the concrete floor.

"I'm afraid your stay here hasn't been very pleasant," he said. "Frederick, can I have some ice for our friend here?"

So they'd switch from stick to carrot for a bit. Kilo accepted the ice pack, pressed it against zer temple, and waited to see what the play would be.

"My name is Andrew Palumbo," the man continued, sitting his fine-suited ass right down on the concrete beside Kilo. Evidently they were going to be chummy. "I understand my cousin has had you in here since yesterday, is that right?"

Kilo gave a sullen nod.

Andrew shook his head, even more sorrowful. "And you haven't told him a thing, and it's easy to see why. You're too clever for that. You understand that telling won't help you. Losing that token was a big blow to the Travs and a colossal embarrassment for my cousin. He'd have to make an example of you even if you handed it over to him, and you're clever enough to understand that."

This was the first time in the entire interrogation that anyone had used the word *token*. Andrew shouldn't have used it either, because he was right: losing it was a reputational problem as much as a logistical one. Either they'd gotten something that made them certain Kilo was the thief, or Andrew was going off script.

When in doubt, stick to your character. "Token?" Kilo said, as if ze was trying to think what that could mean. At this stage, a small-timer would be scrambling to come up with a lie that might satisfy their captors.

"Good," said Andrew, "you're a good actor. And obviously an excellent thief. It'd be a shame to see you rubbed out just because you stole the wrong thing from the wrong man. But I have a way out. You whisper to me where that token is. Just to me. The two boys behind us are on my side, you don't need to worry about them. Then I go out and we let them make a lot of noise while you sit back here with your ice pack. Then finally I tell my cousin I really think you don't know and weren't involved, and he lets you out of here. With the token safe in my hands, Junior's never the wiser. And before long, the head of the Travs isn't someone you've embarrassed, but someone who has reason to be grateful to you. Catch my drift?"

It was obvious. It could even be true. A treacherous lieutenant couldn't expect to get very far on his own, but if he was backing an ambitious cousin in a coup, that made sense. Or it could be that Andrew had his own ideas and was seizing the opportunity. Or, of course, this could be a play arranged by Junior.

Kilo focused on the part that would be most important to the small-timer. "You could get him to let me go?"

"Very soon. And you won't take any more beating in the meantime. That's a promise."

Kilo made zer face say how badly it would like to avoid another beating while ze thought it out. The token was going to be a problem, even if ze did get out of here without any more trouble. Ze would have to find a way to get rid of it that couldn't be traced back to any of zer identities. Ze'd been pushing that problem aside to be handled later, but this was a tempting offer. Handing it over to Andrew would solve all zer problems—if he was really planning to overthrow his cousin, and if he had the juice to pull it off.

Looking over the mimic three-piece suit, Kilo decided the second *if* was the bigger one. "I know all about Junior, and his dad the real boss. Never heard of you."

Andrew tried to keep his face friendly, but the resentment flared up in the backs of his eyes and the corners of his mouth. "But you've taken my money. You did this job for me, so I'm the only boss you should be thinking about." He had to keep remembering to smile. "And of course, once the token is handed over, you'll get the last third of your payment."

That was one thing for him and one against. He knew it was a third of the payment Kilo was still waiting on, so probably he really had been working with Arlo. The heat of his resentment was against him, though. That much anger suggested a lack of confidence. Maybe he could pull off the coup and maybe he couldn't, but Kilo wasn't going to bet on someone who wasn't sure of himself. Also, ze did not like people who misunderstood their working relationship. So two things against.

Right now, he thought he knew Kilo was the thief. That called for some finesse. "What if I couldn't get it right away?"

"Why not? Where is it?"

Ze sent zer eyes darting to the side. "I might have sent it somewhere, to be safe."

"Like where?"

Kilo hesitated. "South. To a... friend in the Florida

Consortium. I could give you his ID and the code word before you let me out." Ze didn't oversell the hitch in zer speech as ze came up with the story—ze was supposed to be a professional—but ze let the desperation in *let me out* land hard.

Andrew's eyes narrowed. "And how did you get it across international borders?"

Kilo pushed panic into zer face and body, let zer whole being scream *caught*. Caught in an addled, last-ditch effort to take up Andrew's offer even with nothing to trade for it. "I— I— I— I have another friend, who's good at that kind of thing....If you just let me out, I can make sure you'll get it."

All Andrew's friendliness melted into menace. "What kind of game are you playing? Do you even know what it is?"

"It's— a token. It's a..." four seconds of racking zer brains, then a sudden revelation. "It's a pass token! It's a—"

Andrew's hand cracked across zer cheek. "If you think it's been unpleasant in here, imagine for a minute what would happen to you if you promised me something you don't even have."

"I'm sorry! I'm sorry. I just thought... please, please let me out of here. I can help you. Even if I don't have the token, I know people, I could help... find things out for you, maybe." Ze let the babble roll out, let the terror mount. As he stood up, ze leaned forward to clutch at his trousers. He pulled away, lip curling.

"Frederick, Jesper. You take it from here." Rage and disgust rolled off of him. Kilo loved a good scene partner. Ze let zer cries rise almost to hysteria as he stalked out and slammed the door, as Frederick and Jesper closed in with their thick-soled boots.

Chapter Four

Vi had already settled it with herself that Tempe wouldn't be coming back and that that was for the best, but nobody had told her eyes. Every time the door opened they went right to it and wouldn't move until they'd seen it was somebody else coming through. She got more annoyed with herself every time, but her eyes had their own program and didn't care how she felt about it.

The upside was that when the two lofts walked in, she didn't miss a second of their entrance. The woman's face was one you could see on concert posters or mag covers, or some nights projected big on the wall of the dive where she'd first become known to Eastport. Now she was known over half the world and making a good start on the other half. And here she was, walking into Vi's bar, one deliberate step after another. She could have been on a magazine right here, every detail perfect from the bronze highlighting her dark brown cheeks, down to the bright orange toenails showing through delicate sandals. She didn't blink or turn her head when a customer at a corner table whispered, "Is that Vaughan Riley?"

The man who followed her in was no mere lackey. Vi didn't know his face, but he held the door for Vaughan Riley with a courtesy that was more possessive than subservient, and when she had taken three steps inside, she waited until he came abreast of her and very deliberately curled her hand into the crook of his arm. The man was tall, blond, and broad-shouldered, and under his finely shaped coat he wore a crimson shirt that might be natural silk.

It wasn't that rich folk never came into Lower Eastport; you just didn't usually see them flaunting their wealth quite so loudly. Even at midday as it was now, their duds would draw the petty and opportunistic criminal element like fruit drew flies. Maybe they were confident in their protection and didn't mind some heads getting broken, or maybe with a face like Vaughan Riley's there was no point trying to be inconspicuous. Either way, Vi's immediate wish was that they'd go somewhere else. She did mind heads getting broken, on general principle and especially in her bar.

"What can I do for you?" she asked when they were still a few steps from the bartop.

"Citizen Ferreira, I presume," said the blond man. "Owner of this fine establishment." His voice was smooth with just a little syrup in it, and he showed a whole row of shining even teeth. He could have sold vacations or jewelry up in the Heights, where they went in for things like silk shirts and teeth. Whatever he planned on selling here, Vi didn't expect to like it.

"That's me."

"My name is Brett Sangster." He paused as if he thought the name might mean something to Vi, but he wasn't thrown when it clearly didn't. "And I imagine Miss Riley needs no introduction."

The famous singer had barely blinked the whole time they were in the bar, and she didn't blink at the *Miss,* which was a bit shocking. Vi didn't know where this Sangster was from, but Vaughan Riley was Eastport born and raised, and here you didn't miss or mister people you weren't sleeping with or giving orders to. And even then, you stuck to *citizen* in public unless you wanted to make a point of whichever relationship it was. As to which it was in this case, Vaughan Riley's face didn't give any clue. She was looking at Vi and the bar with a kind of impartial blankness, not like she didn't have any thoughts, but like any she had were tucked so far back there wasn't any chance of getting at them from outside.

Whatever. Not Vi's business. "So we all got each other's names. Did you come here for a drink or something else?"

Sangster laughed too hard. "We might have expected a famous fighter to be blunt," he said, looking to Vaughan Riley to share in his amusement. She looked back and quirked her mouth an eighth of an inch. Sangster got his hilarity under control and turned back to Vi. "We would very much like to have a conversation with you. In private, if it suits your convenience."

Vi finally got what it was that was bugging her about him. He was doing the thing any salesman did, acting like he was pleased to death to be here talking to you, but at the same time he was so sure he was better than Vi that he didn't mind her knowing it. She'd been in business a long time, and she could take being buttered up and she could take being talked down to, but someone who expected you to pretend along with him that he wasn't talking down was new, and it made her want to smash in those shiny teeth.

"I've got my bar to run," she said.

Sangster looked around pointedly. This early, there were just half a dozen people, all trying not to look like they were watching the two lofts. "I think I can guarantee we will be finished before the rush begins." The sarcasm didn't make Vi feel any warmer toward him.

"Rush or no, I'm here alone until my other bartender comes."

"Then we can return then. What time?"

Hell. The last thing Vi wanted was this pair walking back in when it was more crowded. She sized Sangster up for a minute and decided there wasn't any faster way of dealing with him than hearing him out.

"Let me see if someone can cover." She ducked back into the kitchen where Dusty and his morning assistant were busy on food prep. "Can you spare Bella for ten minutes to watch the front?"

Dusty said yes in a grumble that meant no, he couldn't really, which suited Vi fine. It would give her a reason to cut the conference off quick.

Bella followed Vi out to the bar, but stopped in the doorway, hands frozen comically in the middle of wiping them on her apron. Vi had forgotten there was a star in their midst. Bella gaped at Vaughan Riley for a solid twenty seconds before recovering herself. Vaughan Riley didn't alter the casual drifting of her gaze around the bar, but when it drifted toward Bella she met the girl's eyes and smiled. It was the first real expression Vi had seen on her face since coming in; it was a restrained smile, but friendly.

"We're going to the back for a few minutes. Anything funny happens, anything at all, you yell for Dusty."

Bella nodded. She looked like she wouldn't be able to speak, so Vi didn't ask her to, just motioned the lofts back to her office.

The office was untidy at the best of times, and this week was closer to the worst. Vi kicked a box of sample syrups out of the way and moved the toolbox off the couch before motioning them to sit. It wasn't a very good couch: the fabric was a cheap green plush that had been worn down to a plastic shine in the center of the cushions. Their loft asses probably hadn't sat on that grade material in years, but they kept their faces neutral as they sat down. Vi picked a shirt off the seat of her desk chair and draped it over the back, then sat.

"Okay, we're in private. What's this conversation?"

Vaughan Riley was looking at the charcoal sketch portrait propped against the wall behind the desk. It was of Vi, from her fighting days, and she'd never been able to make up her mind to either hang it up or move it out of the office. In the sketch she was turned three-quarters away, with her shoulders hunched and her fists down, like she was in the middle of getting up after being knocked down. The artist had done a bunch of sketches like it every fight night; Vi had just liked this one.

Sangster followed the singer's gaze. "A portrait of your idol, I see," he said affably. "Miss Riley was a great admirer of yours, Citizen Ferreira. That is why we decided to make you one of the first recipients in my new program."

Vi had been watching Vaughan Riley's face. While her mouth remained composed and serene, something had come smoldering to life in the dark eyes as she looked at the sketch. Belatedly, Vi caught up to what Sangster was saying. "What program?"

"I manage a number of enterprises, and my great life's work is to elevate Eastport and her citizens. I have done this in myriad ways, including promoting Miss Riley across the continent, across the world, and soon above it. But you don't have time to listen to all that. My current project is nearer to home, because we must never forget the people and places that make the daily life of this city so precious. Such as this bar."

"This bar is part of your daily life?"

The sarcasm slid off him like oil. "These institutions are vital to the city. So I am putting forward a loan program, to allow businesses such as yours to develop and thrive. And because you are a favorite of my favorite," he touched Vaughan Riley's elbow as he said it, "I selected you as one of the first beneficiaries."

"You want to give me a loan."

"I see efficiency is one of your strengths. That bodes well for our partnership. The usage of the funds will be largely up to you; I am sure you have projects in mind that would make your bar more profitable. I am, of course, happy to be consulted. Not only my funds, but my business expertise will be at your disposal."

"Normally a person has to go and ask for a loan. Never saw someone walking into a place trying to give one out."

"Naturally, you would be cautious. You will want to review the terms carefully." He pulled a case from his pocket and took out a chip. "All the information is on here. Since you are in a hurry, I won't go through it this morning. You'll find that the loan is modest, but the repayment terms are generous. I hope very much that you'll do me the honor of careful consideration."

Vi took the chip. "Sure. Is that it?"

Her gruffness had no effect at all on Sangster's gleam. "For this morning, our business is concluded. I hope very much that this is only the beginning of a long and mutually beneficial partnership." He stood, touching Vaughan Riley's elbow again. "Come, my dear. We should not interrupt Citizen Ferreira's morning further. Perhaps another day she'll be good enough to give you a demonstration, as a treat." He said the last looking toward the punching bag that stood in the corner of the office. It wasn't for real workouts, but it was good for when a customer had gotten her blood up.

Vaughan Riley stood, looked to Vi, and held out her hand. "It was a pleasure to meet you." It was the first thing she'd said, and Vi almost whiffed taking her hand. The voice was rich, warm, and mellow. Vi wished she could ask her to stay for a drink and see what she was like without the golden businessman in tow.

Tempe had received Rosa's reply to her initial status report. It was just about what she'd expected: regrets that the organization couldn't offer any additional help or insight, confidence in Tempe's ability to handle the situation on the ground. Rosa had also affirmed that Tempe should not try to track down Hannah's whereabouts or wellbeing. The organization would evaluate whether another terrestrial agent could be spared for that purpose, but Tempe was to keep to her original mission.

She would have to do the work of two, not counting her official post as Taillefer Quentin's expert on material quality and terrestrial trade. For ease of movement, she requested an apartment just below the border in Lower Eastport, rather than in Eastport Heights where the rest of the entourage would be staying. She had an official rationale, that it would be tedious to pass through border security every time she needed go down to the lower city to inspect a factory, but no one in Quentin's entourage was inclined to ask questions. There had been enough strained politeness over meals on the solar liner from Eudoxia to Earth; the born Eudoxians were quite content with an excuse to leave Tempe out of casual social invitations.

The first event that required her return to the Heights was a soiree thrown by the Eastport businessman who was courting their trade partnership. To the Eudoxian delegation their host was known as Brett Sangster. To Hannah he had been Canary. Tempe did not expect to gain any concrete information at an event whose main purpose was to please and impress the Eudoxians, but it would at least begin to show her who the man was and where his weak points might be. A person revealed a great deal through what they believed would dazzle others.

She noted with amusement that this was also true of the Eudoxian entourage: as a group they conveyed a very clear message. Fashions on Eudoxia had begun to include terrestrial style elements, transformed through layers of irony and imitation, but tonight everyone in the delegation had reverted to classic Eudoxian style: sweeping shapes, restraint from color, and the rare, proprietary fabrics that would emphasize Eudoxian separateness and superiority. Tempe had chosen a silver-grey blouse with a standing collar and bell sleeves of nimbic silk, one of the oldest and most celebrated products of Eudoxian material innovation. The fabric diffused light into haloes, a pattern of rings that would shift and dance as she moved. Octavia, the financial expert, was wearing a wasp-waisted bodice of true-black, a fabric that absorbed all light no matter the angle, making her silhouette a perfect void that drew the eye again and again. Marcel, the political advisor, also wore nimbic silk but in dark grey, the dancing haloes moving over his tailored torso. Junyi, the cultural consultant, wore a white fabric that appeared plain when you were looking at it, but left an afterimage of elaborate interlacing designs. That material was new enough that Eudoxian branding houses were still battling over what name to give it.

Taillefer Quentin himself was dressed in simple grey, immaculately tailored but with no features to draw the eye or play with light. A true Eudoxian magnate made all his displays by proxy.

Their host received them in his courtyard and showed them into a large garden, brightly lit with golden lamps and starry lights strung through the trees. He was a tall blond man with an ingratiating smile. A Eudoxian doing business did not smile too freely, even on a social occasion, but Tempe could tell that none of her colleagues saw any problem in Brett Sangster's display of teeth. They took it as him humbling himself, which seemed to them perfectly appropriate. None of them seemed to see the power he projected: he smiled because he felt in control and confident of winning the advantage in any challenge.

He greeted each of them by name and with a brief remark indicating he knew their areas of expertise. To Tempe, he said that his head engineer was greatly looking forward to their meeting. He chose to greet Junyi last and walked with him toward the gathered crowd, saying, "I hope to make this an especially rewarding evening for you. I regret that the painter Sol Mendes was unable to attend, as I know you had been wishing to meet her, but I will make a special effort to facilitate that introduction another time. The poet Cassandrine is here, as well as another luminary whose appearance I will keep as a surprise, if you'll indulge me."

A server, in the all-black clothing that was considered discreet in Earth society, approached with a tray of refreshments as they entered the garden. Sangster was not quite out of earshot when Octavia looked around and murmured to Marcel, "They really do let nature grow wild. I thought it might be played up for film." Tempe saw the slightest hitch in their host's step, saw his fingers rub at the lower edge of his coat, but heard no change in the smooth patter he was directing toward Junyi.

By terrestrial standards the garden was quite formal and restrained, but even the mowed lawn and tidy beds showed a profusion of greenery one would never see on Eudoxia. Tempe had always denied being homesick for Earth, but the smell of cut grass made a sharp ache rise in her chest. A fleeting, undisciplined thought crossed her mind: What if I could stay?

She reined it in quickly. She would go where the organization asked her to go. She had already placed her life into their hands and Rosa's, and she needed their supervision even more than they needed her abilities. This job would keep her here for several months, which was plenty of time to enjoy lavish greenery.

This party was also an opportunity to lay groundwork for the months ahead. Sangster might be the immediate target, but the garden was full of Eastport's wealthy and influential citizens. She walked slowly through the crowd, sipping a glass of wine, observing the lines of power in each small cluster of people.

She had studied all the heads of Eastport's administrative bureaus and was surprised by how many of them were here. The secretary of trade would naturally be interested in the progress of the Eudoxian sponsorship agreement, but the secretary of education and the chief transit officer had no such obvious reason to be in attendance. Brett Sangster was evidently very well-connected. He would make a strong ally for Quentin, and Quentin would need Eastport allies to accomplish some of his more delicate and unsavory aims. Cutting this one off at the outset would be important.

To do that, Tempe needed allies of her own. She could not act openly this soon after coming to Earth. Discovering the weapon Hannah had found against Sangster would be one task; she must also find someone to wield it.

It was easy to look for power at a party like this. She watched who approached others and who stood waiting to be approached.

She watched the way bodies relaxed or stood to attention in the presence of others. She watched who turned first in every cluster to accept a fresh drink or bite from a server's tray. Apart from their host and the government officials, she identified three, maybe four, individuals who appeared to stand near the top of the Eastport social hierarchy.

Of these four, one stood out because she was observing the Eudoxian delegation as sharply as Tempe was observing the Earth elites. She looked a little older than middle-aged, hair in neat finger waves, lilac suit perfectly tailored. Like Sangster, and unlike the other high-status individuals, she moved through the party energetically, approaching different groups and speaking to them with purpose rather than waiting for others to move toward her. Tempe saw her speak to both Marcel and Junyi, the latter giving her more words than the former. Curious, she placed herself where she would be easy to approach.

As she waited, she became aware that one of the servers was wrong. He was dressed like the others, but while the others orbited steadily through the crowd, he moved erratically, halting frequently to look around, sometimes appearing startled when a guest took a drink from his tray. Not at all the kind of clumsiness that came from being new to a service job. What was he here for? There was more than enough wealth on display to attract a thief, but he was a little too obvious to be a professional.

She was still watching him when the woman in the lilac suit appeared at her side. Behind her was a younger person, almost pointedly plain and nondescript, who had been following like a shadow as she moved through the party.

"Good evening," said the woman in lilac, smiling. "A beautiful night, isn't it? Citizen Sangster has outdone himself."

Tempe agreed that both the night and the party were lovely.

"We're not formal here, so I hope you'll let me introduce myself. Clemence Dorsey, of Dorsey Imports."

A hungry rival of Sangster's? An import business would certainly be interested in the opportunities offered by a Eudoxian partnership. Tempe extended her hand. "Temperance Carroll. Friends call me Tempe."

"I hope I may, then."

A small white moth dipped over the table and fluttered away toward the lights in the nearest tree. Tempe didn't realize she was watching it until Dorsey spoke. "I hope you aren't startled by our local fauna," she said. "I learned in speaking with your colleague that you don't have insects on Eudoxia."

"We do, but mainly in the horticultural zones. One doesn't see them at parties." A little friendliness, in the shape of a personal revelation, seemed judicious. "It isn't startling to me, though. I grew up on Earth."

"Did you now! I hear it's a struggle to get anywhere in Eudoxian society if you grew up elsewhere."

"It largely depends on having the right friends. And I wouldn't claim much standing in Eudoxian society. I'm here for my expertise."

"And is it rude if I ask what that is?"

"Certainly not." They clearly both wanted to talk about the same thing. "I'm here to advise Seigneur Quentin on material procurement. Quality control as well as provenances. I'm sure you're quite familiar with the complexities of trade lines on this continent."

Dorsey rolled her eyes expressively. "My dear, it's the reason for half my wrinkles." There were, in fact, very few lines in her smooth brown complexion. "I'm sure you have plenty of resources of your own, but we would be more than happy to offer advice if you find yourself perplexed. You can have Ann's link." She motioned to the person behind her, who stepped forward and held out her wristband. "My secretary, Ann Bredon. I'm lost without her."

Tempe took the link. Clemence Dorsey was certainly eager to be friendly with the Eudoxian contingent, and she'd approached the consultants rather than Quentin himself, which showed a subtlety Tempe appreciated. How hungry was she? If Tempe pointed her to a wedge that could be placed between Sangster and Quentin, would she drive it home?

"Has Dorsey Imports ever considered seeking a Eudoxian sponsor?"

Before Dorsey could answer, half the lanterns went out, and one corner of the garden was illuminated with a standing ring of light. In the center, surrounded by the light like a halo, was a woman in a silver dress. The strongest lights were behind her, making her face only a silhouette, but when she began to sing Tempe knew her voice at once. She looked to Junyi, standing a little off, and saw his eyebrows raised in surprised recognition. Vaughan Riley was not widely known on Eudoxia: only those who closely followed Earth pop culture would recognize her. One did not have to know her name to recognize her talent, though; her voice was its own argument. Most of her songs that had reached Eudoxia were upbeat and lively, but tonight she sang a low, crooning ballad. Her voice caressed each line, and the lowest notes stretched out with a trembling warmth that called up an answering tremble in the listener. Without any accompaniment she held the entire garden party captive. No one moved or stirred until the final note trailed off.

Clemence Dorsey sighed as the silence gave way to applause. "There's your answer. Naturally we'd have loved a chance to bid for Seigneur Quentin's favor, but with a talent like that in Brett Sangster's pocket, how can the rest of us compete? Assuming it's true, as I hear, that arts and culture are as essential as goods in this agreement."

They were, particularly for Quentin, who badly needed some friendly human-interest stories attached to his name on Eudoxia. Tempe was beginning to see why he'd settled on Sangster even before arriving. She responded with a smile that was discreet and, if Dorsey chose to read it that way, slightly regretful.

Sangster stepped up to the microphone and in a few brief words of introduction hinted that Vaughan Riley, long a star in the terrestrial sphere, might soon get the opportunity to perform offworld. Junyi murmured something to Quentin that made the magnate nod appreciatively toward the stage.

Sangster left the stage and Vaughan Riley began another song, but Tempe's attention was caught by the server she'd noticed before. On the other side of the garden, he approached Octavia, who was standing apart with a faintly sour look. The server turned his head too far for Tempe to lipread what he said to her. Octavia's eyebrows climbed her forehead as she returned an icepick glare. Then she flicked something—probably an insect—off her sleeve and moved away from the server.

Tempe became aware that Dorsey was watching her watch the server. She smiled quickly. "I wasn't aware that Vaughan Riley was managed by our host."

Dorsey laughed. "Managed is one word for it. I daresay she's his favorite acquisition among many, and he doesn't let her stray far. I had her booked for our silver anniversary gala and paid through the nose for it, and then he and I had a little conflict of business interests, and she was inconveniently ill the day of the gala. Of course, she might really have been ill."

"I see Eastport business relationships are as complicated as Eudoxian ones."

"Now you're being gracious. I'm sure it's obvious that I'm frothing with envy at our good Citizen Sangster, so you shouldn't mind anything I say about him. After all, he's the one who had the foresight to build such a stable of talent. I would never have thought to combine art and industry in trying to attract someone from your sphere." She pointed out a short, elderly woman with a mop of reddish hair, who Junyi had been speaking with before the music began. "I don't expect you'd recognize her on sight, but that's the poet Cassandrine. Another of his acquisitions, although it isn't as widely known. If your artistic colleague wants to bring her up for a fellowship, as it appears he might, he can only deal with Sangster. So how can someone like me complain?"

"You seem like a woman of many resources," answered Tempe. "If this opportunity has passed you by, I'm certain you'll be able to seize another."

"Oh, have no doubt of it," said Dorsey, still smiling. "Now I must stop complaining in your ear—it's terribly indiscreet of me to do it at all. I wish you a very pleasant stay, and do please ask if there is anything I or my company can do for you."

Almost as soon as Dorsey left her side, the server appeared at Tempe's elbow, offering his tray. Up close, the first thing she noticed was that two fingers of his black glove hung limp. Trading her near-empty glass for his full one, she glanced at his face. Mid-twenties maybe, ruddy complexion, the white line of a very old scar on his temple. His manner and posture were decent approximations of a good server, but his eyes were full of anxiety. Another mark of poor craft, inexperience, or both. As she turned her head away and pretended to sip at the new glass, he said in a hushed, hurried tone, "I'm looking for a friend of Hannah's."

In that moment Tempe was thankful to have Octavia's example. She turned back to him, mimicking the incredulous disdain her colleague had shown at being addressed by staff. She kept the same disdain in her voice as she said, "I met a Hannah once."

The server's shoulders dropped visibly in relief. "She said to tell everything I know."

Quentin and Junyi still stood several feet away—probably not close enough to hear, and they didn't seem to be paying any attention to her, but Tempe did not take that kind of thing for granted. She gave him another scathing look. "I don't think it's appropriate for you to speak to a party guest."

"I know. Go to Tommy B 23 and ask for Albert. Bring— shit!"

Looking over her shoulder, his face turned to open fear. Tempe took a fraction of a second to calculate that it would be natural for her also to turn and look. Striding toward them was one of the guards that had stood unobtrusively near the entrance. He was talking into his wristband and looking straight at the server. When Tempe turned her head back, the server was already disappearing into the garden hedges.

The guard swerved around Tempe and pursued him. It all happened so quickly and quietly that Quentin and Junyi didn't even look her way. A few other guests, standing further back and thus having Tempe in their range of vision, looked at her with curiosity but not undue excitement. She made sure her face showed nothing but a slightly irritated bemusement. Tommy B, 23, Albert. She repeated the words in her mind until she was sure she wouldn't misremember them, then went to join her employer.

"Trouble, Carroll?" Quentin asked without turning to look at her. His tone made it clear that the only acceptable answer was no, and the only reason he had asked was to make her aware that the disturbance had not escaped his notice.

"I really couldn't say," Tempe answered coolly. "Perhaps I should ask our host whether such staff perturbances occur frequently."

"No," said Quentin after half a second's consideration. "But tell Marcel of it later."

Marcel would be tasked with probing the incident to discover whether it exposed any weakness that could either be pressed upon to get better terms in their dealings with Sangster or show those dealings to be unwise at all. Tempe hoped the server had covered his tracks well.

Vaughan Riley finished her last song to loud applause, and Sangster approached the microphone once more and extended his arm to her. Tempe watched with interest as the singer, who had been warm and fluid in song, became marble as she reached out and took his arm. Still elegant, still lovely, but cold and immovable. She hated him, Tempe thought. That was interesting.

Chapter Five

Kilo didn't have to fake zer stumble out of the Trav car in the wee hours of the morning or the protective clutch around zer ribcage. They'd gone hard, although nothing was broken and they'd stayed off zer organs. An organization like the Travs would only create corpses it meant to create. But ze'd taken enough to convince them that ze knew nothing about the token, or at least nothing that could be beaten out of zem. Ze didn't bother to check if someone was following; naturally there would be. Like the petty criminal caught out of depth ze was supposed to be, ze went wearily to zer most disposable crash pad and slept the day away.

On waking, ze rolled zer protesting body out of bed and went out for food and an ostentatious bundle of ice packs, drugs, and bandages. The man smoking in the alley wasn't trying particularly hard to look like anything but a major gang gun on watch. Kilo wanted to throw him a wink, but decided reluctantly that it wouldn't be in character.

It was not a run-down and bruised petty criminal that left the building's other exit two hours later; it was a vixen of questionable age with red lips and a skirt that barely covered her ass cheeks. Kilo sashayed into the right kind of club, stole a long coat, and emerged as a wealthy matron whose heels and lipstick signified a clinging to youth, rather than a flaunting of it. By this time ze was as certain as ze could be that no one was following. The last change was for the sake of the destination: ze went into a bar that had a cheap clothing printer in the back, then made zer way to zer most secure crash pad wearing the coveralls and rubber shoes that told of a night full of embarrassments.

The token was still where Kilo had left it months earlier, in a shielded box inside the crash pad's hidden safe. Ze took a quick look inside the box to confirm it was still there, then closed and sealed it again. Getting rid of it was going to be tricky. The token itself was small enough to fit in zer palm, a rounded disc bearing the Trav emblem of a running horse, but it had a level 4 beacon that only Junior or his father could disable. The box blocked the beacon, but a six-inch cube couldn't be slipped neatly into one's pocket or dropped casually by the wayside. And any shielded box of this grade could be traced back to its purchaser, which was the most essential thing to avoid. Kilo didn't give a shit what happened to the token, as long as it didn't lead anyone back to zem.

If ze moved fast, ze could pocket the token and drop it somewhere busy enough to be untraceable. Beat cops normally scanned at level 2, enough to pick up escaped convicts or deadly weapons in the area; they'd only go to level 3 or 4 if there had been a recent theft. The Travs would have scanners running level 4, but not enough to cover the whole sector. Right now they should be focused on Kilo's other crash pad and probably the Riverside Park area. All ze needed was a little luck.

Kilo's ID work had been solid for years; it had been a long time since ze'd moved through Eastport wary of scanning cops. The alert tension, the anxious looking toward every wall and blind corner, took zem back to shakier, hungrier times. So ze was already in a bad mood when ze walked past a daytime dive and saw Loren Caine lounging in the doorway.

"Come in and have a chat," he said.

"No."

Caine smiled, unperturbed. "Then I'll walk with you."

The last thing Kilo wanted was to draw attention, and in this street there wasn't any subtle way to shake him. "If you touch me I'll break your fingers."

Caine just kept smiling and fell into step beside zem. "Do you have the token on you now?"

"I don't work for you."

"I suppose you must have convinced the Travs of that. You don't seem to have suffered too badly from their hospitality."

"I wonder if they know who tipped them off that Arlo rigged his own house burglary," Kilo said. "It's a shame you went to all that trouble and got nothing for it."

"I wouldn't say nothing. We're talking now, aren't we?"

They turned out onto a busy road, a perfect place to drop the token if Caine hadn't been at zer side. If this were the old days, Kilo could have pushed him into the street and let the killer automobiles solve zer problems. Ze dug zer fingers into zer palm.

"Even if I had it, I wouldn't sell it to you. You should've asked before tying me to the Pikes in front of the Trav boss."

"And what would be the point of that?"

The soft complacency in his voice made Kilo's skin crawl. If the Pikes got their hands on the token now, then Kilo would belong to them. Ze would have to, because the Travs would take it for granted that ze did, and ze would need their protection if ze wanted to keep breathing. "How flattering. You make it sound like you'd rather have me than the token."

Caine stopped walking. "Oh, there's no question of that."

Kilo halted next to him in spite of zemself. Caine smiled warmly. "Money and information have limited use. The right person is invaluable." He reached out and very lightly touched zer cheek.

There was a cop puppet two blocks down the street; Kilo couldn't break his finger as promised. The fury of being caught in a bluff momentarily overwhelmed everything else. Ze couldn't shout, ze couldn't curse, ze couldn't beat him down and leave him a pulpy mess on the sidewalk. Ze spun around and began walking away.

Caine didn't follow, only said, "You know how to reach me when you change your mind."

Brett Sangster's welcoming gala had gone late into the night, but Tempe still woke early. On Eudoxia, daylight broke a little before 7 every morning, and she was accustomed to rising with it. Here on Earth in late spring, it was an hour earlier, but her body seemed to be following the sun rather than the clock.

Just as well: she had work to do. She rose, made tea, and sat in the one chair her apartment currently had.

The impostor server was foremost in her mind. Tommy B, 23, Albert. 23 might mean 11 at night, or it might be something like an apartment number. Tommy B was a problem. None of Hannah's contacts had been called Tommy or Thomas, and of course a net search on the name was futile. If the name had been in Hannah's final drop, it was lost to her.

Looking into Clemence Dorsey was much more rewarding. The businesswoman had understated her importance: Dorsey Imports was the largest above-board trade company in Eastport, and it held exclusive agreements with several of the smaller nation-states in the Americas. It must have been profoundly frustrating to her to have Sangster take up the agreement with Quentin before she'd had a chance to begin negotiations. Whether she'd have the capability to wield Tempe's weapon against him could only be judged once Tempe knew what it was, but at least she would have the motivation.

Using the secretary Bredon's link, Tempe anonymously sent some general information on current Eudoxian priorities and trends. Most of it should already be known to them, although Earth perspectives on Eudoxia tended toward romanticism and were generally outdated. Some of the nuances in what she sent would likely be new and useful to them, and overall it would let them conclude that they had an ally in the shadows. Whether they guessed it was Tempe didn't matter overmuch; it would be in their own interest to be discreet. Having gained their attention, she would be able to lay further trails for them as needed.

It was also necessary to do the job Quentin had hired her for. Brett Sangster had promised several new manufacturing processes, the details of which would be handed over to Quentin with an exclusive off-world patent once their agreement was finalized. Tempe did not intend for the agreement to ever be finalized, but she must still perform a thorough evaluation of the techniques on offer.

It made a pleasant change, to focus for a few hours on purely technical work. She went to the manufacturing laboratory and sat with Sangster's head engineer, discussing the minutiae of fabrication and decomposition, the impacts of gravitation and microbiota throughout the stages of reclamation and material output. The engineer had some truly novel solutions to the second- and third-level processing of organic waste, always a problem on Eudoxia. If they passed in situ tests, these alone would be worth well over the estimated value of the technical side of the agreement. She wished she was working under a different magnate; even if Quentin could be persuaded that there was value in entering the sanitation business, he would surely find a way to turn what could be a broad benefit to Eudoxian people into a narrow profit for himself and a select few others.

With gentle reluctance, she said, "The brief we were given indicated a new fabricator design as well. Before we spend all day discussing waste reclamation, perhaps a look at that?"

The engineer blinked. "Ah. Of course. Forgive me. It's easy to get sidetracked on my own pet project." He pulled up a new set of schematics on the table screen and began walking Tempe through the test conditions they'd used to make sure the new design was sphere-neutral.

It was clear within minutes that he was not only less enthusiastic about the fabricator design project, but less familiar with it. Unsurprising; he was clearly a specialist. At a suitable pause, Tempe asked, "I suppose another team did the primary work on this project?"

He was silent a few seconds too long. "Yes, that's right. The lead engineer has departed for other opportunities, so the final testing has been left in the hands of his assistant and myself." He avoided her gaze while speaking and then looked too directly when finished, as if that could make up for it.

"Do you happen to have the lead engineer's contact information? In case I have questions."

"I'm afraid I don't. His assistant could probably answer them—although he isn't in today." He forced a smile. "You may think it's strange that I don't have his link, but we weren't on the best of terms. Professional rivalries, you know."

He was such a poor liar that Tempe felt almost fond. A man made not for intrigues, but for quietly, busily solving problems with material results. She could have pressed and cornered him into giving up whatever he was hiding, but she felt a reluctance to disturb him, as she might when coming across a small animal playing in its natural habitat. There would be another way.

She toured the facility with half her mind on what the mystery about the other lead engineer could be. Her best guess was that the foundations of the design had been obtained through some kind of theft, rendering Sangster's ownership dubious at best. Perhaps there had been no other lead engineer at all.

"And here are our Eudoxian simulators," the engineer said, bringing her to a row of four tanks on the factory floor. "We've nurtured the environments very carefully to make sure our outputs are replicable. This one has been sealed the longest," he laid a hand on the nearest tank, "and if you crawled inside I daresay you'd feel exactly like you were at home."

Tempe hadn't bothered to mention that she was Earth-born. She inspected the samples arranged in a case beside each tank: an array of fabrics ranging from a light gauze to a thick canvas, rods of construction material with differing weights and rigidities, a few droplets of bright gemlike ornamental material. As best she could tell, the outputs were uniform between tanks. "May I take some samples home to bully?"

"Naturally. They should already be printing them, but I don't see... Tara!" he called out.

One of the technicians that had been working on the other end of the factory floor came over, holding a tablet under her arm and looking rather harried.

"Are we printing the samples for the Eudoxian to take back?"

"I asked which set and you didn't say," she answered.

"Didn't I? Oh dear." The head engineer was clearly not an authoritarian, but he threw a glance at Tempe and made an effort. "Well, you should have reminded me. This is an important guest."

Not a bit perturbed, the technician shot back, "I've been on double duty since Monday. Hell of a time for Eightpad to go missing."

"Well, never mind, let's not make excuses. I'll set up the print run myself, go on back to what you were doing."

"Have to start over again," said Tara. "And really, if he isn't coming back then we need to get—"

"All right, all right, we won't bore our guest with personnel troubles." The head engineer looked slightly more alarmed than was warranted, and he all but chased Tara back toward the other end of the floor before coming back.

"I do apologize," he grimaced. "I hope it won't inconvenience you too much to wait while we set up your samples."

Tempe assured him that it wouldn't. She took her time over selecting a sample material, considering which angle to take next. There was something here, but she had to chase it without appearing to be interested in anything beyond materials technology.

She chose her sample, a stretchy fabric that would respond interestingly to stress tests, and while the engineer was setting the machine instructions she asked casually, "Is Eightpad some kind of device you use?"

The engineer blinked rapidly, not looking up from his tablet. "Ah, no, he's one of our technicians. He lived a rather colorful life before coming to our lab and brought that nickname with him. I'd stop them using it, but he doesn't seem to mind, and we do have another Joe, so it saves confusion."

A colorful life, here, was probably a euphemism for gang

involvement. She remembered the two empty fingers on one glove of the server who'd approached her. Eightpad. Possibly a coincidence. But the other technician Tara had said *missing*.

She toyed with one of the construction rod samples, tapping it thoughtfully. "I do wish I could ask some questions of the lead engineer on this project. Will the assistant you mentioned be in tomorrow?"

"I... am not sure," said the engineer. In the corner of her eye she saw him sweating.

"Would it be too much of an inconvenience to give me his contact information so I can reach out directly?"

"Well, in fact, it isn't very convenient..." He quailed under the look of cool surprise Tempe turned on him.

"I beg your pardon," she said. "If there are matters your employer doesn't wish us to look into, of course all I can do is report back to mine."

"No! Nothing like that. Nothing at all." The engineer looked around to see where the other staff were. "This is better discussed up in the lab."

Tempe followed him back to the lab and let him close the door behind her. An attack on her at this point would be madness, but she did scan the room and fix the location of every makeshift blade or bludgeon.

When the engineer turned to face her, the relief on his face said plainly that he'd had time to think of a story. "The truth is, that assistant is the same Eightpad Joe we just mentioned. He's been absent for a few days without notice. I am concerned that his former life may have caught up with him. I fear that if you were able to reach him, you might become embroiled in matters both sordid and dangerous."

"I see," she said, giving him a smile of reserved sympathy. "Naturally we have heard of the more... romantic elements of Eastport society. Is it difficult to get technicians without that sort of background?"

"Well, not precisely," he said. "Young Joe was something of an outlier. Extremely bright lad, lots of potential. Of course you can't help where you're born. My former colleague thought very highly of him, and helped him overcome the deficiencies of his early education. He could go far if he manages to avoid trouble."

"Well, if he does return in the next few days, please do notify me. I'd very much like to speak with him."

Four days after the cop's visit, Arthur commented nervously that it seemed like business had been slow lately. Luce was at the other end of the bar, but her head whipped around, like she hadn't wanted to say it but now that it was said she wanted to hear Vi's response.

"You act like this is your first week working a bar," Vi said sharply. "Slow runs happen. It's nothing to worry about." She didn't know if she believed that herself, but there was no reason for Luce and Arthur to start worrying.

She'd put the chip from Brett Sangster into the top drawer of her desk and was trying to forget about it. Even if she believed it was pure coincidence, him showing up with an offer of cash just when she badly needed some, taking a loan was a great way to make someone feel like he owned you. She'd have liked to toss it right out, but then her only choice for quick money would be the Fontaines.

Nearly everyone in Eastport belonged to somebody. If it wasn't one of the gangs, it'd be one of the Heights corporations or the city government, which were just gangs with more paperwork. All it took was a run of bad enough luck and you had to start taking deals, bargaining away your freedom piece by piece. Vi wasn't cocky enough to think she could escape it forever. She'd kept on her feet so far, but someday something was going to knock her down so hard she'd need a hand up, with all the strings that came along with it. She hoped that day was many years away, and she hoped when it came she'd at least have options. Two bad choices were better than one. So she kept the chip.

She already had one bad option tucked away, one that she'd take ahead of any loan offer or help from the Fontaines. Daly had left Eastport in hot water, panicked enough to sell Vi the bar for a fraction of its worth in ready cash. Months later, she'd found his stash of contraband hidden up behind a ceiling tile. She'd told Dusty and no one else, and they'd agreed to pretend they'd never found it. It was a bad sign, the way her eyes kept drifting to that ceiling tile now. It told her she was starting to get panicked.

You had to keep your head on straight. Bad luck was bad luck, but acting desperate before you really were was inviting more trouble. She only really had two problems: the quarterly rent that was due in two days, and the big whiskey shipment coming in tomorrow. If she could somehow meet both those expenses, things would even out.

She added up the sums at closing time and concluded that she'd have to ask Jonesy for credit on the whiskey. She hated to do it, but she hated all her other options more. Paying rent late would mean heavy fines to the city, and if she had to stuff someone's pocket she'd rather it be Jonesy's. She was one of his best customers, and he owed her a favor she'd never called in. She'd take as much credit as he could give, and if it wasn't enough she'd release some of her order to go to other buyers. If worst came to worst, she'd have to water some of the cheaper booze to stretch it until the next shipment. That was two hits to her pride, the favor and the watering down, but she could take it.

The next morning Roman stopped her as she was on her way to meet Jonesy at the depot. "I looked into what you asked me about," he said. "I couldn't get actual names, but the cop on your beat that night was also on the Hollyhill beat the night Dalton's burned down."

Before it had burned to the ground, Dalton's had been the biggest and most consistently stocked general store in the neighborhood. "Who ran goods through Dalton's? The Travs?"

"Until six weeks ago. Best I can tell, that's when she tried to switch to a smalltime runner."

And a week after that, Dalton's had burned. The cops had called it in in time to keep the fire from spreading to neighbors, but too late to save the store. Eliza Dalton and her grown son had been hospitalized for a week and had hopped a train out of Eastport as soon as they could stand. "What would the Travs want with me?" It would make more sense if it was the Pikes, who didn't have a foothold in this neighborhood yet. The Pelican just down the street was a Trav bar, and this neighborhood was neutral territory. The other gangs would take it badly if the Travs tried to move in too hard on this street.

"I can poke around, see if there are any rumblings about a big move."

Vi grimaced. "And here I thought I'd already worked out the worst-case scenario." A big move here could mean a gang war on Vi's doorstep. She thought it out for a minute, then shook her head. "I don't see it. There's a dozen neighborhoods they'd try to move into before this one. Look if you want, but it's probably just a coincidence. New cop getting overexcited."

"I'll let you know what I find." He hesitated, and then added, "If it's an immediate cashflow problem..."

"I'm not touching Nana's account."

"You know she'd want to help."

"That's why we're not saying anything to her about this." She could see that he thought she was being unreasonable. "Listen. I still say this is all just bad luck, but I'm not new in town either. I don't know how deep this hole gets, and until I find out I'm not having anyone jump into it after me. You know what Dusty promised me when you two moved in."

"We'll take care of her if anything happens to you."

"And right now you've got a nice little nest egg to do it with. That's how I want it. Anyway, it's not that desperate yet. I'm asking Jonesy for credit today, and that'll see us through the week, and then things will even out."

"Let's hope you're right."

Jonesy was already sitting in the depot's front room, where an ever-rotating assortment of small goods lined the walls and people waiting to pick up shipments could sit and drink a passable cup of coffee. He rose when Vi came in, but she motioned him back down again.

"Let's look it over first," she said, trying not to sound as uncomfortable as she felt. She hated asking for favors, hated needing to. Jonesy also looked unhappy as he sat and pulled out his screen.

Her order was all there, everything she'd asked for two weeks ago when cashflow was normal. Half the time there was something or other he couldn't fulfill, which would have saved her needing to beg off some of it, but today couldn't be one of those days. Vi curled up her hands, gritted her teeth, and finally said as casually as she could manage, "How'd you like a shot at paying back that right arm you say you owe me?"

She could tell from how Jonesy took it that something was wrong. He'd always perked up before at the hint there was a little something he could do for her, but today he drooped. "What you got in mind?"

"I'm having cashflow problems. A couple weeks should clear it, but if you could let me take some of this on credit, it'd be a big help."

A muscle in Jonesy's jaw jumped. He curled and uncurled his fingers, then asked, "What kind of trouble you in, Vi?"

"No trouble. Just some unexpected expenses came up, and

you know how tight the margins are. I just need a week or two to smooth it out. Anything you can do would help."

Jonesy shook his head. "That's just what I can't do. I gotta take full payment, and I gotta take it today."

"Why? You strapped too?"

He shook his head again. "That's just how it's got to be."

"Jonesy. What did I do?" This wasn't how it should be going, even if he was running thin enough himself that he couldn't help her. It was too flat and too grim.

"I don't know that. What I know is, I give you credit today, next trip my clearances don't go through, and I'm sunk. And maybe that's getting off easy. I don't want to find out."

Vi got it now. With the sense that she was hanging onto a slim rail over a tall drop, she said, "Someone told you that's how it is?"

Jonesy nodded, not meeting her eyes.

"You got a name? A face?"

"Forgot 'em as soon as they left."

Futile anger stirred in Vi's chest. Not at Jonesy; she couldn't ask him to risk his business or his family. He didn't scare easy, either. If he'd believed the threat, it had to come from one of the big three: Fontaine, Trav, or Pike. They were the only ones who had the pull to block a supplier's clearances through legit shipping channels. Remembering the conversation with Roman this morning, Vi idly traced a T on the tabletop, then looked up at Jonesy.

"I guess you have a better idea than I do what it's about," he said. If that was anything, it was a confirmation, but he wasn't giving her any more. He was good and spooked.

"I wish I did," she said. She shoved back all the panicky calculations and fears that wanted to swarm into the front of her brain. Shoved back a yell of rage along with them. She still had to deal with the shipment. "Then I guess let's look through what I ordered."

Vi left the depot with about three-quarters of her initial order. She hadn't asked whether letting her leave some of the cases was going to get Jonesy into trouble; he'd just let her select what she wanted from the full list and asked no questions. He'd be able to sell them elsewhere in Eastport.

All that meant, though, was that she had 150k still in the account: not enough to cover tomorrow's rent. At least she had the John J. Martin back in stock. She'd taken the full shipment of that; leaving some of it wouldn't have helped enough, and it would have meant losing the exclusive Jonesy gave her.

As she guided the depot's dolly on its spidery legs up the back-alley stairs and into the storeroom, Dusty came out of the kitchen. "All good?"

Vi grimaced. "Had to pay Jonesy up front. Took a little less than my order."

"He'd give you credit if you asked."

"Yeah, that's what I thought." She didn't want to say the rest, but Dusty wasn't going to let her wiggle out of it. "Someone got to him."

Dusty's face went grim. "Got to him like threatened him?"
Vi nodded.

"Against helping you specifically?"

She nodded again. Now there wasn't any way around it. She couldn't tell herself it was a run of bad luck. Someone was trying to fuck her over.

Dusty leaned back against the doorframe. "Well, shit. Okay. At least we know. No clue who it is?"

"Roman said maybe the Travs. Jonesy didn't say it wasn't them. But why?"

"You haven't done anything to piss them off recently?"

"Not that I know of."

"Be a big move if they were trying to horn in on this street."

"Yeah."

"Okay. Roman know about this?"

"Not about Jonesy."

"I'll tell him, yeah? He might be able to find out more."

Vi hated it, but she couldn't argue. "Just not where Nana can hear."

Dusty nodded. "We gonna make rent?"

"Not on time." There wasn't any way around it; no other barrels to scrape. The late fees would put her further in the hole, but that was a problem for another day.

Chapter Six

Tempe was enjoying herself, bullying the material samples she'd gotten from Sangster's factory. She had cut them into strips, carefully marking the origin of each piece, and was inspecting their response to being burned, stretched, left in water, left in a solvent, twisted, and torn. Any unusual material degradation would only show through microscopic investigation of the margins or stress points. It required rigor, creativity, and close observation, and it left her in a calm state of mind.

After she put the samples aside for the day, she found that the back of her brain had been at work on the less tangible problems of the factory and the missing Eightpad Joe. She ought to have found a way to ask if the nickname was because he only had eight fingers. And Hannah had nicknamed her contact October, another eight. It was the kind of association Hannah would make. Eightpad Joe, the eight-fingered server, Hannah's

October. All connected to Sangster. There was nothing to prove it was the same person, but it would do for a working hypothesis.

If she took that as provisionally true, it led to a number of other conclusions. The factory must be involved in whatever Hannah had uncovered. The other lead engineer might have been made to disappear in order to cover a secret. What secret could there be in the design of fabricators that would be worth all this?

Promethean heresy. Theft was a strong possibility. Perhaps Sangster did not truly have the rights to this technology that he was aiming to sell to the Eudoxians. If that was the answer, her next task would be to find the person who did have the rights, then enable or encourage them to contest the agreement.

At best, that would only undermine the technological side of the partnership though. Quentin would be annoyed, but not enough to cancel his agreement with Sangster entirely. What Tempe needed was total disaster on this first phase of their mission: she needed Quentin to have to start from scratch and spend valuable time on finding a new business associate. Hannah knew this perfectly well. There must be more to it than a simple tech grab. Perhaps it was a question of who the tech was stolen from?

She needed to find the server, whether he was Eightpad Joe or not. She still hadn't had any luck discovering who Tommy B was. If the answer was in Hannah's final packet of information, it was lost to her. But if he was Eightpad Joe and had been involved in the Eastport underground, it might also be a name familiar in that world. In which case a net search would be useless, but she might be able to find it out through other means.

She would need to rebuild a network of connections in any case. She didn't have time to start completely from scratch: better to gamble on one of Hannah's contacts. If she happened upon the one who'd burned Hannah, she'd do her best to make it their bad luck instead of hers. She tore out a page from her notebook and started writing out the list of contacts from memory.

Halfway through the list, her wristband flashed a message. She opened it immediately, assuming it would be from someone else in Quentin's entourage. Instead, it was the only other person on the planet that had her link: Kilo, the playmate she'd met on the liner. The message was just one word: Busy?

Tempe hadn't decided yet whether to let the shipboard fling continue after landing. The Tempe of three or four years ago wouldn't have considered it, likely wouldn't have responded to Kilo's overtures in the first place. Self-denial was both instinctual and comforting, but as she looked at the message she heard Rosa's voice: *Don't waste what I've spent on you. You'll be more use to me in the long run if you learn how to be alive.*

She'd been trying, even on days when she wasn't sure what that meant. Already, on a planet that held only strangers and enemies, she'd felt herself petrifying, reverting to old impulses. The encounter with Vi hadn't helped; she'd been glad to see her alive and well, but it had thrown into prominence the difference between them. Vi, who had lived and surrounded herself with life all these years, and Tempe, who had chosen something colder.

She'd rarely felt so alive as in her stateroom on the liner with Kilo. If Rosa were here, she'd say that was reason enough to respond. Tempe finished writing out her list of contacts and then answered Kilo: Not especially.

Kilo, direct and efficient, sent a location pin to what appeared to be an hourly motel. Tempe picked out three contacts to look into, then burned the list and changed her clothes.

She arrived at the motel first and sent Kilo the room number assigned by the scrawny youth at the front desk. They used metal keys, which Tempe had not seen since her childhood. The youth conducted the entire transaction without once looking at her face, which at first she took for skittishness or embarrassment but was probably simple prudence. Metal keys and the option to pay with a preloaded card; some people coming here would want no record, and would not feel friendly toward a desk worker who had looked them in the eye.

The room was sparse and drab, but the bed and shower were large. The walls were bare, almost declaratively so: no pictures or patterns where a camera could hide. The place was clearly designed for one single purpose.

Kilo arrived nearly half an hour later and immediately draped zer arms around Tempe's neck. "Here you are," ze said.

"Here I am."

"Kiss me."

Tempe took the sharp chin between her fingers and turned Kilo's head to place one light kiss on zer cheekbone. Then the other side. She waited for the confident anticipation in zer gaze to turn anxious, then asked, "Do you have anywhere to be?"

"Just here. Won't you kiss me?" Ze bit zer lip and leaned zer whole weight on Tempe. The pleading was uncharacteristic, but Tempe was glad of it. If Kilo was bratty, she'd have to make it more difficult, and today Tempe wanted a little softness. She kissed zem gently, searchingly, still holding zem by the chin to tip zer head the way she wanted it. Kilo's lips parted easily for her. Zer hands roved her body, down her sides, around her back.

"You're very forward today," Tempe murmured. Kilo liked to play coy, liked to invite touch more than extend it.

"Maybe I missed you."

Tempe lifted her head to look into Kilo's eyes. She hadn't taken zem for one to get attached easily. They'd enjoyed one another during the voyage, but Tempe had been fully prepared for it to end when they disembarked.

"I didn't miss you," she said, "but I'm happy to see you."

Kilo laughed, looking pleased rather than offended. Ze liked the things about Tempe that others found difficult.

"How happy?" Zer fingers loosened the sash of her coat, then slid up to her shoulders to lift it away.

It was habit, almost instinct, to feel her pockets when anyone had been near them. Tempe didn't really think anything was amiss until Kilo caught her hands halfway there and brought them teasingly to zer lips.

"Come to bed," ze said. There was not a trace of worry in zer face, only laughing seduction—but it was a little too bright and soft. Tempe freed her hands and cupped the back of Kilo's head with one.

"Sweetheart. What are you doing?"

"Trying to seduce you. Didn't you notice?" Ze held Tempe's gaze, all teasing happiness, as Tempe reached into her own coat pocket and pulled out a small object: a black disc in some kind of smooth material, a little lighter than stone, with a raised emblem in the shape of a running horse.

Tempe shifted her grip to the back of Kilo's neck. "What is this?"

Kilo didn't look down at the object until Tempe asked the question, which showed impressive control. Zer eyebrows rose lightly. "You tell me. It was in your pocket."

Tempe shook her head. "It wasn't there when I entered the motel. You won't make me doubt that. So I think you should tell me."

Kilo's face was always expressive, emotions chasing across zer features, vivid and animated. For the first time, Tempe saw it go entirely blank. Ze looked at Tempe and the disc in her hand with a face perfectly still and neutral. Tempe felt a tiny pain, like the tip of a pin scraping across her heart: even this one thing could not be simple and good.

"It's nothing," ze said after a minute, zer voice flat and half an octave down from the honeyed singsong of zer initial greeting. "I'll take it and go. Just forget it." Zer fingers reached for the disc, but Tempe pulled it back.

"I don't forget things. What is it and why did you try to plant it on me?"

"It doesn't matter. I shouldn't have tried."

"You're right that you shouldn't have tried. You'll have to convince me it doesn't matter."

Kilo gave her a slow, assessing look. "I could take you down."

"Probably. I'm not very strong. Is that what you're going to do?"

"I really did want to see you," ze said, with a wistfulness that would sting if Tempe chose to take it as genuine. "I only tried to plant it on you because you're a Eudoxian, and you just got here. No one will think you're involved in smuggling wars."

"Smuggling?"

"That's what it's for. It was stolen off one of the big gangs. All I'm trying to do is get rid of it in a way that won't land me in worse trouble."

"So you chose to land me in trouble."

"Not much. A little fuss when you cross sectors. You're smart. You'd just say someone must have slipped it into your pocket on the street, and they'd believe you, because why else would you have it? Then it's off both our hands."

Without releasing her grip on Kilo's neck, Tempe looked at the object. Now that her memory was prompted, she recognized the horse emblem as designating one of Eastport's principal crime organizations. "Who stole it?"

"I did. For someone that's probably dead by now. I'm hoping not to join him." Ze leaned zer weight slightly into Tempe. "It's my neck, or a couple hours of inconvenience for you. I didn't think you'd mind."

"But you didn't ask."

"You're not that soft on me. Not enough to say yes if I'd asked. I hoped you might be just soft enough not to give me up, once you realized what had happened."

Behind the pleading shine of zer eyes, Tempe still saw calculation. "If I am, then I'll be tempted to let you go. If I'm not, then I don't really have any right to feel betrayed. That's the idea, isn't it?"

Kilo lowered zer eyes. "Well? Which is it?"

"Who do you work for?"

Zer mouth twisted, a flash of sourness. "No one but myself. Trying to keep it that way."

Whatever problems Kilo had, they weren't hers. She stood still, made herself cold to the pliant form draped against her, thought it out objectively. Kilo was a good liar, maybe even good enough to fool her, but a move against her at this point didn't compute. If someone wanted to remove her from Quentin's entourage, there had been ample opportunities to do so before they embarked for Earth. If someone wanted to uncover the secrets of Rosa's organization, it would be senseless to shake her trust now. Kilo could so easily have lured her into a habit of comfort with zem, making her much more vulnerable a few weeks or months hence. From any angle, she couldn't see what kind of larger game this trick might serve.

She wasn't arrogant enough to imagine that she could see all possibilities though, and she still had no idea how Hannah had been burned. She would have to test it. And their time together had given her the tools she needed. Kilo had given her power and trust that she could make use of, and ruin in the process. Another pin-scratch of regret scored her heart.

"I do work for someone," she said, "and I cannot afford to be soft at their expense. There is no world in which I take possession of this thing for you. Suppose we simply leave it here and walk out together?"

She was already sure Kilo would not take up that option. If

abandoning it somewhere was safe for zem, ze would have already done it. Ze held out zer hand. "I'll just take it back."

"You may have it back, if you pass my test."

"What test?"

Tempe closed her hand around the device. No going back now. "Strip, and get on the bed."

This had been a mistake. Kilo had known it from the moment Tempe seized the back of zer head. In zer mind was Teacher's voice, telling zem exactly where ze'd gone wrong. *Follow your instincts, except when you're afraid. When you're afraid, you follow your training.* Caine had rattled zem, and ze'd made a snap decision, and it had been a bad one.

Tempe stood like a pillar of marble at the side of the bed. Funny that Kilo had first thought of her for comfort—how nice it would be to get lost in her control after holding zemself together against Caine—and only then had the idea to use her to solve the larger problem. Tempe was not comforting now. Her cruelty had always been intimate, warm and breathing. Now she was cold and rigid.

Still Kilo obeyed, taking off zer clothes piece by piece. Ze didn't have a reason to give zemself; it was just easier in this moment to do what Tempe said. It had been a very long few days. Tempe's eyes, scanning over zer body, plainly saw the collage of bruises on zer chest and legs, but her expression did not change.

Kilo got back onto the bed, naked, and waited.

"Hands behind your back," said Tempe. "Do not move them, or this ends."

Kilo obeyed, and Tempe went to her bag, pulled something out, and came back to sit on the bed facing Kilo. In the same marble-smooth voice, she said, "This is work, not play. You won't like it, and you'll be left unsatisfied. Even if I decide I believe you, that's how it has to be."

Kilo knew she meant it, and still zer libido pricked alert at the coldness and promise of cruelty. No help for that. It faded a little when ze saw what Tempe held: a black glove with sharp hard points on each fingertip. They'd tried this toy exactly once.

"I said you wouldn't like it," Tempe said. "I am going to say some names, and you're going to tell me if you know them. Please keep your hands behind your back and your eyes on mine the whole time. Understood?"

Ze could leave. Even this battered, ze was fairly sure ze could take Tempe down in a fight. There was no reason to sit here and take this. Ze didn't move.

Tempe put on the glove and touched a fingertip to Kilo's knee. It made a sharp, bee-sting pain, irritatingly radiant and surface-level, not strong enough to fall into. Zer knee jumped, and ze fought the urge to shake in an effort to dislodge the prickling sting.

"Bai Junyi," said Tempe. Kilo, distracted by the sting, had forgotten the instructions. Tempe took hold of zer jaw. "A headshake will do, but I need a response to every name."

Her hand was so cool and so firm. Kilo longed for a different moment, one where she was touching zem for desire. Ze shook zer head. "Don't know it."

"Good." Her hand left Kilo's face. The bee-sting touch came

again on zer calf, and then again on zer ankle. With Tempe's fingers spread and Kilo fighting to keep zer eyes on her face, it was impossible to know where the next sting would land. "Octavia Martens." Ze shook zer head. "Marcel Dorne."

"No." Ze understood the purpose now. To lie well took focus. Tempe's aim wasn't torture, only distraction, enough to keep Kilo from quite being able to cover the recognition of a name. It might work. It was hard to keep zer head clear while waiting for the next sting to land or trying not to mind the last one.

It would have been an interesting test of zer skills, but in fact the names meant nothing to Kilo. "Azul. Derek Hammond. Arvense. Taillefer Quentin. Rosa Ortega. Brett Sangster. Acero. Hannah Roebuck." Her hand moved over Kilo's hips, arms, torso, stinging at irregular intervals, not allowing any rhythm to develop. Once the sting landed on a bruise, and the pain spread so broad and deep Kilo's eyes shut involuntarily. Tempe avoided the bruises after that. Kilo wished she wouldn't.

She started repeating the names, saying them in the same order once, then changing the sequence. It would have been difficult to preserve the lie, to keep the negation at the same tone every time, to keep from showing any change in tension as ze anticipated one particular name coming up. For once, ze was just as glad to be telling the truth.

By the fifth repetition, it was impossible to stay still. The roaming stings would not let zem rest, would not let zem find an edge to cope. Ze twisted and squirmed away from each touch, and still Tempe looked steadily into zer eyes and repeated the names, watching for a slip. Then the stings started to move up zer inner thigh. Not random anymore, they moved in a steady line, closer and closer to Kilo's groin.

Even in play, even in gentle and soft moments, Kilo rarely let anyone touch zer genitals. Tempe knew this. She wouldn't; would she? Was this testing or punishment? The stinging finger moved closer, and Kilo stopped breathing. She must know that this would be unforgivable. Her eyes, clear and grey, rested unflinchingly on Kilo's. She did know.

The next touch landed so near that the sting crackled out onto the skin of zer sack. "Tempe!" Kilo cried out.

Tempe lifted her hand at once. "All right," she said, peeling off the glove and laying it aside. Kilo fought to breathe steadily, to keep from trembling. She cupped zer shoulders, warm now. "Give me your hands."

Ze unlaced zer fingers and brought them out from behind zer back. Tempe ran her hands down zer arms and up again, bracing, soothing. "I won't ask forgiveness," she said.

"Fuck you," Kilo answered, perilously near tears. Ze should have held out, waited to see whether Tempe would really cross that line. Ze knew how to wash unwanted touch off zer skin. But if she'd done it, that would have killed anything they might still have. It turned out Kilo couldn't bear that. And now ze'd never know whether Tempe could.

Ze bit zer lips around the urge to ask. A child's impulse, asking for reassurance as if words could be believed. But ze didn't fight it when Tempe pulled zem like a child into her arms. Her blouse was soft against Kilo's skin, thin enough to feel her warmth through it. She cupped Kilo's head against her shoulder.

"I... exceeded the bounds of what my work demanded," said Tempe, which struck Kilo as extremely funny. Ze gave a spluttering half-cough, half-laugh and felt Tempe's head move as if to look into zer face. "I won't ask forgiveness," she said again, "but I... acknowledge it. At the end, I was acting from personal impulses."

"No shit." It was funny that she thought that needed to be said. Even funnier that she seemed troubled by it, as if she'd thought she should be able to perfectly divide herself into the agent and the lover. That little bit of shame was a balm to Kilo's own regret. "So I've got your number now. You care about me, at least enough to find out whether I care."

"Mm. It would be easier if I didn't."

Kilo laughed again and burrowed deeper in her arms. "Is that what you people do on Eudoxia? Try to be a perfect working machine with no attachments?"

"No. That didn't come from Eudoxia."

She didn't offer to say where it did come from, and Kilo wasn't going to ask just for the fun of hearing a refusal. "What would you have done to me? If I'd failed your test?"

Tempe's fingers curled around zer shoulder. "If I'd thought about that ahead of time, I might not have been able to give my full concentration to the test."

Kilo was learning more about Tempe in these few minutes than in their weeks of fucking on the ship. "You're more dangerous than I thought."

"Yes."

No wonder ze had been so instantly, powerfully drawn to

her. Already zer body was humming, turning the hated stinging and real fear into their own kind of gratification. It was zer own weakness, but unlike Tempe, ze wasn't troubled by it.

It did, however, make zem think of the last person who'd given zem this particular thrill. "Don't ever try to recruit me for your work."

It was Tempe's turn to laugh. "I truly would not dream of it." Then she shifted suddenly, as if she'd thought of something. "Although—"

"I mean it," Kilo said sharply. "If you wanted to hire me for a contract job, maybe, but we've got to be clear that I work for myself." Ze didn't think Tempe would try to entrap zem as Caine had—but then ze hadn't seen it coming from Caine either.

"We had better avoid mixing work and play in future, I think. But there is something I've been trying to find out without success. Does the name Tommy B mean anything to you?"

You never got anywhere being too helpful too quickly. "There's lots of Tommys in Eastport. Lots of B-somethings too."

"I'm aware," Tempe said dryly. "The person said it as if I'd be expected to understand it, but it's not a name in any of our mutual acquaintance. I thought it might be someone familiar in the Eastport underground."

"Didn't they know you're new in town?"

"Time was short. Are you probing, sweetheart?" There was no menace in her voice, but there was a definite warning. Kilo twisted to bat zer eyes at her.

"Can't help being curious. Was it a person they were saying, or a place?"

"It could have been a place."

"It was. It'll be in your tourist guide as the Thomas Alexander Fontaine Memorial Arcade. Lanes A through G, but if you didn't get a stall number I guess you'll just have to wander lane B."

There was a little satisfied easing in Tempe's expression. Probably she had gotten a stall number. Kilo grinned. "It's fine if you don't want to tell me. I would never probe. Stalls on the main floor change up all the time anyway. If there's something particular you'd better go soon." Ze traced a circle on Tempe's wrist. "And if someone tries to send you downstairs, think twice and keep sharp. Main floor stays pretty clean but there's all kinds of business underneath. Your tourist guide won't tell you that either."

"Much obliged."

She held zem a little longer in silence, then stood up. "Stay behind at least five minutes. Do not follow me out. Agreed?"

"Don't suppose you've changed your mind about taking the token along."

Tempe didn't bother to respond. The token sat visible on the bedside table, and she still checked all her pockets very carefully as she put her coat back on.

Kilo couldn't help asking. "Is this it for you and me?"

Tempe's stillness was like a tree's now, not a statue's. The folds of her coat stirred ever so slightly as she took a breath in and out. "If I decide it's not, you'll hear from me."

Chapter Seven

Vi knew something was wrong the minute she woke up, although it took her brain a few more minutes to catch up to why. There were voices in the kitchen, and one of them was Dusty's. It was bright daylight; Dusty should be in the bar kitchen. He was almost never upstairs in the daytime.

She liked to take her time getting up, but once she realized what she was hearing she rolled out of bed, tugging on a T-shirt as she left her room.

All three of them were there at the kitchen table, Dusty, Roman, and Nana, holding mugs of coffee and looking up at her with grim faces. Nana stood as soon as she appeared and went to the coffee maker.

"What happened?" she asked.

"The bar's closed," said Dusty.

"What do you mean closed?"

"City shutdown for unpaid rent. Went down this morning and saw the notice. Front door is deadlocked."

"Bullshit."

"Go on down and check."

"I didn't mean you." If Dusty said it then it was true. Vi ran her fingers through her hair, which was still sticking up every which way. A shutdown this fast?

"You did pay the rent last quarter?" asked Roman.

"Yes!" She tapped into her wristband and projected it onto the table-center screen. "Go look in my city records. No other delinquencies this year. No notices." But when she opened up the bar's city account, the first thing she saw was a brand-new notice: This establishment is under a temporary closure until overdue payment is received...

Roman scrolled through the account history. "Okay," he said after a minute. "How often do they do a full shutdown after one overdue payment?"

"Never. Why would they, when they can just collect late fees? What good does it do them to have me shut down?"

Roman nodded. "So someone's got a lot of pull."

Nana came to Vi with a steaming mug and pressed it into her hands. Once Vi had taken it, she wrapped her hands around Vi's, warm from the mug, holding them tight.

"It'll be okay, Nana," Vi said. "I'm sure it's just a mistake. I'll get it sorted out." She darted a warning glance to Roman.

Nana attempted to smooth down Vi's hair, and then signed, "Be careful."

"I will. Don't you worry about a thing."

She had to repeat her reassurances when Luce and Arthur showed up for work. Luce immediately started peppering Vi with questions about what she was going to do, what Luce could do, who was responsible. Arthur looked like he was on the verge of tears.

"I'm getting it sorted out," Vi repeated firmly. She was as worried about Luce going off and storming City Hall as she was about Arthur having a breakdown. "Meanwhile we're going to take this chance to do a serious cleanup."

"We still have a job?" Arthur asked.

"Did I say you didn't? This is temporary. We'll be back in business as soon as I get the payment in. And for the next couple days you two will have plenty to do to scrub and polish every inch of this place. If you run out of things to clean, there's the wobbly chairs to fix, and Dusty may need help dealing with the perishables." She said it firmly, as if this had been her plan all along, and it worked on Arthur. Luce was still mad and worried, so Vi put her in charge of working out the cleanup plan with Dusty. The key to a wound-up Luce was aiming her in a useful direction.

With the staff settled, Vi went back to the office and shut the door. There was no one left to reassure, which left her stuck with the grim reality: she had no good way out of this. There was no safe, sure way to raise the money she'd need, especially with late fees stacking up every day. She needed a big chunk of money and she needed it fast.

She saw the day looming closer, the one where she'd have to sell her independence to keep going. Someone was trying to get her there faster. The Travs? The Fontaines? This Brett Sangster or someone behind him? She pulled open her desk drawer and stared at the slim navy-blue chip lying there. She should have Roman look into the offer and Sangster. She'd have to, if it came down to a choice of taking his loan or taking help from the Fontaines. But not yet. She still had one move she could make on her own.

She stepped back out into the hall and heard Luce and Arthur chattering and busy, unlikely to come disturb her for the moment. Then she locked the office door and pushed up the ceiling tile in the corner where Daly had hidden his contraband.

It was all still there. Five rolls of metal coins, heavy and solid in her hand. They were wrapped in sleeves of stiff paper, varying in height and width, slightly uneven as coins of different sizes had been rolled together. She could see the first and last coin in every roll, some of them still showing the original stamped design and some worn smooth over the centuries since they'd been minted. The values they'd originally had were meaningless; the underside had its own system of assigning value to the different sizes and metals. She did know that the cheapest coins ran around 5k each, and even if one of these rolls was the cheapest kind, the others weren't. Each roll had to hold at least 100k, maybe a lot more.

Daly must have been well and truly fucked to leave the city without even taking the time to change these for legit money. Or maybe he just didn't know anyone he could trust to change them on short notice. That was Vi's problem too. She'd be happy to have them off her hands, but getting caught carrying or selling this much coin would put her on the hook for involvement in smuggling. It had never been worth the risk before. Now she figured it was, if she could find somewhere to sell them.

Rebecca would know, and it was tempting to go straight to her. But to go to Rebecca was to go to the Fontaines. Even if they weren't the ones fucking with Vi now, if she went to one of their people, they'd have it on her forever. Next time they needed a favor from a respectable bar owner, they'd have the evidence of Vi changing several rolls of coin to back up their request.

She put the coins into the one desk drawer that locked, then went to the kitchen. Dusty was alone in there for the moment—Bella had a sick kid at home and hadn't been sorry to take a couple days off. Even as Vi was planning to get everything on track, she'd made the mental calculation: with Bella staying home she could stretch Luce and Arthur's payroll that much further if worst came to worst.

"Does Roman know about what Daly left in the office?" she asked when the kitchen door was closed behind her.

Dusty stopped in the middle of cubing a cut of beef. "I didn't tell him. You said forget I'd seen it."

"Yeah, I know. I'm thinking it's time to remember."

Dusty resumed his chopping and didn't speak again until he'd slid the cubes into a bowl. "I can't think of any better ways." He didn't sound happy about it, but there wasn't much to be happy about. "Will it be enough?"

"Yeah. Some left over too. If I can sell it. That's why I asked about Roman."

"I don't know as he'd know where to go. Ten years ago he might've, but the scene's changed since then."

"Yeah." Anyone changing coin ten years ago would have moved or died or changed allegiances by now.

"No harm asking him."

Vi shook her head. "I don't want to involve him if I can help it. Especially if he doesn't know already. You just keep on forgetting you've seen it, and we'll leave it at that."

Dusty washed his hands and turned to her. "Vi. What's happening... I'm worried it'll get worse."

"And what am I supposed to do about that?" Vi snapped. "Can't see the future. I just have to take shit as it comes." She was pissed because she shared his worry, and she knew he knew it.

"I just think you should have someone watching your back."

"That's what I need you for. Watch out for the bar and for Nana."

"I said *your* back."

"I'll be fine. Never gone down yet without getting back up."

Dusty looked like he was preparing another argument, but Luce came through the swinging kitchen door just then, and Vi took the opportunity to slip back out.

Vi was hauling things around in the storeroom, mostly because she needed to put her muscles to work or explode from frustration, when Luce came in. "Hey boss. That person's lurking out front."

For some reason the first person Vi thought of was the oily golden-haired Sangster. She'd been imagining throwing fists at a lot of people, but his was the only known face. "What person?"

"Your friend." Vi's heart skipped a beat before Luce continued. "The slinky one with a grin like a knife."

"Oh." Heat bloomed treacherously in the pit of her stomach. "It must be late." Kilo usually didn't come around until after dark.

"I was thinking maybe we could break for dinner soon."

Vi grunted and followed Luce out to the front, where she could see Kilo's shoulder leaned up against the glass outside.

"Arthur, Luce, call it a day. We can pick it back up tomorrow." She stalked up to the glass and knocked sharply on it. Kilo turned and grinned. Ze pointed to the door, made a twisting motion with zer hand, and raised zer eyebrows. Vi quickly sliced a hand across her throat. She didn't know if Kilo could really open a city deadlock and didn't want to find out. And what was ze doing lurking here where it'd draw her staff's attention? She jerked her head toward the back. Kilo's eyelids lowered slowly, like a self-satisfied cat's, before straightening up and slinking off out of view.

Arthur wanted to hover and ask questions about what would happen next and how long they'd be shut down, but Luce bustled him out the back. Vi tried not to think about how much of Luce's hurry was because she knew what Kilo usually came by for.

It was the usual thing this time, too. Kilo emerged from the shadows once Luce and Arthur had turned out of the alley. Vi stayed in the office doorway.

"Does this mean I can come in?" ze asked. "Or am I still demoted to alley fucks?"

"Since when did you ask?" Vi said, backing up from the door.

Kilo sprang lightly up the steps and slipped inside.

"You almost look like you're happy to see me."

Happy wasn't the word for it, but she pulled Kilo to her with hunger. This was what she needed, something nasty and simple. Kilo was sharp and wicked in her arms, clawing down her back, biting at her lips. Hot and easy and fierce.

There was a moment of pause when she pulled Kilo's shirt off and saw a patchwork of brown and purple bruises over zer ribs. She stared, a surge of furious protectiveness welling in her chest. Then Kilo slapped her across the face, light but stinging.

"Focus up, barkeep. That's not your business."

She caught Kilo's wrists and pinned them up against the wall. "Better watch your hands."

"Better do something to keep me busy."

She kept her strap in a drawer in the office; this was where she got the most use out of it. She bent Kilo over the sofa and fucked zem until they were both jelly-legged and spent. At the end, panting, she kissed the sweat off zer neck, nosed at zer damp hair, felt zer heartbeat fluttering under her hand.

Kilo murmured something that sounded like "Reliable barkeep," but refused to repeat it. Vi pulled out, not too gently, and went to get a towel out of the toy drawer. Next to the towels was the little bowl of candies Kilo had always liked to suck on after fucking. After taking off the strap, Vi fished one out and tossed it to Kilo.

Ze caught it and flipped over on the sofa. "You kept these, I'm touched."

"Forgot about them."

Kilo grinned. The sour-sweet smell hit Vi's nose from halfway across the room. Ze popped the candy into zer mouth and wriggled zer bare shoulders down into the sofa cushions. "How long was I away before you put them in a drawer for safekeeping?"

Six weeks; long enough that she'd gotten upset seeing them lying out, not so long that she'd given up on Kilo ever coming back. "Luce probably did it."

"Didn't know you let Luce look in your toy drawer. Or did you start fucking her while I was away?"

"None of your business." She spread the towel over the other end of the couch and sat down. Kilo immediately dug zer toes under her thigh.

"Cold," ze said, with an unapologetic grin.

"Bullshit, it's hot as fuck in here." She closed her hand around Kilo's ankle, playing with the slide of skin over bone and tendon. For a few minutes there was only the sound of the candy clacking against Kilo's teeth.

Somewhere in the stretch of silence, Vi made a decision. "If someone was looking to change some coins, where would they go?"

Kilo sat up at once, languid gaze sharpening. "Barkeep! Where did you get your virtuous hands on coin?"

"Didn't say it was me."

"It better be. If I give you a name, it's not for some stranger to use."

Of course there wasn't a way around it. "I found them. Wasn't ever gonna use them. Now I don't see a better choice."

"Not an honest soul to help you out? Not even that cop who drinks here?"

Vi bit her tongue in time to stop from asking how Kilo knew about Officer Daniel. "I don't know what you're talking about."

"You can't lie for shit. Better work on that if you're going to dip into the underside."

"I'm not. If I was, I'd sell them to one of the gangs. I just want to get them off my hands and get enough to re-open my bar."

"Okay. Let's see 'em."

Vi snorted. "I'm honest, not stupid."

Kilo's laugh sounded bizarrely pleased. "Barkeep does learn. But how much coin we talking?"

"It's in rolls."

"Rolls, plural?" Kilo whistled. "Then you want to see Norma. Hooker would do as well, but you'd hate talking to him. Norma's all business."

Vi put on her tank top and sat down in the desk chair. "Great, a name's really helpful. I just go down to the weeds and shout for Norma until someone answers."

Kilo stood up, still naked, and straddled Vi's lap. "So rude, and I'm just trying to help." Ze stroked the sides of Vi's face. "I'd be hurt if I didn't know how much it kills you to even be asking me. Norma sees customers on Thursday and Friday afternoons at Tommy Q17. Other days in other places too, but that's the one you could get into. Don't take her first offer, but if she comes up by more than ten percent, take it." Ze touched Vi's nose. "Try not to look too above it all. She might not be as understanding as me."

Vi hadn't meant to grab hold of Kilo's hips, and didn't realize she had until ze made a little suggestive grind. "Put your clothes back on. We're done for tonight."

"I was just wondering when I started fucking mainly topsiders. You're the second person this week I've sent to the Tommy on shady business."

Kilo had mostly given up mentioning other lovers since ze realized Vi wasn't going to get jealous. It was important to keep that up. "What's the other one look like? I'll warn them if I see them."

Kilo laughed. "I'd love to see how she handles you. She looks like a schoolteacher but she's wonderfully cruel."

Something about the way zer voice warmed did spark a little jealous flare in Vi's gut. She grunted. "I'll leave you to it then. Norma, Q17?"

"Southeast elevator's the closest. Buy me something nice to thank me. Barkeep's first underside deal, I'm so proud." Ze managed a darting kiss before Vi shoved zem off her lap.

The Thomas Alexander Fontaine Memorial Arcade was a roofed shopping center occupying several blocks in the lower downtown. According to tourist guides, which Tempe had consulted after speaking with Kilo, it was a destination recommended for "the traveler prepared to rub elbows with a broad segment of Eastport society." The rubbing elbows was literal: every lane of shops was full of people moving like a muddy stream, with eddies and convergences and the occasional large obstruction when a shop's wares were attractive enough to bring a mass of people to a standstill. The shops were simple stalls, some bearing a sign overhead to give some indication of their contents, some relying only on word of mouth or line of sight. Some of the stalls appeared to be little more than a rummage sale, a collection of whatever secondhand goods the proprietor had managed to get their hands on. Others offered handmade wares or particular services. Knowing how fundamental smuggling was to Eastport's economy, Tempe wondered how many of the goods sold were strictly legal.

The stall at B23 bore a crooked sign advertising wristband upgrades. The shopkeeper clocked Tempe's before looking at her face. "Excellent prices on trade-ins!" he said brightly. "Money in minutes, several forms of payout available."

"I'm not looking to trade in my band," she said. "I'm looking for a friend."

He took the disappointment in stride. "Your friend got a name?"

"Albert," she answered.

"Maybe you'd like to come in back and see our high-grade samples." Without waiting for an answer, he moved to the curtain hanging over the back of the store and slid open the metal grate behind it.

"Thank you," she said. She did not step all the way through until her eyes had adjusted enough to see the shelves lining the room, the rear door, and the single man sitting on a folding chair inside. It was indeed the server from the party. She stepped in and heard the metal grate close behind her.

A second folding chair was waiting for her. Sitting in it placed her knees a few inches from the server's.

"To start with, Hannah told me your code name. What is it?" he said.

"Let's not start there," Tempe said. "If she told you mine, she must have told you hers. You tell me mine, and I'll tell you Hannah's. Will that do?"

He thought it over for a second and then nodded. "Fair enough. You're supposed to be Acero."

"I am. And she was Azul."

"Was?"

That was Tempe's own bad habit. "I hope she still is. The last message I received from her was several weeks ago."

"Yeah. She disappeared around then. I have the stuff I told her, and one more thing I didn't get to pass on yet. I'll give you all of it if you'll get me out of here."

"I'm willing to help, but I don't have any connections yet. Do you know why she had to disappear?"

He shook his head. "I hadn't even busted into the— I hadn't done the last thing she asked me to do yet. And I don't think anyone was onto me for a while after that. I wasn't her only dance partner, figured it was something to do with one of the others."

He was speaking naturally, neither avoiding eye contact nor forcing it. He seemed anxious about his situation but not about her, or whether she believed him. Provisionally, she accepted the statement as likely true.

"Then I can't rely on any of the people she sent me. How can

I help you?"

"All I need is money on a card. I can find my own way out."

"If you leave town, you're no good to me."

"If they snuff me I'm no good to you either, am I? I'm not doing any more jobs, for you or her or anyone. All I've got is information and you can have it all, once I've got enough cash to skip. You don't need me to testify or any of that bull, the stuff will be proof enough. And I couldn't give you the whole formula if I wanted to; that died with Stephen."

She was trying not to give away the extent of her own ignorance. What did she know? He had broken into some place as part of the job. There was a thing or things remarkable enough to be proof of something. And the mention of a formula. "Stephen was the one who developed it?"

"Yeah. I guess Hannah didn't give you his name."

"She didn't give any names. Including yours."

"Yeah, yours neither, she just said someone who was coming with the Eudoxian bunch. And one time she slipped and said she, so I knew it was you or that other lady."

"I'm Tempe. Professor Temperance Carroll." She held out a hand.

The rhythms of courtesy were easy to fall into. He took her hand. "Joe Melnick."

Joe. There it was. "Money isn't a problem, Joe, but I'll need to be sure of getting what I need. You were Stephen's assistant?"

"Yeah. He and I worked on it alone; maybe some of the others guessed but no one knows for sure. She said she didn't need the how it was made, just the what and where to find it. She said that'd be enough."

Not a simple matter of intellectual property theft, or the critical questions would have been when and for whom. "Had she seen it herself?" she tried.

"Nah. She was trying to get a look at the boss's coat, but she hadn't found a good way. She took my word for it, though. It's as good as the original, or Stephen wouldn't have been satisfied."

There was a note in his voice, confidence and pride and warmth, that led her to her next stab in the dark. "You worked under Stephen for a long time."

His lips tightened. "Would have been six years this winter. She promised she'd make the boss pay. You still gonna do that?"

Odds were good that the boss meant Brett Sangster. "I aim to, if I can get your help."

He shrugged. "Stephen was good to me, and he shouldn't have gotten axed just for doing what the boss asked him to. I want his hide for that. But not as bad as I want to save my own. Stephen would've agreed with me." He smiled wryly. "Or if he wouldn't, fuck 'im."

"Fair enough. So I give you the money, and you give me..."

"Where he's keeping it at. Like I said, I found it a little while after Hannah disappeared. Been waiting on you to show up."

From out front there was a scuffing of feet on the floor, four distinct sweeping sounds. Joe's head snapped up. "That's the sign, guns on the prowl. They know I'm here, they just don't know what room. You want your info you'd better come through quick. Downstairs, unit P36. I want two cards, 10k each."

He was out the rear door before she had time to negotiate.

Chapter Eight

Tripp had been working for the Travs going on four years. His mom had made his big brother promise not to let Tripp get involved in any of the gangs, but they were both gone now and Tripp hadn't made any promises to anyone. Working for the Travs wasn't like she'd made it sound anyway. Most days Tripp didn't do anything but stand guard at the main house, looking sharp when the boss came by and sometimes chasing down a stray noise that always turned out to be a dog or a raccoon. On nice afternoons the old man would roll out to the courtyard and Tripp would sit with him and play cards. Not the hard-knuckle bloody life his mom had feared. Sometimes he wished he could see more action, but then he thought of her, guiltily, and decided it was alright to stay at the main house as long as the boss wanted to keep him there.

He liked going on depot runs. It was a chance to get off the compound and have a smoke and a drink while the clerk fetched their shipment out of the back. He especially liked going on depot runs with Alonzo, who sometimes worked the compound and sometimes dogged the boss, and usually had good gossip.

"You should've seen that punk Andrew, swinging his dick around like it was too big for his pants," said Alonzo, picking up the story he'd begun on the way over. "He even tried to give me an order, me standing right there at the boss's shoulder. I thought the boss was going to deck him."

"He should've," said Tripp. One of his big fears was getting promoted off the compound and onto Andrew's guard duty. He'd do whatever job he was given, because that was how you stayed comfortable and alive, but if a knife was headed for Andrew's throat he'd be sorely tempted to just let it find its target.

"Not in front of company. Especially not that Sangster. Talk about swinging dicks. That guy—"

Alonzo shut his mouth as a man walked in the door. Tripp sized him up automatically: older middle age, normal clothes, coming alone. Probably some kind of shopkeeper. The clerk came out of the back room and greeted him by name, then said to them, "This man's goods are on ice, I'll get them first if you boys don't mind waiting a little longer."

Tripp and Alonzo both shrugged, and the clerk gave a little half-bowing nod and returned to the back. "New clerk?" said Alonzo.

"I guess so." Tripp hadn't really registered it. "She was here when I came on Friday too. They change around sometimes."

"She's kinda slow."

"Doesn't bother me any."

"Nah, I guess not." Slow meant more time to sit back and shoot the shit.

The clerk came out with a single box on a dolly and signed it over to the new customer. "It'll just be a couple more minutes," she said to Tripp and Alonzo.

"Take your time," said Alonzo. As the clerk disappeared into the back, he said, "I miss the girl that was here a couple months ago. She was a looker."

Tripp's taste didn't run to pretty girls, so he shrugged. "What was it about that Sangster?"

"Ah." Alonzo grimaced. "Probably shouldn't talk about it." He liked to do this, liked to play coy just when he was getting to the good stuff.

"No one here but you and me," said Tripp. "You know I don't talk."

Alonzo shook his head. "No details, but he's giving orders like he's at the Grand Hotel. He's got the guys out delivering messages and picking up packages for him, okay, but now the package has to be dropped off at a specific place at a time he'll be good enough to tell us later, and never mind if it means the boss has to cross another professional."

In the language of the underside, a package was usually a person, dead or alive, while any kind of smuggling handoff was discussed in terms of meeting a friend. "What kind of package?" Tripp asked, leaning closer.

"The kind that stays where you put it. My point is, there's favors and there's orders, and if it's still favors the boss is doing for that Sangster, the man better have saved his firstborn kid or something."

"Why doesn't he tell him to jump in the river?"

"That's what I'd like to know. He ever come to the main house?"

"That Sangster?"

"Yeah."

"Just the one time, couple months ago. You were there." Most of the Travs had been there, with the slick Heights man the only outsider. No one Tripp talked to knew what had been said in the family meeting, but common opinion was that the boss hadn't been happy with the outcome.

Alonzo grunted. "I was wondering if he'd been cozying up to the old man."

"Not him. Andrew comes around a lot, though." It didn't take any special kind of brain to see that Andrew thought he should be running the Travs instead of his cousin.

"They play cards?"

"Yeah."

"Who wins?"

"The old man." He almost always did, whoever was playing. Tripp had beaten him exactly once, and the old man had been even more pleased about it than Tripp had. Junior beat him less than half the time. Andrew never had, that Tripp had seen.

"That's something at least."

Tripp wanted to ask more, but another man walked in. It was probably time to get back anyway. Alonzo looked back toward the counter. "Where's that clerk gotten to?"

He had to rap on the counter, and she emerged from the back looking harried. "Sorry, boys. One of the dollies giving me trouble. I've got your shipment."

There was a steady run of other customers after the two Trav guns left, keeping Wendy Liu the depot clerk busy for the next hour and change. Wendy was a floater, licensed but not assigned to any one depot, filling in as needed. She'd been working depots here and there for years, not very consistently but enough that her credentials checked out to anyone inclined to go digging. She was one of Kilo's most useful aliases.

When the depot was finally empty again, ze assumed the clerk's usual bored slump and turned over the day's haul. A lot of promising information from the two chatty guns. Ze'd been wondering if Cousin Andrew wasn't zer best bet after all—as pissed as he'd been, no doubt he'd be happy to accept the token, and maybe he'd keep Junior too busy fighting for his spot to waste effort on making an example of Kilo. But the name Sangster had pricked zer ears. That was one of the names Tempe had spoken while her claws roved Kilo's body. Ze didn't know whether he was an ally or an enemy to Tempe, but from the sound of it he was both to Junior.

Better than fueling an internal Trav battle would be getting the token back to Junior in a way so favorable to him that he'd have no interest in looking deeper. And if ze could fuck over this Sangster in the process, ze'd either be helping Tempe out or getting payback on her... appealing either way. Kilo sunk Wendy Liu's chin into her hands so ze wouldn't have to manage zer smile for a minute. This could get interesting.

Everyone knew the Tommy Arcade had an underground, but regular topside citizens didn't venture there unless they were desperate. Vi had planned on never being that desperate. It felt like a bad dream, standing by the southeast elevator with rolls of coin burning in her pocket.

She'd worn a line in the floor going back and forth trying to decide whether to bring all the coin or just some of it. If she brought it all and something went wrong, that was it and she was fucked. But what if she only brought a couple of rolls and they turned out to be worth less than she thought? She'd have to come back, have to stand for a second time in the shadow of the elevator bank, looking over her shoulder every other second. In the end she'd brought them all. It would be a relief to have them gone from her office.

No one else rode the elevator down with her. It went a single level then stopped, letting her out in a narrow hallway with a sickly greenish light. The underground wasn't laid out in rows like the upper level, there were a lot more turns and corners. People coming down here didn't want clear lines of sight. She heard footsteps from other halls a few times but didn't see anybody.

Q17 stood in the middle of a hallway, third of four doors in its wall. Nothing except the numbers to indicate who or what was inside, and most of the doors were shut tight. Q17 itself was a little ajar. Vi knocked softly, trying not to push the door further open.

She didn't know the protocol, but she wasn't going to waltz in first thing. Getting no answer, she knocked harder, and the door creaked an inch inward under her knuckles. Still no answer. Fuck it. She pushed the door open.

It was a small square windowless room, with two chairs and a small folding table. A shelf against the back wall, mostly empty. No furniture big enough to hide a person. Which meant the only one in the room was the body on the floor.

The body was sprawled on its stomach, face turned toward the door, eyes half-open and lightless. Vi knew what death looked like, but she still had to check. She took two steps in and touched the splayed hand. Cold. On the head she could see what looked like the edge of a bloody mess, and she didn't feel the need to look closer. She was no detective.

This didn't look like a Norma, although Kilo hadn't given any description. It looked like a man, maybe in his twenties, with light brown hair. The hand Vi touched was missing two fingers, long-healed stumps where the ring and little finger would be. Maybe another prospective client that had somehow offended Norma and gotten clubbed before she fled. Didn't matter. Wasn't Vi's business. She got up and turned to the door.

A cop puppet stood in the doorway, filling nearly the whole space with its shining bulk. There was no chance of getting past and no way she could outrun it if she did. She gritted her teeth against the urge to protest innocence before she'd even been accused. It never helped to overexplain to a cop.

"Name and citizenship," said the cop flatly.

"Victoria Ferreira. Eastport citizen." What were the chances of it being a coincidence, a cop here just in time to catch her with a corpse?

"Citizen Ferreira, you're under arrest."

"I just got here. I found him like this. I don't even know who he is."

"What is your business here?"

The rolls of coin were heavy in her pocket. If the cop searched her she'd get taken in just for having them.

"Meeting a friend."

"Friend's name?"

Nothing about her situation would improve by dragging the mysterious Norma into it. She spun her brain trying to come up with another name.

"Temperance Carroll, citizen of Eudoxia." The voice came from the hallway, and Vi would have known it even if she didn't know the name. What the hell was *she* doing here?

The cop seemed just as surprised. He stood stock still for a full count of ten before saying, "Eudoxia. Don't hear that one much."

"Please do scan my ID." Tempe's voice was cool, unbothered. The cop turned halfway and extended his scanner hand. Tempe lifted her wrist to meet it. After a silent moment, she spoke again. "Citizen Ferreira and I arranged to meet here privately. If you are taking her in for questioning, I must insist on coming as well. And naturally I will want to speak to the chief on duty."

The cop was silent. Whoever was driving it had to be thinking furiously. Eudoxia was full of very wealthy people, and a lot of them had interests in various Earth governments. Treating an Eastport citizen high-handedly was one thing, but meddling with the wrong citizen of Eudoxia could have deep consequences. "Citizen Ferreira was caught kneeling over a dead body."

"I saw her in the hallway only a few minutes ago. I expect if you investigate the scene, you'll find the body has been here longer than that."

There was a lengthy pause. Finally the cop turned back to Vi. "ID."

Vi held up her wristband. If he wanted to scan her now, that meant he wasn't planning to take her in right away—at least she could get away and get the damned coins off her. He scanned it, then stepped into the room. "Don't leave town until we've decided if we want you for questioning."

"I wasn't planning on it," Vi answered shortly.

Tempe appeared in the doorway once the cop had vacated it. "Then I take it we are free to go."

"For now," said the cop. He stood looking down at the body like he didn't know what to do with it.

"Is there anything else you need to do here?" Tempe said quietly to Vi. Vi, stupefied, shook her head and followed Tempe out.

Vi couldn't find her tongue until she was in the elevator with Tempe, riding back up to the arcade's main floor. "What are you doing here?"

"Business." Tempe's expression was blank as she looked at

Vi, whatever she was thinking or feeling tucked deep away. "Who did you really go to meet?"

"Someone who could help me get some quick cash."

"Was it the corpse?"

"It was supposed to be a woman. I guess maybe she killed him and ran."

"No. She didn't." The elevator came to a stop. "This is interesting. I'd like to hear more. I have one more stop to make here; will you wait for me and then give me a few minutes to talk in private?"

"Of course." She followed Tempe into the B lane of the arcade and stood just out of earshot while Tempe talked to a guy at a stall. They didn't talk long. Tempe laid a card on the counter and received something small in exchange, then she returned to Vi.

"A private car, I think, if that suits you," said Tempe.

"Sure." Vi led the way out of the arcade to the nearest cabstand, where people were piling into a public car. Tempe tapped the scanner to call a private one.

"You've figured out your way around pretty well," Vi said. All the curiosity she'd learned to tamp down was bubbling up. What had Tempe had gotten from the guy at the stall? Why had she been in the Tommy underground? Why had she stepped in to help Vi? It was usually safer not to know things, but with Tempe here she was having trouble remembering that.

The private car rolled up on the track and stopped in front of them. Vi followed Tempe in and sat on the bench opposite her. "You pick the destination," Tempe said. "Anywhere it will take a little while to get to."

Vi put in an address that would take them up toward High Street. While she was entering it, Tempe pulled a small dome-shaped device out of her bag. She set it on the floor between them and pressed a button on top. The air took on a thick, unnaturally silent quality. "I'd rather talk in a bubble, to be safe."

Vi had heard of this kind of device but had never seen one in use. "No one can hear us?" Her voice sounded strange, ringing louder in her head than outside it. Tempe's sounded hollow, as if it was coming from a distance, but every word was clear.

"No one, including recording devices."

"Handy."

The car jerked into motion, and the window screens showed Eastport sliding by. "Do you mind if I change the view as well?" Tempe asked. "I don't like false windows."

Vi shrugged, and Tempe scanned through the view options until the large screens around the cab showed them driving along a sunny beach. "That's even more false," said Vi.

Tempe smiled. "Always prefer the obvious lie. It reduces cognitive strain. So you didn't recognize the dead man?"

"No."

"Did Hannah ever come to your bar with another person?"

"Hannah? No, she always came alone. What does this have to do with her?"

"I'm trying to understand that. What's interesting is that that corpse was only moved into that room about half an hour before you got there."

"How do you know?"

"I followed it. They moved him there from a different room on the same level. I thought that was strange, so I waited to see what would happen next. Your appearance was nearly the last thing I expected."

"I'd never been there before. Just my luck to find a dead body my first time underground."

"Do you think it was luck?"

Vi twisted her fingers together, staring at the little white dome on the floor. "Sure. Someone puts a body in the room I'm headed for, and then a cop happens to be right around the corner to nab me for it. That's the kind of luck you get when someone who holds strings is pissed at you. Only I don't know who it could be or why." She met Tempe's eyes. "And you being there. Was that luck too?"

"What do you suspect?"

"I don't know." She ducked her head, ran her hands through her hair. "The thing is, there's only one person in the city I can think of who's got a real reason to hate me." She hadn't wanted to think about this. Hadn't let herself wonder if it really had been coincidence, Tempe showing up the same night the cop did. Thinking about it now felt like bands of iron were closing around her chest. She pushed the rest of the words out in a rush. "So if you're working some kind of revenge plot, you're doing a good job, and I can't complain. I won't fight it either. Only I hope maybe you could let the rest of my people off the hook. And I hope we can end it now, however you want. I'm fucking tired."

"Vi. I promised you once never to lie to you."

"Yeah. I remember." Vi had made promises too.

"I keep that promise for me, not for you. It is important, for me, to have someone I've never lied to."

"Okay."

"If I intended to hurt you, I would tell you. To do anything else would be... erosive. I can't afford it." She gave a thin smile. "I have hated you. I have never considered taking revenge on you. Whatever is happening to you, I have no knowledge of it beyond what I've seen today."

Vi's lungs let go of all their air at once. "Okay. That's good. That's good."

"It is possible, though, that our problems are connected. Will you tell me more about yours?"

Vi told her everything, from the cop's unexpected audit to the present. She left the names of people out, populating her story with "friends" and nameless descriptions. When she was finished, she saw Tempe turning the pieces over in her mind.

"That loan offer. You didn't think of taking it instead of coming here?"

"I don't trust it. And the more desperate I get, the less I trust it."

"Could I know the name of the man who made the offer?"

"It was Sangster. Brad or Brent or something."

Tempe leaned back against the seat. "I've heard of him. And the singer? Vaughan Riley, perhaps?"

"Yeah. How come you've heard of him?"

"He has intersolar ambitions." She was tapping her fingertips against her thumbs in a steady sequence; a habit she'd always had when thinking hard. "He's been acquiring talent in a number of areas, working his way into sole control of their outputs. That makes him impressive to a Eudoxian looking to work with a terrestrial partner."

"What kind of talent?"

"Artists like Vaughan Riley, a few technical innovators."

"Not so much bartenders or ex-fighters."

Tempe smiled. "Eudoxia is just starting to admit that terrestrial music and art might be worthwhile; they're a few years out from importing gladiatorial spectacles. Although..." her eyes narrowed, and the tapping of her fingers sped up. "No," she said after a minute, firmly. "Your prestige here simply wouldn't be worth that much. If they were going to do that, they'd just send up a bunch of nameless toughs; Eudoxians wouldn't know the difference."

"There go my dreams of intersolar fame."

"Regardless of the reason, I do think it must be Sangster targeting you. You were right not to take that loan."

"I guess the smart thing would be to go to the Fontaines, throw in with them. At least with them you know where you are."

"Why should you throw in with anybody?"

"Everyone does, in the end. Probably stupid of me to think I could be different." Anyone else, anyone from Eastport, would get it. They'd be telling Vi she should have caved long ago.

Tempe was looking at Vi speculatively. "What was your impression of the singer, Vaughan Riley?"

"She was strange."

"Strange how?"

"Felt like she was barely there. I couldn't tell if she hated him or hated being downtown or was scared out of her skin or what."

"Do you think it was true that she was a fan of yours?"

She remembered the cool pressure of Vaughan Riley's hand, the way her eyes had rested on the sketch. "Maybe, yeah."

"I wonder if you could get her to do you a favor."

Vi knew that look: the narrowed eyes and small private smile that meant Tempe was making a plan. It had thrilled her once. "Whatever this is, I'm trying to get out of it, not deeper in."

"Do you think that's possible?"

"It has to be. I just need to hang on until Sangster or whoever decides I'm not worth it."

"You're being stubborn, Vi." She said it gently, and there was a trace of warmth that Vi didn't dare imagine might be fondness.

"What else can I do?"

She should have known Tempe would have a specific answer. "It happens that you and I have the same enemy. I need some information that would be difficult to obtain without help. For Vaughan Riley it should be simple and carry very little risk."

"So not no risk."

"Does anything come with no risk?"

"Don't split hairs. I'm not going to persuade someone who says she's my fan to get herself in trouble just to help you out."

"It would be helping you as well. Maybe her too. Once I have what I need, Sangster will have much bigger worries than snaring you."

"Were you paying attention before? If it really is Sangster against me, then he's got enough pull to make the city shut me down after one late rent day. And he's got one of the major gangs in his pocket. You just got here, and that's the guy you pick to go to war against?"

"War is overstating it. But I would not be fighting if I didn't know I could win."

"That's the difference between you and me. I don't get to pick what fights I end up in. In the ring it was just me, and I could go all out no matter what. Out here I have people to protect. There's no winning, there's just living another day."

Tempe looked at her silently. The car slowed, connected to another one with a soft thunk. Vi looked out the fake window at the bright sun and palm trees, feeling Tempe scanning her face.

"You've changed more than I thought," Tempe said at last.

"I haven't. I just got smarter. I know to stay out of shit from the beginning, instead of getting halfway in and finding out I can't follow through. You should be glad about that." There was a sore spot in her chest like a boil ready to burst. She tried to turn it into a laugh. "What are you even thinking, asking me to get involved?"

"Over the years, I've worked with people I trust less than you."

Vi shut her eyes. It shouldn't hurt. The part of her that cherished Tempe's trust should have died a long time ago. "Find someone else."

"What will you do?"

"Whatever I have to. Worst comes to worst, I'll sell the bar and start over somewhere else. Nothing I have is worth that much."

Tempe didn't answer. The car rattled along gently. Finally Vi made herself look at Tempe's face again. It was composed, thoughtful, inward. Once upon a time she'd loved when Tempe retreated into her own mind: Vi could look at her uninterrupted, and eventually she'd emerge with a trove of surprising thoughts that she'd give to Vi and no one else.

Whoever got to hear Tempe's thoughts these days, it wasn't Vi and wasn't ever going to be again. She cleared her throat. "I owe you for today. I didn't deserve your help, and I can't repay it."

Tempe startled out of her thoughts. "And?"

Vi shrugged. "That's it. I just wanted to say it, so you'd know I know. You can hate me some more, that's only fair."

Tempe looked faintly amused. "Do I need your permission to hate you?"

"I guess not." She felt embarrassed now. She didn't know how to explain why it felt like something she needed to say. "Just letting you know we're in agreement. Maybe you should rethink the revenge thing. If someone's going to take me down, I'd rather it be you."

"I'll think it over." Tempe held out her arm. "Will you take my link in case you do want to talk further?"

"For revenge?"

"For anything."

She should refuse. If she was going to be consistent and firm in her decision, she should force them both to accept that there wouldn't be any more contact between them. But as the car detached from its convoy and slid into a station, she found it was not possible to turn down the thin thread of connection. She extended her own arm, grimly amused that people called her stubborn when she couldn't even stick to one negative resolution.

Chapter Nine

The stop Vi had chosen was nearly an hour on foot from home, but she decided to walk anyway. She needed time to think. She couldn't get her mind off whatever Tempe had been going to ask her to do. Now that Tempe wasn't here trying to talk her into it, her own brain took up the job. The idea of fighting back called to every muscle in her body; she felt a surge of energy just at the thought. It would feel so good to be doing something.

It had felt good seventeen years ago, when Tempe had first found Vi raging at one of the Home's routine injustices and whispered, *Want to do something about it?* It had felt good for two years, enacting scheme after scheme, seeing something wrong and fixing it from the shadows. It had felt good right up until the moment they'd pulled her into the Headmaster's office and shown her how much they knew. Two pages of the Headmaster's big book were filled with their secrets: not everything, but so many things they thought they'd gotten away with undetected. While she was still gaping at the list, they'd shown her how easily Tempe could have an accident, as a few other girls had over the years. And worst, they'd shown her Nana. They'd shown her what Nana had been at pains to conceal in every letter, the squalor she'd been living in, the illness she'd worked herself into while trying to scrape enough to buy a house so that they would give Vi back to her. She almost had enough now, they'd said, but there could be an accident there too. It was easy to make money disappear. It would be easy to make a case for prolonging Vi's minority, keeping her at the Home another two or three years. Would Nana survive it?

Vi had given them everything. Even now, she couldn't imagine making a different choice. Watch them crush both Tempe and Nana, or give up the plan and take the freedom they offered? They'd promised to release Tempe too, to sign both of them into Nana's custody. Looking back, that was the part Vi had been foolish to believe. Maybe they'd have let Vi go back to Nana, but Tempe was the real danger to them, and she had no family outside to complain if she disappeared. They'd have had some other plan to deal with her. No one had expected her to press the detonator.

That was the difference between them. In everything she undertook, Tempe knew what the cost might be and didn't hesitate to pay it. Vi couldn't be like that. Not when it was more than her own body on the line. She wasn't cut out for this kind of fight.

She shook off the memories and the fighting impulse that

would lead her nowhere good. She had more immediate problems. If the corpse at the Tommy really had been a setup for her, then someone had known she'd be going to Norma's at that time. Was Kilo working for Sangster? She wanted to think it couldn't be, but that was just her being stupid. Kilo zemself would laugh, say something like, *Of course I'd sell you out, barkeep, if the money was good enough.*

It wouldn't even have to be money. Ze could have been threatened, like Jonesy. Then that would be one more person in trouble because of Vi.

She didn't realize her steps were drifting into the bike lane until a cyclist swerved around her, cursing. She cursed back, just on principle, and then stopped under a cabstand to pull herself together. At least get enough of a grip to walk in the lines, or what good will you be to anyone? Her ears were still ringing from that device of Tempe's, but that was no excuse.

That device of Tempe's. Aside from Kilo selling her out, the other possibility was someone listening in. Sangster had been in the office, could he have planted—

It hit her like a brick. How stupid could she be? That fucking chip. It had been sitting in her desk the whole time.

She ran half the way home and went straight in through the alley. There it was, in the drawer where she'd left it. Like it couldn't do any harm if she just ignored it.

First there were the coins to deal with. Conscious of every small sound, she put them back into the locked drawer. She stared at the chip like it was poison. Act normal. Check in on the bar first. To Dusty's look of inquiry, she just gave a tight shake of the head. He wouldn't ask anything more where Luce and Arthur might hear. She complimented the two of them on their work—it was going to be hard to come up with much more for them to do—and then went back toward the office, grabbing the chip on her way upstairs.

At home, Roman was reading quietly on the sofa. She didn't see Nana.

"Is she resting?" Vi asked.

"She's working," he answered. "She's been inspired the last few days, she—"

"Okay." If anyone was listening, the last thing Vi wanted was for them to know a single thing about Nana. "It's you I came back for, actually." She set the chip down on the coffee table. "I got this loan offer a little while ago. Can you look at the contract details and tell me if it seems okay?"

Before she'd even finished speaking, her hands started to move with their own message: "Can you find out if this chip has... an ear?" If there was a sign for electronic bug, she didn't know it. Roman caught her meaning.

"Sure, I can take a look," said Roman out loud. Signing, he said, "Be right back."

He went through into his and Dusty's half of the apartment. Vi crept around to see Nana bent over her table. The grey head came up, and Vi darted in to kiss her cheek. "Don't let me interrupt. I just came to pick Roman's brain about something."

Roman returned with a small box and screen. Setting it up on the coffee table, he slid the chip in. Vi hovered, trying to judge the answer from his face. It was his hands that spoke, though.

"Yes. And a signal out."

"Can they hear us now?" Vi signed.

"Yes. What should I say about the contract?" Vi didn't recognize the noun and frowned until he fingerspelled it. She threw up her hands, too furious at the idea that someone was hearing her every word to think through what words would be prudent.

"It's a generous offer," said Roman out loud. "Give me a few more minutes to look at the fine print."

He let her pace an angry lap around the room, then signed, "I think you should string them along. Sound interested. Find out what the game is."

What was the game? She was no closer to that than she had been this morning. "What do you know about this Sangster?" she signed, spelling the name.

"Nothing useful," Roman signed back. "I can dig."

Even after talking with Tempe, a part of her had wanted to believe that maybe this wasn't as bad as it seemed. Maybe there were other, separate explanations for the continuous barrage of trouble, and if she laid low for long enough it would all blow over. The bugged chip burst that bubble. The loan offer was a trap, and the corpse planted for her to find was a bigger one. If they could get the city to shut her bar after a single day late on rent, what were the chances they could get her arrested for murder? Even if they couldn't make the charge stick, they could hold her for days, maybe weeks, while her debt to the city ran up. And there wasn't a fucking thing she could do about any of it.

A sharp snap of the fingers pulled her out of the storm in her head. Nana was standing in the doorway to her studio, scowling. How long had she been standing there watching them talk? Vi scrambled for an explanation, a way to assure her there was nothing to worry about, but Nana signed, "Did you say Sangster? Brett Sangster?"

Vi nodded.

"He's been messaging me."

The storm turned to deadly calm. "Messaging you?" Vi signed back, to make sure she'd seen it right.

Nana nodded.

"Saying what?" Using her bar, even her life, was one thing, but if they were using Nana to get to her…

Nana fetched a screen and handed it to her, projecting from her wristband onto it. Vi read a string of messages from Nana's professional inbox. The first few were a conversation, Sangster introducing himself with warm compliments on her art, leading up through several exchanges to a proposal for a business deal. Nana had declined, politely but definitively. Sangster had expressed surprise and urged her to reconsider, leaving the terms open for negotiations. After her second refusal he had become condescending, hinting that her age and lack of business experience made it difficult for her to understand the value of his offer, and suggesting that she seek advice before he withdrew the opportunity. She had responded tersely: It seems your time is valuable; you need not waste any more on this stupid old woman.

After that he had returned to flattery, ceasing to mention contracts or deals but inviting her to be his guest at a soiree, where she would have an opportunity to meet a Eudoxian curator who admired her. She had declined this as well. His final message, sent a few days ago, had mentioned again the immediate financial benefits he could offer. Nana had not bothered to reply.

Vi read it all with a cold clarity. Her mind felt uncommonly quiet, uncommonly sharp. She distinctly remembered Tempe talking about Sangster acquiring talent, acquiring ownership of talent, selling culture to Eudoxia. Nana was the one they wanted, Nana and her art. The world flipped inside out: they were using Vi to get at Nana.

"Don't accept it," she signed to Nana.

Nana raised her eyebrows and just pointed at the tablet with pursed lips. Vi got it. She'd already refused and stuck to it. "I'm not actually stupid," Nana signed.

"You should have told me," she signed.

Nana's eyebrows climbed even higher, her mouth puckered even deeper. "What should you have told me?" Her hands moved with sharp emphasis.

"I was handling it," Vi answered. Nana folded her arms, her gaze boring into Vi. It made Vi feel about eight years old, even though Nana had to look up to stare her down now. She sighed explosively. "Someone's been making trouble. I didn't know why. I didn't think it had anything to do with you. I didn't want to worry you."

"I was already worried. You think you're grown up, you can handle everything alone now?"

I can, rang stubborn in Vi's mind, even though she knew better. It would be so easy for them to take her out of the picture long enough to come for Nana. They could do whatever they wanted; she'd found that out when she was a child and had worked hard since then to make sure no one would have a reason to come for them. But she hadn't stopped Nana from painting. It was embarrassing to realize: even knowing that the paintings sold well, she'd still thought of it as a rewarding hobby, something her Nana did to pass the time. To the outside world she wasn't Nana, she was Sol Mendes, and evidently that meant more than Vi had ever realized.

"He wants that agreement," she signed finally. "He wants us to need it. He's been giving me money trouble so we'll need it." Her hands hovered in the air after the final sign. She hated to add a worry, but if they arrested her Nana would need to understand. "He put me near a dead guy. He might use that too. If that happens, don't believe anything they say."

"What should we do?" Nana asked.

Vi looked at her: small, wiry Nana with the cropped grey curls, with the lines dug deep into her face that folded up when she smiled. The hands that spoke, that made beautiful art, that soothed Vi's head when it ached and salved her bruises when she fought. Nana who had worked and worried and carried Vi in strong arms until Vi was big and strong enough to carry her instead. They could come for anything else, but if they came for Nana that was the end.

"String him along," she signed to Roman. To Nana, she answered, "I'm going to trouble him back."

After letting Vi out of the car, Tempe set the destination for her apartment. She should have expected Vi's refusal; it should not be making her chest roil with frustration and disappointment. It was so hard to look at Vi and not see the stalwart partner of her youth. She had always responded to Tempe's ideas with a spark in her eye and a flex of her limbs, like she was itching to jump into action. It hurt to hear the defeat in her voice, to see how strenuously she held herself back.

There was no need to ask what had happened. That day in the Headmaster's office had broken Vi as badly as it had broken Tempe.

But you should still be fighting. Tempe wanted to hold her down and carve it into her arms. Tempe was: Tempe had found the guardrails she needed against her own horrible choice that day and had found her way back into the fight. Vi could do the same. Vi must do the same. It was very obviously killing her not to.

She took a deep breath, trying to refocus. She had not come here to save Vi. The last thing she needed was another personal entanglement. Hadn't the last encounter with Kilo been enough to remind her of the dangers?

She almost wished she'd failed to notice the token ze'd slipped into her pocket. Or that Kilo had let her violate zem at the end. Either way would have made for a clean break, however ugly. Something plain and unforgivable, a definite end. Instead she felt sticky threads wrapping tighter around her, spun out of the way ze had nestled into her arms afterward, out of zer easy acceptance of Tempe's ruthlessness. They would see each other again; she knew it, even though she'd pretended not to.

One murky liaison was plenty. She and Vi had already harmed each other enough for one lifetime. Vi's refusal to be further involved was better for them both. The roil in Tempe's chest was just noise, easy to tune out if she chose.

Fortunately, there was new intelligence to occupy her attention. Tempe had approached the shopkeeper at B23 hoping to get a little more information, like where Joe had lived before or anyone else he might have spoken with. He'd done her one better by setting a chip on the counter.

"Left this with me. Said if anything happened to him, it'd be worth something to you."

Tempe had slid him one of the two cash-laden cards she'd brought for Joe, and the shopkeeper had handed the chip over in exchange. "He said to tell you one more thing: give 'em hell."

Back in her apartment she connected the chip. All it held was a pair of coordinates. She pulled up a city map and found that the location was in a warehouse district. Not only that: the coordinates appeared to pinpoint a particular warehouse. Whose warehouse was an easy guess, but she didn't live by guesses.

It took an hour of digging through public records to confirm it: that warehouse belonged to Brett Sangster, held under layers of shell ownership. Not fully secret, but discreet. Getting into the warehouse shouldn't be overly difficult, once she was sure what she was looking for. Between Joe's hints and Hannah's choice of the word *Promethean,* she had a strong guess, but she should be certain before arranging a break-in. And she would still need to find a way to put the information into hands that could help deliver the final blow. Clemence Dorsey was the right person for that; Tempe had watched her make a few quiet, savvy business moves in response to the anonymous information Tempe had sent to the secretary Bredon. If Tempe gave her an opening, she would take it.

She was maddeningly close. In the car, a complete plan had come to her, one that would get her the confirmation she needed and bring Dorsey-Bredon along. But it hinged on Vaughan Riley's cooperation, and she doubted she could win that on her own. Given a month or two, perhaps, but Quentin was eager to sign the agreement with Sangster and move on to his other business here. Sangster was giving another grand party in two weeks' time, and all the Eudoxian entourage had been given to understand that their final assessment of the agreement should be completed before that date. If Tempe couldn't scuttle the partnership by then, it would be too late.

Her wristband flashed. She opened the incoming message, and her mutinous heart leapt at the sight of Vi's name.

I'm in. What do you need me to do?

The Cerulean Spa combined luxury and discretion, two elements that were essential to the mistress of a gang boss. Clara Godard had been coming every two weeks since Junior first established her in his household, and by now she was familiar with the other faces and bodies that came to be plucked, soaked, peeled, and massaged. When a new face appeared, she watched with interest; you never knew what connections might lead to useful information.

So when she saw a new boy trying to order a drink at the juice bar, she looked up from her reading and paid attention. He was slight in build under the fluffy robe, East Asian, beautiful face but too short to be a model. Actors and singers that came to the Cerulean were usually famous enough to be recognized, and Clara would certainly remember that face if she'd seen it before. Probably someone's new kept boy, then. He looked young, possibly too young, but that wasn't any of her business. When the drink was passed across the counter, he held out his wrist to pay automatically.

"No scanners," said the server pleasantly. "You have a payment card, do you not?"

The boy blushed. "Oh, of course. It's... my first time here, I forgot."

Clara felt a twinge of amused sympathy. The spa was a dead zone for wristbands, but it was easy to forget if one hadn't often been to places like this before. The boy felt in his pockets, which was of course foolish since the robe belonged to the spa. "Is it... I think it must be in my locker."

"Take your time," said the server. He and Clara shared an indulgent look as the boy departed. She remembered the feeling of having been newly picked up by a man rich enough to afford a place like this, trying desperately to look like she belonged.

The boy returned after a few minutes looking even more mortified. "I'm so sorry," he whispered so softly Clara had to strain to hear, "I think I must have left the card at home. Can I—

can I pay you the next time I come?"

"It's no problem. We can simply charge the account that booked your appointment."

"Oh." The boy curled in on himself in misery. "Could you—couldn't you please just let me pay it next time? I don't want him to—he just gave me the card yesterday, he'll be annoyed that I forgot it. Couldn't you please? I'll pay double, even, next time. I'm booked here again next month."

Terrified of offending his new patron, whether because the man had a temper or because the boy was afraid of being dropped as easily as he'd been picked up. Clara stepped up to the counter and extended her own card. "Allow me."

"Oh!" said the boy, looking up at her with miserable, hopeful eyes. "Oh no, I hate to trouble you."

"No trouble at all," Clara said as the server swiped her card. Leaning in a little, she said, "We hate to annoy our gentlemen friends, don't we?"

The boy stammered gratitude, and she gave him a sisterly pat on the shoulder. "You'll get used to things, don't worry."

He had good manners, leaving her to go back to her seat and her reading. She caught him sending a few shy, grateful glances her way, but he didn't disturb her again.

A few nights later she was at her usual bar waiting to meet a friend, and the bartender said her drink was on the gentleman at the corner. She looked up, already prepared to calibrate the politeness of her rejection, and saw to her surprise the boy from the spa. He seemed much more at ease here, looking fabulous in a mesh top and long spiked earrings. He gave her a small wave and a large smile but didn't try to approach her.

Twenty minutes later she was bored and antsy and annoyed at the friend who'd flaked on her without so much as a word. She went over to the other corner of the bar where the boy from the spa still sat drinking something electric blue in a rocks glass.

"There was really no need to pay back the drink," she said.

"I feel bad owing people," said the boy. "And you really saved my ass the other day."

"I never let anyone buy me a drink whose name I don't know."

He sparkled and held out a hand. "I'm Alex."

"Clara. And if you really want to pay me back, how about coming to my booth? I've just been stood up, and I don't feel like drinking alone."

Alex was a delightful drinking companion. He told his life story, which was more or less what she'd expected and not too dissimilar from her own. She liked how he covered hardships and impoverishment with a veneer of glamour, liked how some of his stories were obviously embellished or borrowed from friends. He was witty and snide, and underneath it she saw the vulnerability. A boy who'd had to learn to pretend to be sharp and impermeable. He wasn't practiced enough yet to hide it all the way, how badly he craved security and affection. Didn't they all?

She found herself exchanging confidences in turn. Nothing indiscreet, no names, but once she learned who his current patron was and that he could have no likely connection with Junior's rivals and associates, she spoke in vague terms about her current headaches. It was a relief to be able to talk about it; even with her friends she had to be guarded, since they would know exactly who she was talking about and you never knew who some of them might be talking to in their turn. She would never tell anyone the things Junior confided in her, late at night with his damp head resting between her breasts, but her own worries she could share. Junior's power meant someone was always trying to unseat him, which would leave her in a perilous position if anyone succeeded. It was clear to her that his cousin Andrew wanted his position, and also clear that that horrible blond businessman had much too strong a hold over the entire organization. She'd tried to help Junior out by making up to his old man, but she'd misjudged her approach and now he disliked her. It was maddening to have her future rest on power games that she couldn't play. Her tools were allure and intimacy, trust and facades, and all this was being played out with money and information and influence. Worst of all, she liked Junior, liked him almost deeply enough to give it another word, and liked relying on him. She didn't want to have to choose between staying with him on the edge of a knife or abandoning him.

    She didn't tell Alex most of this. She didn't think she did. She did get quite drunk and vehement and a little teary by the end of it, but she wouldn't have made it this far if she didn't know how to hold her drink and her tongue. At least she was certain she gave no names and no facts. And Alex was so green he barely seemed to understand some of what she was saying. He was still just grateful to have a luxurious apartment and only one man to please every day; she remembered being like that once. She hoped he would never have bigger worries than that. She told him so, tearfully again, patting the back of his hand. She told him he must reach out to her if he had any troubles or any questions, and only in the car on the way back home did she realize she'd never gotten his link.

Chapter Ten

Once a month at Burke's Bar and Lounge, Eastport's biggest bosses and tycoons played cards in the upstairs saloon. It was the main reason Ramiro the headwaiter had ulcers. Every month, the night before the game, he lay in bed with visions of mob guns opening fire and laying waste to the top level of Burke's; of a bigwig mysteriously dead at the card table and furious interrogations directed at himself and his staff; of any number of mishaps that could end with the most powerful eyes in the city turned angrily upon Burke's. He cared for the reputation of Burke's almost as much as he cared for his own hide: he had been working here since before he bought his first razor. He was proud of its venerability, proud of the stars that had begun their rise on its stage, proud even of the sterling reputation that made it the only choice for the card game that made him so anxious.

There was always a little something that went wrong; he

stood guard on card game nights to ensure small mishaps would not become large ones. Tonight, he'd had a waiter call out at the last minute and been forced to put on a boy he'd only hired earlier this week. He liked to have his most reliable staff on duty for the card game, but at least the new boy was quick at the job. Naturally Ramiro would not have him serve the card room, but he could handle the downstairs all right.

The card players would begin arriving in half an hour. Ramiro had just finished his inspection of the room and was returning through the main hall when he heard a crash behind him. He spun in time to see the card room door swing shut. Doubling back, he found a girl with bright pink hair and a clingy champagne-colored dress swaying slightly and holding herself up by one of the chairs.

He caught her by the shoulders. Her head rolled up toward him and her eyes slowly focused. "Hey," she slurred, "what're you doing in the ladies' room?"

"This isn't the ladies' room," he said, pulling her away from the chair by force.

"But I hafta—" she gulped and started to fold over.

Panic fueled Ramiro. He picked her up bodily and shoved her through the door of the nearest restroom. He heard a stall door crash and a miserable retching sound.

He took another quick look at the card room on his way back downstairs, straightening the chair the girl had disturbed and making sure nothing else was out of place or missing. In an excess of caution, he took back the ice bucket that he'd just filled and placed there a few minutes ago.

Marysia, who'd been working at Burke's nearly as long as he had, laughed when she saw him refilling it. "What, was one of the ice cubes deformed?"

She did not take the card game seriously, which was why Ramiro always had to work these nights in person. "A drunk customer stumbled into the card room."

"Right, of course, a secret plot to poison the ice. Good thing you're on the case."

"Refilling an ice bucket costs very little. I left the customer in the upstairs ladies' room. Go check and make sure she's come back downstairs, and hasn't left a mess anywhere." He handed her the full ice bucket. She took it with an eyeroll and a mocking salute.

Kilo pulled the waiter's uniform back on over the gold dress. The heels, lashes, and pink wig went into the trash. Makeup scrubbed, cheek pads in to form the round face of the new waiter, and hair combed down into an unprepossessing bowl cut.

Placing the token in the room had been the tricky part. Ze'd already left the shielded box under a decorative table in the hall, where it would be overlooked but easily found later. It would be child's play to sneak upstairs at some point during the busy night, retrieve the token from where it was stuck behind the bar cart, and place it on zer target. Then ze would be home free.

Burke's lounge was lush and intimate, round booths with

seats in emerald velvet, the red and violet light making every face both warmer and less distinct. The singer, alone in a spike of white light, held the stage and filled the air with a soft tenor crooning. Likewise alone, at a hightop table in the corner, Vaughan Riley sat listening.

In posters and videos she was radiant, the glitter of her eyes both beckoning and defiant. In Vi's bar on Sangster's arm she'd been still and remote. Here at Burke's, she looked vivid and alive again, but entirely turned inward. She was still beautiful, the violet light shining richly off her curved lips and high cheekbones, but her eyes were like wells, taking in and letting nothing out. The only thing she radiated was a wish to be left alone. Even as Vi and Tempe watched, they saw a hopeful-looking man take two steps toward her and then about-face at a single glance, retreating to the other end of the bar.

"Hope she's a big enough fan not to chase me off," Vi muttered.

Tempe laughed softly. "I don't believe you don't know how to hold a beautiful woman's attention."

Vi turned to her, startled. Tempe was looking up at her with her chin on her hand, speculation in her eyes. With everything that had changed between them, this was somehow exactly the same. Or, not exactly: back then it had been all unnamed hunger and wordless understanding. Vi had learned the words since then, and of course so had Tempe. She had a sudden gnawing desire to ask the names of everyone Tempe had ever touched. For Tempe to ask her the same.

"Am I wrong?" Tempe asked, shaking her back to the

present. She couldn't ask for an exhaustive recounting of Tempe's love life. She couldn't ask whether she counted Vi as her first anything. But she could let Tempe see what she'd made of herself. If curiosity was going to eat her, let it eat them both. She picked up her drink and strolled toward Vaughan Riley's table.

All three hightops immediately adjacent to Riley's were vacant. Vi went to the one that was just a little forward of it, not blocking Riley's view of the singer onstage but enough to cross her line of sight. She leaned her elbows on the table and gave all her attention to the stage as the song wound down. When the audience began clapping, she turned her head.

Vaughan Riley was looking at her. She kept looking as Vi met her eyes, unruffled. Vi gave her a nod and then turned her head back to the stage.

A few more glances back, strategically timed, and in almost all of them Vaughan Riley was looking at her already. That was enough for an opening. At the end of the next song, Vi turned and stepped toward her.

"If you're trying to place me and you think it might be awkward to ask, I'll spare you. I'm Vi, and you stopped by my bar a little while ago."

The corners of Vaughan Riley's lips curved up. "I remember you perfectly well. From long before you owned a bar."

Vi took that as an invitation to come all the way over to her table. "Do me a favor, pretend you're only saying that to be nice. I don't know how to deal with it when someone says they're a fan. You're probably used to it, but I only get it once every four or five years, and it throws me every time."

"Then I won't say it. Perhaps we're both fans of Andre." She nodded toward the singer onstage.

"I could say yes to be sociable, but I only just learned their name from you. Truth is I don't listen to much music. I don't say that to sound like a challenge—I just don't want to be embarrassed when you find out I can't name more than three or four of your songs."

"Please don't start naming my songs. What brings you to Burke's, then?"

Dancing around a subject had never been Vi's way. "Honestly? I was hoping to run into you."

"Were you." Just a trace of rigidity crept into her smile, and she held Vi's gaze levelly for several seconds. Onstage, Andre began a new song, and Vaughan abruptly snapped her attention to the stage. "This is one of their best, I want to listen."

Vi waited in silence through the end of the song. Vaughan had said it was a favorite and maybe it was—she certainly gave it her full attention—but there was a line between her brows, and she did not smile throughout the song. When it was done, she picked up her drink.

"I want some air. Come along if you want."

Vi followed her down the hall past the toilets, to a door that stood casually half-concealed behind a tall potted plant. It opened onto a short metal-grill platform that obviously had once had steps leading down to the alley, though now it was surrounded by iron railing on all three sides.

"They keep this door locked most nights," Vaughan said, leaning against a railing and looking up to the scalloped edges of the roof. "I get special privileges. I sang here every week before I got a recording contract. People would come to hear me, but just a few people, and after the show I'd come and sit at a table and chat. They'd give me my first drink on the house. Just one drink. These days they put whole bottles in my green room."

"Do you miss it?"

Vaughan took out a cigarette and offered one to Vi. She hadn't smoked in years, but after a second she took it and lit them both. Vaughan took a drag. "Thanks for not asking if I should be careful of my voice. I allow myself one a month. Sometimes two. Do you miss fighting?"

"Parts of it."

"What parts?"

"Knowing what I was doing. If I won or lost a fight I pretty much knew why, and I knew what I had to do to get better. And if I made a mistake, I was the only one who got hurt."

"I remember your fight against Apple Kennedy in '45. Odds were twelve to one against you, and I only had a couple hundred that I couldn't really spare, but I put it on you. And then you went down and everyone thought it was over. I'll never forget how I felt when you stood back up."

Vi hadn't been playing cool; she really didn't know what to say when people brought up her old career. "Guess you were telling the truth about being a fan."

"Oh, yes. Did you think he made that up?" Just in the one word *he,* Vi heard the same coldness she'd seen in the bar. "He told me we were going to see you and offer you some help, like a little treat for a pet."

"Who's the pet, you or me?"

Vaughan gave her a sharp sidelong glance. "I meant me, but it could be you. Or anyone who gets close enough."

Like Nana. She wondered if Vaughan had brought her out here to warn her off, and what Sangster would do about that if he knew. "Do you hate him?"

The tip of Vaughan's cigarette glowed. "I can't afford to hate him. He makes sure of that."

"I worked under a shitty boss when I first came to town. He liked to say the meanest shit and watch you swallow it because you needed the pay. I don't think he saw us as pets, but if we were dogs he would've kicked us. I couldn't afford to show it, but I still hated him."

"Sangster doesn't kick, not as long as you know you're on the leash. He brings around treats. And he keeps his word. I told him when I signed with him that I wouldn't let him fuck me. He likes people to assume he does, but he's never touched me except for show."

Maybe Vaughan wasn't warning her off after all. "Do you think it's worth it? Being on the leash?"

"Who isn't on some kind of leash? I was in debt before I signed with him. I might have ended up tied to someone else, maybe someone who wanted more than arm candy. And I sing for millions now. I'm about to get an offworld tour. However you look at it, I made a good deal." Her hand was clenched tight around the banister.

"I guess so," said Vi. "You did the smart thing, right? The smart, careful thing. I've been doing that too. I've been thinking for years that no one's got a leash on me, except the whole damn city does. I've got to be smart and careful every day, so no one decides they need to come at me. Can't do anything I want to do. The kicker is, when they decide they want it bad enough, they'll come at me anyway. So what the hell was I doing staying to heel all that time?"

Vaughan looked at Vi steadily as she took another long drag. She held it in this time for several heartbeats. Smoke curled out of her nostrils, then she turned to the side and tapped off the ash. "There was one time I wasn't careful. Back on my first tour, out on the West Coast, there was this boy. Sweet boy, hazel eyes, nice hands. He chatted me up after a show, and I took him to bed. And the next day they found him dead in his apartment. Sangster brought me the news clip himself, said he thought I'd want to know, said the kid seemed special to me. The rest of it was in his eyes. I haven't let anyone else touch me since."

Silence hung while Vi took that in. Before she'd figured out how to reply, Vaughan spun back around and gave her a sly, glittering smile. "So I don't advise you to make a move on me, Vi Iron Fist."

Vi stepped closer. Vaughan's gaze dropped briefly to the open collar of her shirt, then daringly back up at her eyes. Vi let her hand rest on the railing just outside Vaughan's. "Is that true?" she said. "He'd kill anyone who touched you?"

"I haven't tested it out. Maybe it's only men he cares about. Maybe I could do it so he'd never find out. I was shook, that day, so I've been careful. Smart and careful, just like you said."

"Are you as sick of being careful as I am?"

Vaughan closed her eyes. "Yes."

Her mouth was curved and berry-red. Vi knew she could kiss her right here, knew it for an invitation. She leaned her face nearer and felt the rise of Vaughan's chest against hers. She hovered for a breath, then slid her cheek against Vaughan's. "Do you want to be free of him?" she whispered.

Vaughan's whole body stiffened. "Now that isn't funny."

"It's not a joke. Yes or no?"

"There isn't a way out. He holds too many strings."

"What if someone cut them?"

Vaughan pulled her head back and looked up into Vi's face. "You're serious."

"That's what I came for. Don't get me wrong, you're beautiful, and I'd gladly make a move on you if it wouldn't mean ending up dead in my apartment tomorrow. But I'm here because you might be able to help me. It all depends how much you want that offworld tour."

"I want a lot of things. Mostly I don't want to end up dead in *my* apartment. Can you promise me that?"

"I can't promise anyone that. But I wouldn't be here if I thought that was a risk. Did you hear me before? I'm more or less a coward. Just trying to be a little less."

"And what would I do, if I wanted to be a little less a coward?"

"I'm told there's a coat he always wears. A friend of mine wants a look at it."

Vaughan's eyes narrowed thoughtfully. "That coat... what is it about that coat?"

"You'd have to ask my friend. She seems to think there's something she can use against him, if she gets her hands on it."

"That sounds absurd." She ran her fingers along the point of Vi's collar. "Except I've seen how precious he is about that coat. This friend of yours... reliable?"

"Unfailingly."

Vaughan's brows went up. "Just a friend?"

"Maybe not even that. But I trust her. If she says she'll do something, she'll do it. Even if you wish she wouldn't."

"Seems like I'd have heard of someone like that. Who is it?"

"She's not from around here."

"So what happens? I get the coat, I let your friend have a look at it—where?"

"I'll ask her where. She says a few minutes is enough. Then you take it back up, or whatever you want to do. We don't want him to know anything's been done."

Vaughan shuddered lightly. "No. That we don't." Her lashes flicked as her eyes went back up to Vi's. "I think my cowardice could just about stand that. But do I get a reward if I do it?" Her voice dropped low.

"What do you want?" Vi asked. There wasn't much closer she could get, but she moved her thigh forward to slide against Vaughan's. Vaughan's lips parted, and she held Vi's gaze.

"Don't give it to me yet," she breathed. "He's got me that spooked, I'd be afraid he'd see it on me even if I fixed my lipstick."

"Afterward, then." Vi couldn't take her eyes off the round lower lip.

"Afterward. We can both be brave." She curled a hand

around Vi's forearm, ran it up over her bicep and back down, before pushing Vi back to stand up off the railing. "I always thought it'd be interesting to meet you. I was right about that."

Vi counted a hundred before leaving the terrace and going back into the bar where Tempe was waiting. The singer Andre had left the stage, and the band was playing croony slow-dance music. There was no sign of Vaughan.

"She went up?" Vi asked under her breath, and Tempe nodded. "She said she'd do it. I guess she'll try." Now that Vaughan was out of sight, every nerve in Vi's body was on edge. Whatever happened next, Vi was responsible.

"Your anxiety's standing out like a red light," Tempe murmured. "Shall we dance?"

Vi stifled a shocked noise; it came out like a muffled squawk. "That won't make me any less anxious."

Tempe smiled. "It will give it cover." She held out her long, cool hand, and Vi let her lead to the area in front of the stage. Tempe put her arms around Vi's neck and leaned in near her ear. "If you stand at a bar broadcasting anxiety, you draw attention. If you're dancing, you might just be worried you're not a good dancer."

"I know I'm not a good dancer," Vi said. She was overwhelmed in every part of her by suddenly having Tempe in her arms. They'd slept like this every night for five years, and the loss had been unbearable, and then she'd borne it anyway.

"You're squeezing me," Tempe said.

Vi didn't loosen her arms. "Can't hold you any other way. You're the one who wanted to dance."

Tempe was still for a fraction of a second, then she laid her head down on Vi's shoulder. "I didn't think it through."

It was good Vi couldn't see her face. One assault on her senses at a time was plenty. It was enough—it was too much—to know by the way Tempe melted against her that she was also shaken. Whatever time and betrayal had broken between them, Tempe's body still answered Vi's instinctively. "Talk about something else," Vi said roughly.

"How did you come to own a bar?"

That was a good, concrete question. "Worked for it for years. Was saving up all my prize money on the side, looking for a chance at something better. Then the owner got into hot water. He signed the bar over to me in exchange for a ticket out of town. Sometimes I think it's the worst deal I ever made. You know how much of a hassle it is, running a bar?"

"I truly don't. Would you do something else if you could?"

"Never thought about it. It's my bar now anyway." Over Tempe's shoulder she saw Vaughan enter the lounge, a suit coat draped over her shoulders. She squeezed Tempe's arm. "She's here. She did it."

"Well done," said Tempe, sending a blaze of satisfaction through her chest. "You go to her first. Tell her to go to the restroom and I'll meet her there. Then you come back out here and wait."

Vi started to move away, but Tempe held her by the arm. "Hold on till the hallway is clear." A woman had just gotten up from a table near them and was passing by where Vaughan stood.

Once the coast was clear, Vi went to Vaughan. "Did you have any trouble?"

"It looks good for a man when his lady friend needs his coat to warm her pretty shoulders. I can't be away long, though."

"My friend says to meet her in the restroom. She's the blonde standing where I just came from."

"I saw you dancing with her," said Vaughan. "Where will you be?"

"Out here, I guess. Less conspicuous. Will you be alright?"

"The faster it goes the more alright I'll be."

Vi went back to the bar, trying to figure out what "not anxious" would look like. She ordered another drink, just for something to do with her hands. Tempe did not look her way, seemingly absorbed in something on her wristband, and then a minute later moved casually toward the hall.

One minute passed. Two. Five. Vi gripped her drink, the glass sweating in her fingers, counting her sips so she didn't just down the whole thing in her nerves. Then from the hall came a high-pitched yell. She let the glass fall and was running before it hit the ground.

There in the hall was Vaughan, coat still draped on her shoulders, flanked by two men that were unmistakably somebody's muscle. One of them gripped her by the elbows, the other pulling something from the pockets of her coat. She was spitting out a patter of haughty outrage, but her eyes when they met Vi's were flooded with panic.

That was all Vi needed. She went right for the first guard's stomach, making his grip on Vaughan's elbows soften. Then she spun and swung for the second one, so he wouldn't get any ideas about grabbing Vaughan before taking Vi down. Doing it left her ribs open, and the first guard hit them hard enough to crack. The pain sharpened her focus. It had been a long time since she had a problem she could just take a swing at. She kept moving, kept the guards dodging, landing hits where she could. In the corner of her vision she saw Vaughan running toward the door. Good. That was all she needed. The guards were going to take her down, no question, but she could buy time. Her fist hit muscle and satisfaction blazed. *I'm a problem, I'm your problem, fucking deal with me.* They kept trying to get clever and pin her or go for their stunners and she made them pay for it every time. She'd always been known for being fast and hard with her fists. Finally they gave up and aimed for the knockout. She went defensive, covering her face, backing toward the wall. Every second would count. They backed her all the way into a corner, and then finally one of them managed to get his stunner out. She threw out one more reckless strike just for the satisfaction of it before the world crackled black.

Ann Bredon stayed silent in the bathroom stall at Burke's, listening to the sounds of fighting outside. The only other occupant of the bathroom seemed to be doing the same. Ann was fairly sure Professor Carroll knew she was hiding in a stall, but if she did not speak Ann would not either. One should always follow the informant's lead; besides, it was possible she was wrong, and it was someone else who had dropped the hints that led Ann here.

She'd already learned plenty from the evening's outing. She'd hidden herself in the stall before the other two women entered and had overheard the whole of their conversation. Citizen Brett Sangster's coat was lined with nimbic silk, according to Professor Carroll, and her voice had sounded suspicious rather than impressed. *'It makes one wonder where he got it, and why he chooses to wear it so discreetly.'*

With plenty of time on her hands, Ann Bredon scanned back through her employer's master records. Dorsey Imports handled all manner of goods, including plenty of specialty fabrics, but she found no records of nimbic silk, imported or exported, any time within the last ten years. That didn't prove anything except that it was exceptionally rare, but the choice to wear it as a lining was stranger than perhaps the professor even realized. Ann knew Brett Sangster, as she knew all of Clemence's important rivals. All of Eastport's elites were conscious of status, but Sangster in particular liked to display his prizes where they would be seen and remarked upon. If he had obtained some yards of a rare Eudoxian fabric, she would have expected to see it around his neck or folded into his breast pocket, somewhere where knowledgeable observers could see and whisper to each other about the wealth and connections that had allowed him to acquire it. The lining of a coat might in theory be shown off, but to Ann's knowledge Sangster had never shown off his. She'd never heard so much as a rumor that he wore nimbic silk.

Ann waited in the bathroom for several more minutes after Professor Carroll left. When she emerged, there was no one in the hallway, although an empty plinth and some scattered petals on the carpet showed that a vase had suffered from the earlier violence. Walking toward the exit, she heard angry voices up the stairs. One of them was Citizen Sangster's, and she drew a little nearer, lingering to listen.

"You must think you're one slick son of a bitch, Junior." Sangster's voice. Much rougher than Ann had ever heard him use at business and society functions. It had always been rumored that he'd come up in Lower Eastport and pulled himself into the Heights, but she'd never entirely believed it until now.

"The token was in your pocket, and that box is registered to your name," came a voice Ann did not know. "Until you can provide a satisfactory answer for both, any agreement between us stops. I think no one will fault me for this."

"You say it was in my pocket. I say one of your men put it there while pretending to grab my singer."

"That claim would stand up better if you didn't have a shielded box waiting to carry it."

"I'll find out who left that box. How well did you cover your trail? You thought you could set me up in front of these fine witnesses. How impressed will they be when they find out you tried to play me and them? This is how Junior Palumbo treats his allies; everyone take note."

Ann stifled a gasp. Junior Palumbo was the boss of the Trav gang, and that meant she was overhearing a much more dangerous conversation than she'd thought. Heart pounding, she turned away from the stairway as casually as she could. She didn't know what would happen if she was caught listening, and it wasn't worth finding out.

As soon as she was safely out on the street, she tapped a message to Clemence. Whether she'd gone to bed already or not, she would want to hear about this at once.

Chapter Eleven

On first waking up, Vi thought she was back in the Home dormitories. The hard mattress and papery crackle under her head were right. The bright light pounding through her lids was wrong though, and there was no chill at her back, and her arms were empty. She shifted, and the sear of pain in her side brought her to full awareness.

She opened her eyes and saw bars. She was lying on a thin mat on the floor, in a small bare room with sullen yellowed walls. Across through the bars she saw another cell like hers, empty. Moving made her head throb, but she forced herself up and onto her feet. She had to brace against the wall for a full minute before she could stagger to the bars.

There wasn't much to see. The three cells across from her were empty, and she couldn't see any further than that. She banged on the bars and yelled, "Hey! Who's there?"

A small chorus of shouts and jeers answered her, mostly male voices, all distant. Gripping the bars, she staggered to one edge of the cell and then the other, looking and listening for any sign that Vaughan or Tempe was locked up next to her. If they were, they were unconscious or unwilling to answer.

She reached for her wrist automatically, only to find that they'd cut her wristband off. Her arm looked strange and naked without it. She wrapped the fingers of her other hand around where it should have been and pressed down a rising feeling of panic. No way to connect to anyone, no way to find out what was going on outside. And no hope that she'd just been slung in here for a night for rowdy behavior. They didn't cut off your band unless you were under real charges.

She squeezed her eyes shut, resting her head against the bars. What had happened? The last she'd seen, Vaughan was running toward the exit, and Tempe was nowhere in sight. The men had been dressed like mob guns. What had they pulled from Vaughan's pocket? Something small and dark, held in the gun's fingers. Tempe had said she only wanted to look at Sangster's coat, nothing about slipping something into it. Tempe had never lied to Vi. Never yet.

Her head was pounding. She desperately wanted to lie back down, but she wasn't sure she'd be able to get up again. Whatever happened next, she wanted to face it standing. She wrapped one arm through the bars and leaned back against the wall.

The next thing that happened was a pair of cop puppets coming down the row of cells with food. She could hear the clomp of their feet and rowdy hails from the more populated area. She seemed to have been thrown down at the far, empty end of the jail. She listened hard; the cops moved steadily toward her after feeding the prisoners at the other end. No sign of them stopping at any other cell within several feet of her.

They made her back away from the bars before they would slide the tray in on its slot. She asked what she was in for, what time it was, how long it would be before anyone came to talk to her. She might have saved her breath. They ignored her completely and walked away while she was still shouting questions.

The meal was a flat nutritional loaf, the kind they handed out at welfare. She hadn't missed the taste, but she choked it down. If she couldn't do anything else, she could at least work on getting back to full strength. On the same principle, after eating she lay back down on the mat and tried to force her spinning mind to settle down and rest.

She must have dozed off. Some time later she was startled awake by the same clomping sounds coming toward her cell. Just one pair of feet this time. The cop came into sight, stepped close to the bars, and waited.

"You gonna talk more than the other two?" she asked finally. She didn't feel like making an ass of herself by yelling at metal again.

"I've been thinking of corn cakes and honey," the cop answered.

Officer Daniel. Vi staggered up to her feet and went to the bars. "What the fuck is going on? Why am I here?"

"You assaulted two men at Burke's."

Vi snorted. "First time I've heard of someone being charged with assault against mob guns."

"Witnesses say it was sudden and unprovoked."

"Did witnesses also say they were holding a lady against her will?" She'd thought it out, and this was the story she was going to stick to: talking to Vaughan had been all flirtation, nothing else, and she'd attacked the guns because Vaughan looked threatened. That should hold, unless Vaughan herself contradicted it, in which case Vi was fucked.

"That isn't the worst of it. I looked at the files. They're putting together a murder case against you."

Vi shut her mouth before blurting out, *the guy from the Tommy Arcade?* Instead, carefully, she said, "I haven't killed anybody."

"Didn't say you had. But they're putting together a case, and it looks to me like they have what they need to win it."

He didn't say evidence. You didn't need evidence if you had a motivated judge and a couple of liars on the payroll. Vi clenched her hands around the bars. "I didn't fucking kill anybody."

"Listen to me, Ferreira. I'm here because I hope to keep eating corn cakes and honey for a good long time. You might think you can get out of this on the strength of what did or didn't happen. I'm telling you I've looked it over, and you can't. So I hope you'll choose the smartest way out."

"What the fuck is that supposed to mean?" She was starting to think she knew, and panic and hatred rose up in her chest. "If you really want to help, how about you stop them from sticking me with something you know I didn't do?"

"This goes above my head. I'm sorry." He started walking away. Vi slammed on the bars of the cell and swore, but he didn't turn back around.

More hours passed. Vi paced the cell, testing the scope of her injuries. Nothing too dire, mostly bruises. The ribs might or might not be cracked. Her left ear was ringing slightly, which she was used to ever since a particularly rough fight in her prime. It would go away in time, unless it didn't; she'd been warned that too many hits might make the damage permanent and leave her the ringing as a constant companion, but no point worrying about that now.

The only marker of time was the arrival of another nutritional loaf, brought by cops as uncommunicative as the first ones. Not knowing what was going on outside was driving her out of her mind. It might be afternoon or evening, and she didn't even know if the events at Burke's had happened yesterday or the day before. She hadn't felt this helpless since she was first taken to the Home, twelve years old and terrified and unable to reach out for Nana. She'd gotten used to it back then, gotten used to living for weekly letters and putting aside every worry about what might have happened between them. Could she get used to it again, if they threw her into prison for murder?

Footsteps down the hall again, lighter and non-metallic. She scrambled to her feet and went to the bars. A pair of shining black shoes, pleated slacks. That goddamned coat. Brett Sangster stopped in front of her cell and looked her over complacently.

"I won't waste time telling you how much easier this all could have been. I hope you are sensible enough to be reflecting on that on your own. Your story was inspirational: an illegal underground fighter turned honest citizen and respectable business owner. If you'd taken my first offer, you could have risen even higher. Now look: a few setbacks to your business, and you turn back to violence and lawlessness. Truly heartbreaking."

"You made up the story. If you don't like it, try a different one." She couldn't get her mind off the coat: what did it mean that he'd gotten it back? Was Vaughan safe? Had she given them away?

He continued as if she hadn't spoken. "I worry what will happen if you go to prison. I worry your violent tendencies will only increase. I worry you may become so uncontrollable they have no choice but to send you offworld."

Vi's blood froze. She hadn't even imagined that possibility. Plenty of places on the continent would ship any murder convict to Mars, but Eastport saved its transportation sentences for egregious cases. Or, of course, for convicts who really really pissed off the wrong person.

She could handle herself in prison. If they sent people to harass her, she could give as good as she got. If someone really wanted her dead they would get her eventually, but that was true anywhere. But could she stop them setting her up? A prison would be full of guys like the corpse in the arcade, guys someone would be happy to turn into a body just to make trouble. She had no idea how she'd defend against that.

Sangster continued, sounding even more pleased with himself. "If only you had a more reliable, stabilizing influence at home. But after speaking with your only living family member, I'm not confident that she can guide you back to the right path."

She'd nearly forgotten again: this was all about Nana. "So she turned you down again."

"It seems that your grandmother will only be guided by you, rather than the reverse. Which leaves us with few alternatives. Because I have sympathy for you, I have offered to supervise your rehabilitation. You will work for me, under house arrest on my premises. In time, with good behavior, you may earn back your liberty."

"Work for you? Ha."

"Anything you do from now on will be under my direction. If I want you to go to prison, you will go to prison. If I want you transported, you will be transported. But that would be unpleasant for you and a waste of potential for me. Better for both of us if you can work for me, in comfort and fairly compensated. Perhaps in time you can return to your bar. And I will grant you the privilege of speaking with your grandmother every day."

"Speak with her about how she should sign on with you, you mean."

"About whatever you like. I'm confident that in time she'll be persuaded, one way or another. Whether she makes the choice feeling comfort and security or terror and grief is really up to you."

"She knows as well as anyone that a golden cage is still a cage."

Sangster smiled coldly. "Certainly. And if you really prefer the iron one, so be it. But think carefully. You live at my pleasure now, and your chances to please me are fast running out."

Not long after Sangster left, the overhead lighting dimmed. Vi didn't lie down; she paced her cell, thoughts swirling. It could all be a lie. Sangster might not have the power he claimed. Officer Daniel's warning might be false, whether he was lying or deceived. But she had already been here too long if the charge was going to be simply assault against the two guns. And Daniel was no beat cop; anyone in a position to pressure him already had more than a little leverage. And how much would it really take to sway one judge and a couple of witnesses against a lone citizen with no protectors to back her up?

The threat was plausible. And if it was true, what then? She wanted to spit in Sangster's face; she wanted to shout that an honest prison was better than a gilded one. But the threat of transportation stopped her cold. If she went to Mars, she'd be cut off from everyone. She'd have to hoard video messages received once a month at best. And Sangster could still use her to threaten Nana into doing what he wanted. Whatever she was enduring, she'd hide it from Vi, and there would be nothing Vi could do in any case. Nana would live out her old age worrying and fearing for Vi. They probably wouldn't see each other again before she died.

She fell eventually into a restless, miserable sleep and half-dreamed, half-remembered the second worst day of her life, the day they came to take her to the Home. They'd brought two men, because even at twelve that was what it took to handle Vi, and the grief and fear in Nana's eyes was seared into her memory. She'd opened her mouth to cry out, and that had frightened Vi more than anything because she'd never before seen Nana try to speak. Then, with tears streaming down her cheeks, Nana had stood up straight and signed: Be good. Wait for me.

When the cops came in the morning, alongside her meal they brought a supervised release agreement on a tablet. She read it through, as if she had a choice. Hadn't she always known this day would come? She'd expected more warning. She'd expected at least to be able to choose who to sell herself to. The Fontaines would have been better than this.

Maybe eventually she could find her way to a more tolerable servitude, but for now there was only one way forward. This was the truth she'd learned fifteen years ago: that she did have a price. And Sangster had found it.

They didn't hurry about processing her surrender. The midday meal came and went, and she was still kicking her heels for what felt like a whole day before a cop finally came with cuffs to bring her to the discharge room. A man was waiting for her there. He was about her height and not much bulkier, dressed in dark jeans and a plain black shirt, close enough to what mob guns wore but not the same. He saw her sizing him up and smirked.

"Boss says if you want to knock me out and make a run for it, you're welcome to try, and I shouldn't twist an ankle chasing you."

She understood why when she'd been checked out. They didn't give her wristband back, not even the cut band to carry. She stood there stupidly waiting until the grim woman behind the pane barked, "Waiting for something?"

"Can't I even check my band, see if there were any messages?"

The woman looked over to the side, bored. "It's in the pile to be wiped. Might have already gone through."

Sangster's guy leaned in. "Why? Someone in particular you were hoping to hear from?"

Even if Tempe had messaged, it would be too risky to look at it with someone peering over her shoulder. "I guess not."

So she had no money and no identity. Without a wristband, she couldn't even get into a car alone. She couldn't cross sectors, and she couldn't reach out to anyone for help. She hadn't exactly planned on making a big getaway once she was out of jail, but it was stifling to realize that even if she tried, it would be near-impossible to get anywhere.

They took a private car. It was a long, dull ride, Vi pacing the little box of the carriage while her escort read on a screen. He asked her one time if she wanted to read the news, with a little jeering smile, and she told him to fuck off.

A while later he opened a bag and tossed her a sandwich. "Got to take the slow lane through the border. We'll be here a while."

Of course they were going to the Heights; that was where Sangster lived, and she'd be even more stuck without a band up there. Up there, there were scanners in the doorway of every shop. She'd never been through the slow lane at the border check, and the monotonous start and stop every few feet made her sick to her stomach.

Finally the door opened to admit a crisp official with a flat screen in hand. She looked up blearily while Sangster's man gave him the documents. Then she had to stand up and get her picture taken before the official left and the car jerked forward.

She was too stubborn to ask the time, but it was fully dark by the time they arrived at Sangster's mansion. It was the kind of house Vi had mostly seen on screens, tall and imposing, two wings coming forward on either side like pincers to draw a person in. There was a track running off the main road so the car could stop right in front of the door, so lofts wouldn't have to waste their precious steps crossing the big front courtyard. Under the left wing was a big cutout arch where another set of tracks ran, because it wasn't enough to have a private car, you also had to park it out of sight of the house. Fill in the front courtyard and that arch, and you could have six or eight families living here comfortably.

Sangster was waiting in the front hall with his gleaming smile.

"Welcome! Here at last. I trust the journey was comfortable?"

"I want to talk to my grandmother."

"It's already late," he said. "Not knowing when you would arrive, and wanting to be respectful of an old lady's sleep, I asked her to send you a recorded message. You'll find it in your room. I'm sure you want to wash and rest yourself."

What Vi wanted was to talk to Nana, see with her own eyes that things were well at home and let Nana see she was alright too. But it didn't seem like objecting would get her anywhere, and she wasn't keen to give him more chances to show he was boss. Sangster waved over a neat young woman in a plain dress who led Vi upstairs, down a long hallway, and into a small bedroom.

"Toilet and shower's across the hall," said the young woman.

"If you need anything to eat, tell me now, otherwise nothing till breakfast at seven tomorrow. You're not to wander around the house alone."

Vi sent her away and crossed into the bathroom. When she saw her own face in the mirror, she was a little glad she wouldn't get to call Nana tonight. She was grimy and haggard, eyes baggy and a nice shiner over her temple. Hardly a reassuring sight. At least by tomorrow she'd have washed and maybe slept.

She showered, for once taking as long as she wanted. If Sangster cared about water overages, he could put it on a timer like normal people did. She disliked the sweet floral scent of the soap, but that was good. Whether she was going to be here for a week or a month or a year, she didn't want to get comfortable, and there were plenty of comforts. The towels were thick and soft and covered even her height from shoulder to knee.

In her room she found the little stand-up screen with a black box plugged into it. It was a restricted access portal, linking out to a couple of the big news sites and a library of dramas and nothing else. Roman probably could've hacked it to get broader access, but Vi was stuck with what they gave her. She found the file named Sol Mendes and today's date.

The video showed Nana standing in the doorway of their apartment, a strained smile on her face. In the background was Roman, looking toward the camera but not saying anything. A voice behind the camera said, "Go ahead."

Nana signed, "We're all fine here. I'm glad you're out of jail. They say I can talk to you tomorrow. Be good, and don't worry." Then she turned and nodded to Roman, who flashed a grin and a thumbs-up.

That was all, barely fifteen seconds. Vi watched it over and over until her eyes leaked and her head ached and she fell asleep.

Vi ate breakfast alone in a little sunlit room on the ground floor. The breakfast table was quite a sight: eggs and sausages and potatoes and an ostentatious bowl of fresh fruit salad, including some fruits Vi hadn't seen in years. It would have been a real test if she'd had to choose between indulging in this spread or another nutritional loaf, but there was no plainer food on offer, and her belly had to get full somehow.

Sangster came in when she was halfway through her second cup of coffee. Vi answered his pleasantries with a grunt. She'd eat the breakfast, but she wasn't going to kiss his shiny shoes over it.

He didn't seem bothered by her attitude. "Your decision to join us is well-timed. Recent events have left me inconveniently short of muscle. When you've finished breakfast, I'll have Nita show you downstairs, where one of my former employees is being questioned. I don't imagine you have experience performing interrogations? For now you can simply observe. Ritchie is very good at his job; you can learn a lot from him."

Vi was pretty sure she knew what 'questioning' meant, and she wasn't wrong. Nita, the same young woman who had shown her to her room last night and down to breakfast this morning, led her to the basement. It was fitted out as a gym, with punching bags and other workout gear. There was a side room done up in shower tile, from which she heard thumps and whimpers.

"In there," Nita said, pointing to the shower room and then

backing up the stairs like she wanted to get away quickly. So some people in Sangster's employ were still squeamish.

Vi wasn't squeamish, but the sight of the man on the floor turned the breakfast in her stomach. He was curled up in the corner of the shower, sopping wet and whimpering. His face was purple all over and split in several places. Blooms of blood spread pink over his shirt and swirled through the water on the floor.

Ritchie, it turned out, was the guy that had brought her up from jail yesterday. He was wearing a tank top and heavy boots today. No weapons, unless you counted the boots, but he looked like he was doing plenty with just his hands.

He nodded at Vi. "Boss said you'd be down after breakfast. Bobby here bought a shielded box in the boss's name, and he thinks he doesn't have to say who paid him to do it." He set a boot over one of Bobby's ankles. "We're here to teach him he's wrong."

"I told you!" Bobby shrieked as Ritchie pushed his weight forward over the ankle. "No one paid me, I did it for the boss, it was on my list!" There was a crack, and Bobby gave a little shrieking sob.

Vi didn't think he was lying. He didn't look like much of a hero—he looked like a guy who would say just about anything he could to make this stop. And Ritchie, lifting his boot with a remote, predatory smile, looked like a guy who was having fun.

"Seems a lot of fuss to go to for a box," she said, trying to sound casual. "What makes you think someone paid him off?"

Ritchie turned cold eyes on her. "I guess you do have a lot to learn. The only one here to answer questions is him." He aimed a lazy kick at the foot he'd just stood on. "Boss tells me what he wants to know, I get the answer. That's it."

"Does your boss want him dead?" The way Bobby was holding his stomach, even after having his ankle broken, said he'd been kicked there more than a few times, and who knew what kind of damage was underneath.

"If he cared about that, he wouldn't have put him down here with me." Ritchie squatted down and got his fist around the collar of Bobby's shirt. "Tell you what, Bobby boy. If you die on me, then I'll believe you really don't know anything. How's that for a deal?"

Bobby just cried.

She'd seen guys beaten about this badly. Never in Mikey's ring, but in some of the others, the kind where the money from one night would set you up for half a year, assuming you could walk and talk and shit at the end of it. There had been days when she'd wanted nothing more than to pound something into a pulp, wanted it badly enough to walk into one of those rings, but she never had because it would have broken Nana's heart. And even in those places, you'd know the person you were hitting had walked into the ring just like you had, with the same odds and for more or less the same reasons. She'd never had the stomach for this kind of thing.

Not much she could do now, whatever her stomach thought about it. She liked her chances at taking Ritchie down, but then what? Haul the unfortunate Bobby out of here and go where? She couldn't buy so much as an ice pack with no wristband, couldn't even walk into a store, so what good could she do him?

This was always what people told themselves. 'I won't be able to help him, and I'll just get myself into trouble for nothing.' This was how it started, standing by and watching an evil thing happen and telling yourself there's nothing you can do. She knew that well enough, but that didn't make it not true. She couldn't figure out any way with more than a one in a hundred chance of doing some good. Maybe this was how it would be: she'd stand in worse and worse spots and do the same math and end up being the one beating a guy, telling herself there was nothing else she could do. Or maybe she'd hit a line somewhere, something that made her decide it was worth the one in a hundred chance. A real hero would make that call here and now, for Bobby, a stranger who might be any kind of shitbag for all she knew. Vi's chance at being that kind of hero had been and gone fifteen years ago.

Ritchie kept at it, mostly with his boots. Sometimes for a change he'd haul Bobby half off the ground and bash him into the shower fixtures, or turn the water on full hot until he was red and shrieking. He didn't stop until Bobby had been silent and ragdoll limp for a good minute or two. Then he stepped out of the shower, wiped his boots, and washed his hands in the sink.

In the mirror he caught Vi's eye and held it, unblinking. He waited until he'd dried his hands and turned around before saying anything. "You said something wrong, back then."

Vi was feeling a little slow in the head. It was hard not to turn and look at the huddled mass on the floor of the shower. "What?"

"You said *your boss*." Ritchie stepped over and clapped her on the shoulder. "He's your boss too."

She would have liked to peel off and hunker down in her room until someone came to find her, but Ritchie's eye on her made it clear he expected her to follow. They went to an office where Sangster was talking to a cop in plainclothes. The door being open, they stepped inside and waited.

"This is the only waiter that night who wasn't on Burke's regular staff. He got in on a word from a cousin who works there, but now the cousin's saying she's never heard of the guy. The ID cracked as soon as we gave it a serious look. Don't have a name or whereabouts yet, but I'll let you know as soon as we do."

There were two images on the screen, a slightly blurry still from a security camera, and an ID photo. Both showed a young Asian man, slightly pudgy, unattractive haircut. Vi stared at the screen until Sangster turned around.

"Did he say anything?" he asked Ritchie.

"No, and not likely to. Guess he wasn't paid off after all."

Sangster turned back to the cop. "Then you should also look for a hacker who got into my employee's agenda."

"Got it," said the cop. He confirmed a few more details, then stood to leave.

Sangster shook his hand. "I appreciate the assistance, officer."

"Always happy to help out a good citizen like yourself. I'll let you know as soon as there's news." The cop bent his head down not quite far enough to be a bow, but too far for a nod.

"I hope your time with Ritchie was instructive," said Sangster to Vi. She focused on his left cheekbone, because if she looked right in his eye it got harder not to hit him. "Anything else to report?"

"No, sir," said Ritchie. "Bobby's still down in the showers. He won't be walking out."

"Go tell Kurt to deal with him. Ferreira, come." He pointed to the chair the cop had been sitting in.

Vi's feet stuck to the floor. Ritchie gave her a shove that made her stumble, and walked out chuckling. Feeling like her legs were made of lead, Vi went over and stood behind the chair.

"Sit," said Sangster. "You've been very cooperative this morning. I appreciate that. As I said, I will always reward cooperation." He turned his screen toward Vi. It took her much too long to realize he was making a call. "Sit," he said again, hissing slightly. "Didn't you want to talk to your grandmother?"

Not now. Not with the smell of Bobby's blood still in her nose. But the call was already connecting. Nana's face filled the screen. Vi sat.

"Hi, Nana," she croaked. She swallowed and tried to push the corners of her mouth into a smile. "I'm here, I'm safe. How are you?"

"We're fine here," Nana signed. "How long can we talk?"

Vi looked to Sangster and asked, "How long do I have?" He was standing, and she had to look up to ask. He smiled down with a benevolence that churned her stomach.

"Take your time," he said. "You're not in prison." He beckoned at the door, and Nita came in. She went to stand in the corner of the room while Sangster and everyone else left.

"I'm not in prison, he says," Vi said to Nana, trying to find a comfortable edge of sarcasm. "So that's nice."

"Are you eating well?"

"Too well, and my bed's too soft, but I'll cope somehow. Tell me what's happening at home."

The quick, certain movements of Nana's hands were as reassuring as the words. The bar was still closed; Dusty had been bringing in Luce and Arthur for a couple of hours every day to work on cleaning up. Nana had had a bad pain day two days ago but was much better now. She and Roman had started reading a new book series in the afternoons. The price of flour was up fifteen percent, she was glad she'd bought that big bag a couple weeks ago. She hadn't signed any contracts with anyone.

"Sounds great, Nana. You all just keep doing what you're doing."

Nana nodded, eyes hard. "Will you be able to come home?"

"I don't know. I hope so. I'm kinda stuck here for now." She lifted her bandless forearm. "It's okay though. It's very comfortable. Don't worry about me." She tried to banish the bloody body on the gym floor from her mind's eye, afraid Nana would see it in there somehow.

"He wants you to make me sign. What will he do?"

"I guess that'll be a fun surprise. Let's not worry about it for now. I'll talk to you tomorrow, okay?"

"Tell me if you need me to do anything."

"Of course I will. You and Dusty and Roman just keep looking after each other."

"Be careful."

Vi couldn't keep the smile on any longer. "You too," she said, and ended the call.

Nita walked her back up to her room. She immediately crossed the hall and threw up into the toilet. Afterward she lay on her bed, head spinning. Faces ran in a carousel through her mind:

Bobby's swollen cheek and slack mouth, Ritchie's complacent grin, the lines on Nana's forehead. And the one she'd shut out of her mind immediately, for fear Sangster or the cop would see. The face on the screen when she'd walked into Sangster's office. The ID photo wasn't anyone she knew, and the profile shot off the security footage was similar enough to it, so maybe she was just spooked and imagining things. But at the first glance of the security shot, she'd been certain it was Kilo.

Chapter Twelve

There was no one to beat up the next day, and Ritchie was off on some errand. Vi had spent all night in fretful nightmares where he threw a body at her feet and demanded she finish the job, and she turned it over to find that the battered face was Kilo's. Hearing he was out hunting for someone made her miserable and jumpy. She prayed she'd been wrong about the person on the footage.

The man summoned to take her around today was called Kurt. He was taller than Vi by half a head and bulked out to match. His right ear had a notch taken out of it up at the top. When he caught Vi looking at it, he grinned and turned his head to show a long, straight scar running back from the ear. "Ever seen what a metal bullet can do?"

"Not to someone still walking."

He nodded. "Man who fired that thought a gun in his hand

meant he didn't have to worry about me. I'm still walking, like you say, and he isn't. Pity is, I didn't want any trouble with him in the first place. Don't want any with you either."

"Wasn't planning to make any," she said.

"Then we'll get along fine."

The morning was spent supervising a hired grounds crew, keeping all six men in sight as they worked over Sangster's big back garden. At first it was nice to be outdoors, but after a couple hours Vi was hot and bored and wished she was the one hauling stumps out of the ground.

"Do we get a shift change ever?" she asked Kurt.

"No one to change with. Boss wants Sal with him and Ritchie's doing what he does. Now we don't have the Travs loaning us their guns, everyone's working around the clock until he hires more people he can trust."

The sidelong look told Vi that what he meant was, they couldn't trust her and it was a drag. "I didn't ask to come here."

"Well, you're here now. Guess we'll see if you make our job easier or harder."

"Guess we will."

In the afternoon the grounds crew left, and Vi and Kurt went in for lunch. Again there was a bowl of fresh fruit, more tempting than jewels after a long hot morning outside. She wondered if the large helping she'd had at breakfast the previous day had been noticed.

"You always eat like this?" she asked.

"Yeah," Kurt said. "What, you think you're getting special treatment?"

Vi shrugged. After finishing half the sandwich he'd piled high with roast beef off a platter, Kurt said, "I don't know where you came up, but for me this is gravy. Fill my belly every day and lay down easy at night. Do what I'm asked and get paid, simple as that. All my life I never thought I'd have it so good."

"How about the kid that got beat to death? Did he have it good up until yesterday?"

Kurt didn't blink. "Guess it wasn't good enough for him. Guess he got ideas about something else he wanted."

"What if he didn't? What if he really didn't do anything or know anything?"

"Then I guess he got unlucky." He took another bite of sandwich, chewed, and chased it down with limeade. "I like my luck the way it is. I see anything that makes me feel like it's gonna turn, I might get jumpy. You get that."

"I get it."

After lunch, Kurt said they were going for a depot pickup. Getting a look at the road in daylight didn't make Vi feel any better about her options. They were on the side of a hill, the road running up and down in front of the mansion, just one set of tracks and the whole road only wide enough for a single car. Even if she could sneak out and had somewhere to go, she'd be scrambling down a steep incline and hoping there was room to dodge if a car came by.

Knowing it was futile didn't stop her trying to judge the distance they rode to the depot. They made a couple of sharp turns and stopped once to let another car pass the other way. Without her band she didn't even have the time, but it seemed like upwards of ten minutes before they were at the depot. Maybe three or four miles. Not a good prospect on foot.

The depot was easily twice the size of Vi's at home. It'd have to be if it was serving rich folks for four miles around or more. The inside waiting area had the same rickety seats and aging coffee machines, though.

"Guess the lofts don't come get their own shit," she said to Kurt.

She didn't hear his response, because just then the depot clerk turned around. The name tag said Wendy Liu. The face was of a plain, average woman, older than young but younger than middle-aged. Except that the face was Kilo's.

"Name?" said the depot clerk.

"Sangster," Kurt answered. Vi couldn't do anything but stare. She'd seen Kilo in disguise before—back in the early days ze got a kick out of showing up at the bar and seeing how long it took Vi to recognize zem—but she'd never seen zem working. Zer fingers tapped on the keypad and zer face had the exact brisk, slightly bored look every depot clerk wore. Like this was all routine, like ze'd done it thousands of times.

Kurt hadn't been in the room when Sangster was looking at the photos from Burke's. Maybe he wouldn't recognize Kilo even if he had, but the risk was too big. Ritchie was out looking for zem right now. What if he'd been the one to come to the depot today?

"Five shipments in," ze said, looking at the screen. "Couple of them have been here past four days." The sour twist of zer mouth was exactly the one Vi's regular clerk wore when she hadn't been able to make a pickup promptly.

"We've been short-staffed," said Kurt.

Kilo shrugged. "Gonna need a hand digging them out. Just one of you, space back there is tight."

Kurt gave Vi a shove to the shoulder. "That'll be you, then. You got a rear exit?" he said to Kilo.

Zer brow wrinkled. "Staff only. You want to smoke, step out front."

Kurt shook his head. "I just want to keep an eye out, make sure that exit stays staff only."

Kilo appeared to clock Vi's lack of wristband and gave them both a slightly nervous look.

"She won't cause any trouble," Kurt said. "Just keeping an eye out."

"Harming depot personnel or interfering with stock comes with a minimum two years and a lifetime security flag," Kilo said, sounding like a public service announcement. Ze glanced again at Vi's bare wrist, where the flag would be recorded if there was one.

"All I'm worried about is her running. Not that I think she would. Just trying to guard my luck."

Kilo swallowed, looking slightly nervous, but only slightly. "You sit here, you'll have a good view of the rear exit and the storeroom door."

That seemed to be enough for Kurt. He sat down with a cup of bad coffee, chuckling at the glances Kilo kept throwing Vi as ze led her back to the storeroom.

Once the door closed behind her Vi grabbed Kilo's arm. "You

have to get out of here," she hissed. "They're looking for you."

Kilo turned and gave Vi a perfect customer service smile. "Who could be looking for me? I'm just a depot clerk. Come on, we don't have much time." Ze switched on a dolly by the door and led on through the narrow shelves filled with boxes.

Vi kept the grip on zer arm, following. "You don't understand. They've got your picture. I think one of their guys is out trying to hunt you down."

"Good hunting to him," said Kilo. "Here we are. One of your shipments is up there behind three other boxes. I made sure it would be."

"Do you know what they'll do if they catch you?"

Ze sighed and abruptly let zer weight fall back against Vi. She caught zem instinctively. Leaning back on her chest and looking up, ze said, "I'm touched, barkeep, but do you think I just hatched? Do you think I make my living picking pockets? I'm working here." Ze patted Vi's hand and then stood back up. "Glad you're anxious to help me, though, because I do need something."

"What were you even doing at Burke's?"

"Work while we talk. I was wrapping up a quite delicate job. You and your friend fucked it up for me."

Vi froze in the middle of lifting a box down. "What friend? I was there alone."

"You weren't dancing alone."

There had been a time, again back in the early days, when Vi had gotten into a habit of looking for Kilo everywhere she went. She never should have gotten over it. "I dance with people sometimes."

"And yet you've never danced with me." For a second the unfamiliar businesslike tone dropped away, and it was the provocative voice Vi was used to. "Forget that. I've already talked to Tempe, so you can drop the chivalry."

Vi set down the box she was holding and carefully reached for the next one. "If I knew who you were talking about... what did she say?"

"Lots. You two fucked up my plan and I fucked up yours. Not as badly, unless a person cares how long you stay indentured to the golden boy up the hill, which I guess you do. There's a plan, but we need someone on the inside."

"We?" She had to be careful. She couldn't accept that Kilo was speaking for Tempe just because she wanted to. "I don't see her working with someone like you."

Kilo's lips curled up. "Oh, barkeep," ze said in a soft, nasty voice. "How I wish we had more time to chat."

"What the fuck does that mean?"

Ze let the smile linger for a second before flipping back into business mode. "It means we should be back out with your pal in less than two minutes. That box up there is one of yours. Put it on the dolly and focus up. Right now, rich blondie has you under his thumb, he's gunning for me, and Tempe wants him taken down for reasons she doesn't feel like sharing. That's at least two enemies he should be losing sleep over, if he knew what was good for him."

No need to ask which two. She'd seen Tempe in action, and she might doubt Kilo's loyalties but never zer competence. "I can't do much where I am."

"We don't need much. Just two things. First: I don't know how or when it might come up, but if you get a chance to do Junior Palumbo a favor, take it."

It took her a second to place the name. "Junior Palumbo... the head of the Travs?"

"Acting head."

"The Travs are the ones who got me into this mess."

"Whatever they did, it was because blondie told them to, and he and blondie aren't such good friends right now."

"Fuck that. That enemy of my enemy is my friend shit doesn't work in Eastport. Everyone's got too many enemies. He still fucked me over, why should I help him?"

"She said to say, because he's our Ada Mackie."

She hadn't heard that name in fifteen years. There was no plausible way Kilo could know it, except the obvious one. "You really are working with Tempe."

"She wouldn't tell me what it meant. I guess you know, though."

Even Teacher Mackie herself had never known that her success in gaining the post of assistant head was due to the quiet machinations of two pupils. They hadn't liked her—years at the Home had given them ample reason to resent every one of the teachers—but she'd been better than the alternatives. And in the end, she had tried to do the right thing, for all the good it had done. "Yeah. So what's the second thing?"

"I'm giving you a little toy. Once it's connected, it will give me everything I need, but to connect it needs to be within five feet of the target for at least fifteen minutes."

"And the target is?"

"Blondie himself. It needs to be within five feet of his wristband and no one else's in that time. Handily we don't even have to brick yours." Ze glanced at Vi's naked wrist. "Usually this is a seduction play, but you can probably come up with something less distasteful." Ze opened zer palm and showed a round disc, a little thicker than a poker chip and a nondescript grey in color. "You can just keep it in your pocket. When you're ready to start, push and hold the button for three seconds, then just keep the man's attention for fifteen minutes."

"I'm not good at lying."

"I know." Ze patted her arm with a condescension Vi would resent if she had the time. "Don't think of it as lying. Think of it as being someone else."

"Who, you?"

Kilo laughed. "You couldn't if you tried for a lifetime. Think about what he wants you to be, what he went to the trouble of getting you into and out of the joint for. Be that person. Forget that you're anyone else."

"What if I can't do it?"

"Then we have to find another way. Maybe we come up with something that works before he catches me and crushes you, maybe not."

The dream of Ritchie dragging Kilo in and demanding Vi finish the job swam sickeningly in her vision. "You should run."

Kilo stepped in between her and the shelving and looked up, eyes hard and black. "I'll run when I feel like running. I don't usually work with people, barkeep, but I figured if I asked you to do a job, something important to me and you, you'd find a way to get it done. Did I figure wrong?"

Zer chin was pointed up, directly at Vi's heart. Ze looked so sharp and so fragile all at once. Vi's chest gave an agonized throb. She seized Kilo's jaw and kissed zem hard and deep. For once Kilo yielded to her immediately, opening to her mouth, melting against her chest. Zer hands crept softly around her neck, tender and trusting. As if they were real lovers.

When Vi let zem go, ze blinked and smoothed back zer hair. "Wendy Liu would never," ze murmured. "Did that help?"

"I don't know." Vi felt shaken. She would still rather scoop Kilo up and run. If there were any chance of getting anywhere, she would. "After I make the connection, what do I do?"

"Hide the disc, somewhere on the property, anywhere it won't be found. Leave the rest to me. Just make sure to do it before the big gala next week. And remember what I said about Junior."

"He's our Ada Mackie."

"Someday I want to hear all about how you and Tempe know each other."

"Give me the disc."

"Already did." Ze flashed a grin and started walking briskly toward the storeroom door.

Vi felt in her pockets and found the round shape. "Fucking..." she started, but Kilo was already opening the storeroom door.

"I'd prefer you don't swear in my depot," ze said in a flat tone of clerkish disapproval.

Kilo met Tempe in the back room of a variety store. The owner was named Julius and he looked about a hundred years old. He didn't greet Kilo, but when ze had gone through into the back, he locked the door behind zem. The place had been Tempe's pick; for someone new in town, she had a lot of ground information.

Tempe was poring over something on a screen and making notes in the little paper notebook she carried around. Kilo took a seat on a box in the corner of the room. "I got it to her."

Tempe finished writing a line, then looked up. "How is she?"

"Spooked. At first she didn't think she was gonna do it."

Tempe nodded, like this wasn't a surprise to her. It had been a surprise to Kilo. Ze'd expected Vi to jump at the chance to do something, not need to be honeyed into it. The honeying wasn't a problem, but the idea that Tempe might know Vi better than Kilo did was irritating.

"But she will," Tempe said.

That had never been in doubt. Kilo propped zer chin on zer hands. "She was real worried about me. Wanted me to get out of there, never mind what happens to her."

"Mm," said Tempe. She was looking back at her screen.

"She's fun. Doesn't want to care about me, but can't help herself. When we first started fucking I kept stealing things out of her office, and she kept letting me back in anyway."

Tempe didn't stir a hair at that.

"So you knew she fucks me."

Tempe looked up. "I'd guessed." She ran untroubled eyes over Kilo's face. "Were you hoping I'd be jealous?"

Jealousy would have been fun, but it wasn't the only game. "Which of us would you have been jealous of?"

It was a tiny hit, but ze scored. Just a fraction of a flutter of Tempe's eyelids. She folded her hands and took a full breath, in and out, before speaking. "Then were you hoping I'd also be worried about you?"

"Fuck you," came out of Kilo's mouth before ze could stop it. Too angry, too exposed. Ze turned zer snarl into a blade-thin smile. "Why should you worry? You're a stone-cold professional, and this is business. If they drag my body out of the river tomorrow, you won't shed a tear."

"I rarely cry," said Tempe. "And yes, this is business. I know the risks you run, and I want you to go anyway. Wouldn't it sound hollow if I said I was worried?"

"I'm not in this for you." Kilo was the one with zer face on a security recording. Sangster and Junior should have left Burke's each certain that the other was screwing them over, but Tempe's move had created enough confusion around what really happened that everyone was looking for the truth. Ze only had so much time before someone's teeth closed around zer throat. "Just like you're not in it for me."

Tempe stood and came toward Kilo. Softly she put her fingers under zer chin, tipping it upward. "Then we understand each other. I'm glad I can do my job and help you at the same time. If something goes wrong and I have to choose between rescuing you and doing my job, I will keep doing my job. Given that, does it really matter how I feel about it?"

It shouldn't matter. Kilo couldn't afford to have it matter. That didn't make a difference to the twisting feeling in zer chest. "Vi would choose to rescue me."

Ze said it because it might be true and because Vi was the one soft spot ze'd found on Tempe so far. It landed better than ze'd dreamed. Tempe went very still, the blood leaving her lips. "I know that very well."

It was almost too good a success. Kilo had a sense of something monstrous, something ze didn't want to poke awake at this delicate moment. It could wait. Having struck such a big prize, ze could afford to show a little underbelly. "It does matter. I'd like to know that you'd be at least a little bit sad while you threw me to the dogs."

Tempe's hand thawed against zer face. She stroked zer thumb with her cheek. "I would be. More than a little bit."

Kilo turned and nipped her hand. "Then you're lucky I'm as good as I am."

Marcel made Tempe wait, standing, while he sent three different messages. It was not the trial he thought it was; becoming a statue in a room was one of her oldest skills. There might come a time when she needed to insist on the level of respect any born Eudoxian would expect as a matter of course, but at this stage in the game it was convenient for her colleagues to look slightly down on her.

Finished with his work at last, he raised his head. "Still here, Carroll? What is it?"

"I've found something concerning in my investigation of Mr. Sangster's factories. I am not sure whether it's worth bringing to Seigneur Quentin. I would appreciate your opinion."

"Of course. My own duties are nothing at all, I am perfectly at leisure to help you perform yours."

Hitting the right grade of humility was delicate. To apologize at this point would be placing herself too low down. "Since you have worked with Mr. Sangster the most closely, I thought you might be able to provide additional insight or context to what I've found."

"Very well. What is it?"

"As you know, his fabricators are designed to mimic conditions found elsewhere, including Eudoxia. The stated aim is to demonstrate that his materials and formulas are worth buying for our own use. I have found indicators, though, that his factories may be using the same technology to reverse-engineer materials believed exclusive to Eudoxian manufacture. Specifically, I think he may be attempting to make nimbic silk."

Marcel responded as any Eudoxian would: a flash of pure outrage followed by disdain. "Nimbic silk, by definition, can only be fabricated in the celestial environment. Even if your speculation were true, what he would be trying to make is a paltry imitation."

"Of course. Pardon my misspeaking."

"What basis do you have for this absurd suspicion?"

"There are lacunae in the factory records, signs of research projects that have been covered over. And—there is a coat he always wears. It seems precious to him, like an emblem of status. I happened to overhear a servant discussing it, and I suspect that the lining is of nimbic silk. Or, as you say, an imitation."

"Did you not consider the possibility that he purchased genuine nimbic silk for the lining of his coat?" Marcel's tone suggested a profound weariness with having to do his colleagues' thinking for them.

"I thought, if it was genuine, why would he wear it somewhere so secret? Using it as the lining would almost seem to be... in the nature of a private gloat."

Marcel had been working with Sangster nearly every day and was secure in their relationship as he understood it: Sangster an able resource eager to gain his favor. Tempe watched him consider for mere seconds, and then reject, the idea that Sangster might be secretly disdaining him in return.

"And this is the only basis you have? A few missing records and a bit of amateur psychology?"

"I am still looking for more direct evidence."

"You'd do better to stick to your actual duties. Don't waste my time like this again."

"I apologize." She kept her gaze fixed deferentially on Marcel's collar. It was so easy to set up an arrogant man. In the unlikely event that he'd taken her concerns seriously, he would have become the first ally in her long campaign. Now he was her first target.

Chapter Thirteen

Before talking with Kilo, Vi hadn't thought to ask why there was so much garden work being done. Over the next couple of days, she kept her ears open and gathered that Sangster was throwing a party for a bunch of Eastport elites and that he had some business riding on it. A Eudoxian delegation would be coming; most of the garden work seemed to be for their benefit, cutting back the greenery into more sparse and formal patterns, laying white gravel paths all over the lawn.

Vi would have taken it for a problem in her own brain hearing "Eudoxians" and thinking "Tempe," except that Kilo had told her to have the link established before then. With that, she gave it at least seventy percent odds that Tempe would be coming, even discounting for her own bias. Something was happening at or after the party, and it counted on Vi having linked the little disc to Sangster's wristband before then.

The first few days she just waited and hoped an opportunity would arise. He'd been eager enough to corner and talk at her before she came under his roof. Now that she was here, though, he only spoke to her in passing, and only to give instructions. Most days he wasn't even there to initiate the call with Nana. If not for the job Kilo had given her, she'd have been thankful for this. Most of her time was spent with Kurt, who she was getting to like. They sparred in the gym a couple of times, and when he found out Vi could beat him any time she wanted, he didn't get sore in his manliness, just grinned and asked her for pointers.

She could get used to this. She could see how it would happen. Get comfortable enough with the cushy bed and the expensive food, never having to worry about where it was coming from. Do normal work most of the time so that when you had to beat up a Bobby you'd be thinking about how to get it done as fast as possible and get back to your regular life, instead of wondering how you'd ended up with this being your job.

On her own, she'd probably have started some shit the minute she caught herself feeling like this wasn't so bad. Remembering what Kilo had said, she picked up that feeling and looked at it all the way around. This was his plan, make the cage so easy and comfortable she forgot to see the bars. Then at some point he'd ask about the contract again, and the choice to submit wouldn't look so bad. She tried thinking like that person, holding the disc in her pocket like a talisman against it turning true.

Only Sangster didn't ask her about the contract again, and as the days passed and the big party grew nearer, she decided she had to make her own chance. She seized a moment when she was just finishing breakfast and he was walking toward his office.

"Boss," she began, trying not to grimace around the word, "what would happen if my Nana signed the contract?"

He stopped in his tracks and turned a look of surprise on her. She knew right away that she had been too sudden, too abrupt. But after a second his plaster smile spread out.

"Why don't you come sit with me and we can talk about it? Bring a cup of coffee, if you like."

He sent Kurt out to get started supervising the yard workers. Sal, who was usually on his personal bodyguard duty, got a look from Sangster and took up a casual post just outside the open office door. Funny, the idea that she might try attacking Sangster. If there was a chance of that getting her anywhere, she'd have done it days ago.

He sat in the armchair at the back of the office and invited her to sit in the desk chair. *Five feet,* she thought, rolling it over. It was good she'd taken him up on the coffee; having to set it down on the same side table he was using made an excuse to be that close. She'd already practiced hitting the button on the disc from outside her pocket. She glanced at the clock and pushed it.

"I'm pleased you're finally willing to discuss it," Sangster said. "I'm certain we can come up with an agreement that benefits us all. I am a little curious why the sudden change of heart."

She didn't have an answer ready for that. "Isn't that why you brought me here? To change my mind?"

"Certainly. I'm only surprised that it worked so quickly. Is it that the conditions of my household are so agreeable, or that the gravity of your situation is finally becoming evident?"

There was a trap in the question. She couldn't see what it was, but she knew it from the glint in his eye and the purring smugness of his voice. She was not cut out for this kind of game. The silence stretched on while she tried to figure out what to say. Too long for a reply, but only a fraction of one of the minutes she needed to keep him here for.

Sangster's eyes started to narrow, and Vi blurted out the first safe truth she could think of. "I'm worried about her."

"About your grandmother?"

She nodded. About this she didn't have to pretend. "How am I supposed to know how things really are over there? Every day she says she's doing fine, but she'd say that anyway."

"Do you suspect something particular might be wrong?"

What would be the best answer? She hesitated, again too long, and then said, "No. I just worry."

She didn't think he believed her, but maybe that was okay. Maybe if he thought she was hiding some worry about Nana, he wouldn't think she was hiding anything else. "If it eases your mind, I can assure you that I have eyes on your former home. I would know of any unusual activity."

That did not ease her mind. Taken another way, it could be a threat. She looked down at her hands and said, "Thank you," not trying to make it sound sincere.

"Perhaps I can send a physician to confirm her good health." He was watching her closely.

"She wouldn't let him in. She doesn't trust strange doctors." That was also perfectly true.

"An escort to visit the one she prefers, then."

Vi hadn't meant this conversation to be so focused on Nana. The less he interacted with her, the better. "I just want to see her. I'd feel better if I could see her. If she signs the contract, can I go home?"

Sangster leaned back in his chair. "Originally, I would have had no reason to say no. But you and your grandmother have been so persistently defiant. I would be concerned that, once reunited, you would try to find some way to shirk our agreement. You would fail, but it would be a further waste of resources. I've already spent quite a few on you."

"Then what would happen? What would the contract be promising, and what would we get?" This was her plan, if you could call it that: get him to talk about the agreement in as much detail as possible, until the time was up.

He considered her for a moment. "We can discuss that, but what is the hurry? There are several subjects I'd like to talk about with you, now that you've abandoned your tantrum and are ready to talk reasonably."

Vi curled her fists and took a deep breath. She could take an insult. Whatever he wanted to talk about, that would just buy her more time. "Of course."

She knew she wasn't being convincingly agreeable. She'd just barely managed to unclench her jaw. But he didn't seem to mind; if anything, he seemed pleased that she was so obviously restraining herself. His eyes went to her fists and lingered there a moment before returning to her face with a bland smile. "At the Thomas Fontaine Arcade, you were found bending over a corpse. Your claim was that you went there to meet a friend. The person who identified herself as that friend was a Eudoxian named Temperance Carroll. I'm very curious how you came to be friendly with a Eudoxian, and what you were there to meet with her about."

There was just enough warning in his mention of the arcade, of the corpse, that she thought she managed to keep the shock off her face when he dropped Tempe's name. She didn't know what she should be putting there in its place, though. She should have been prepared for this. Of course the cop would have reported Tempe's interference. What could she say? How could she cover it? Her brain stuck and spun and wouldn't give her anything.

"There's nothing to be afraid of," Sangster said, almost cooing as if to a scared animal. "Remember that you're in my custody. You won't be prosecuted for anything unless I permit it."

He thought she was stupid, she realized. He thought she was stupid enough to forget that he was her biggest enemy, that if the hand of the law had come down on her it had been on his orders. And that broke her mind free enough to remember that he already knew everything she'd said in her office. "It was a lie," she said, speaking dully and sullenly. If he wanted to think she was stupid, let him. "I didn't go there to meet any friend. I went to change some coin."

"How fortunate for you that someone appeared just in time to claim your friendship."

"I guess."

"Who is Temperance Carroll?"

Don't panic. Be stupid. "She said she was a Eudoxian."

"Yes, I know that much. How do you know her?"

"She just showed up."

"You had never met before?"

Vi shook her head. What else could he possibly know? Nothing from her youth would be on record here in Eastport. If he'd had eyes on the bar since the cop's visit, he might know that Tempe had been in once, but how could Vi be expected to remember everyone who had ever visited her bar? And if he knew they'd been together at Burke's, surely he'd be starting with that.

"Why did she step in to help you, then?"

"I don't know." What would be plausible? What would Tempe want her to say?

"She must have asked you something."

"I was scared shitless, I don't really remember."

"Try."

He wasn't going to let her get away with nothing. Vi frowned, concentrating. It was the dead man that had taken Tempe there; did he know that already? Was the man connected to him somehow? How could she satisfy him without telling something he didn't already know? "She just asked some questions about why I was there and what I'd seen."

"What had you seen?"

"Just the empty room and the dead guy. I'd only just gotten there when the cop showed up."

"Did she ask about the corpse's appearance?"

If he was asking, he probably already knew. "Yeah. I guess maybe that's why she helped me out, she wanted to know about him."

"What did you tell her?"

There was no way to avoid the obvious. "He was a youngish guy, white, missing two fingers from one of his hands. That's what I saw so that's probably what I told her."

"What did she say to that?"

"Nothing really. She kept pretty buttoned up. I think she was annoyed I couldn't tell her anything more."

Sangster leaned forward in his chair. "Did she mention my name at all? Or did you mention it to her?"

"Your name?" Vi tried to sound slow and thick and perplexed. "Why would that come up?" He held her gaze, searching. Her bones said it was time to switch from defense to attack. "Who was the dead guy? Why did a Eudoxian want to know about him? Why do you?"

"Don't concern yourself with that."

"If I'm on the dock for his murder seems like I should at least know who he was."

"As I said, you will only be prosecuted if I deem it necessary." He picked up his coffee mug and settled back into the chair.

"You're not going to report me for having coin?" She was starting to find a little satisfaction in playing dumb.

"Again, only if I find it necessary." He was getting impatient now. "And on that subject, let us discuss what I will ask of you and your grandmother."

Fifteen minutes was a long goddamn time. They were barely halfway through it and Vi felt like she'd run two miles. She sat and listened with gritted teeth while he laid out his plans for her and Nana's future. He would invest in the bar, which was a nice way of saying that he'd own it and her. He assured her that he wouldn't interfere with the day-to-day operations, but would from time to time weigh in on important decisions. The scope of what counted as important was conveniently vague. He didn't need to say that the bar would be available to whatever gang he wanted to buy favors from.

As for Nana, he would take over responsibility for the sale of her work, including soliciting commissions and gallery showcases. Someone in the Eudoxian delegation was apparently a big fan of hers, and meeting him would afford her new worlds of opportunity. It all sounded very fine. For an artist hungry to be famous, it might even be worth it. But Nana painted what she liked, when she liked, and she didn't go out and meet people unless she felt like it. Vi wasn't going to have that changing as long as she could stand on her own two feet and prevent it.

She truly didn't know much about art sales and commissions, and she asked every question she could think of, trying not to look like she was watching the clock. At last fifteen minutes were up, and she had to fight the impulse to spring out of the chair.

He noticed it. "Something the matter?"

Vi grimaced. "Need to use the restroom."

"Of course. I hope, now that you've understood my plans more clearly, you'll help persuade your grandmother to agree to them."

"I don't know. I'd like to talk with her in person. Can't I go see her? You can send your guys with me. Not like I can get far on my own anyway."

He studied her, frowning slightly. "We shall see. Before this

Friday's event, I cannot spare anyone, but after it... as long as your behavior is as satisfactory as it has been, I think a visit to your old home can be arranged."

She swallowed the implication that this was her new home, thanked him, and tried not to look like she was running out of the room.

Alone in her bathroom, she took out Kilo's disc. The single little light on its side now glowed blue. She closed her eyes and breathed in and out. She'd done it. She hadn't let them down. She poked around the bathroom and tucked the disc into the back corner of a cupboard, behind supplies that wouldn't need to be restocked for a couple of weeks. That would keep it safe at least until the big party. She hoped neither it nor she would be here long after that.

This was only Tempe's second field report to Quentin. She had made both of them meticulous, leaving only a few gaps for questions to which she could immediately supply complete answers. He was a little bored in these meetings, which was all to the good. Let him develop the habit of thinking of her as overly scrupulous and entirely predictable.

As he was about to dismiss her, she cleared her throat. "There is one other thing..."

"Well?" He was in a good mood today. A gift of fresh fruits had arrived this morning, including types one did not find in any legit Eastport grocery. Tempe had been unable to subtly discover who had sent them.

"I beg your pardon. It may be nothing, but if my suspicions are correct it would be of grave concern. Marcel didn't think it worth bothering you about, but I've been uneasy in my mind."

"I have another meeting in four minutes."

"I'll be brief." She described, as she had to Marcel, her suspicions about the nimbic silk. She put a little more confidence behind them, mentioning that the head engineer had accidentally let something slip about reverse-engineering fabricators and adding detail to the description of the coat lining that she pretended to have overheard. Quentin looked just as skeptical as Marcel had.

"Mr. Sangster has been nothing but deferential and obliging," he said. "He must know that to even attempt such a thing would be an unforgivable offense. Why would he risk it when we can give him so much?"

"Yes, sir," Tempe said. In truth, she doubted that he did know just how great an offense it was. It was difficult for terrestrials to fully grasp the finer points of Eudoxian self-importance. "As I said, it may be nothing. But even the slimmest possibility seemed too disastrous to overlook. If he was making it for his own private use, that would be offensive enough, but if he were to use his trade agreement with us to sell his own mockery under our name..."

"Nonsense," Quentin spat. "He could not hope to get away with such a thing. You said Marcel does not share your concerns?"

"No, sir. Given how closely he and Mr. Sangster have worked these last weeks, I had hoped for his insight into the man's character. Perhaps he has given it truly, and I should not have bothered you."

"Indeed," he said with deep sarcasm. "You would do well to listen to your more experienced colleagues."

She didn't need him to become suspicious of Marcel now. The seed was there, and once Sangster was exposed it would begin to take root.

She had enough now for her own purposes. She could pretend to discover the warehouse at any time, and that would put an end to the deal between Sangster and Quentin. She herself did not have any need to ruin Sangster beyond that. But he had Vi in his grip and Kilo in his sights. She could endure seeing either of them destroyed; she could endure anything. To fight for them was a personal indulgence. She hoped Rosa would approve.

To escalate the offense enough to ruin Sangster, she would have to manage both the timing and Quentin's mood. She clasped her hands and adopted a deferential persistence he would find irritating. "I still cannot be easy in my mind. Pardon me for being overprotective of your reputation and mine. If you could see fit to lend one or two agents that I might send out to investigate Mr. Sangster's warehouses. It would have to be done in secret, of course."

"Break into his warehouses? Are we to present ourselves as thieves and sneaks?"

"I would of course take full responsibility in the event we were discovered."

Her terrestrial birth helped here. Quentin could bear her disgrace very comfortably if it came to that. He considered, saw that she was not going to move from her supplicant posture, and tapped his desk three times. Silently, his chief of staff entered.

"Christopher. Who was the footman you had to discipline the other day?"

"That was Jacob, sir. He was found asleep twice while on duty."

"Send him to wait outside this office. Professor Carroll will have a task for him."

"Yes, sir." Christopher departed.

"You may have one man," said Quentin. "Should you be discovered, or even suspected, it will be clear that you acted entirely on your own." He looked pleased with himself, as he should. Whatever doubts Tempe had raised about Sangster could be neatly dispelled, and at the worst he could discard her and Jacob as easily as paring a fingernail. Tempe thanked him, and stepped outside to meet her agent.

Chapter Fourteen

The first few guests came in ordinary cars. Private ones, naturally—no one who rated an invite to Sangster's party would take a shared car—but standard street vehicles. The fifth car to arrive was a personal one, shiny and black with an outline of a running horse on the side. Vi thought she recognized the emblem, and Kurt beside her gave a low whistle.

"Look sharp," he said to her, while tapping something into his wrist.

"Travs?" she asked.

"Yep." His band buzzed a response a second later. "Huh. Sal says they were invited." He rolled out his shoulders. "That's good. Didn't have tangling with mob guns on my list for today."

First out of the car were a couple of guns wearing plain black. Then came two young men, both dressed in neat three-piece suits. The taller one Vi recognized from media photos: he was the Trav boss, Junior.

The last person to exit the car was an old man in a wheelchair. His legs were covered with a blanket, but the suit coat he wore had been shaped to fit neatly over thin shoulders. His hair was white, his cheeks lined, but the eyes looked hard and sharp out of deep sockets.

"Shiiiit," Kurt whispered. It sounded more like awe than alarm. "That's the big man himself, Robert Senior. He never comes out anymore. I heard he hasn't left the Trav compound in five years. People been saying he might be secretly dead."

Sangster came into the courtyard to greet them. Word had it that he and Junior were out for each other's blood, but from his smile you'd never know it. He started in on a syrupy welcome, and Robert Senior cut him off.

"You say you have information I must hear. I have come. I will hear it without delay."

Sangster's smile was not dimmed by the interruption. "Your presence is an honor; I would not dream of being discourteous. I do hope you will agree to stay and enjoy the festivities, but first we will speak in my office. Ferreira!" he called out, startling Vi. "Lead the way."

Kurt gave her a *better you than me* grimace. She stepped forward, nodding at the two Trav guns, and said, "Uh, this way."

She stepped aside at the door to the office, letting the others enter. Sangster was the last in, but instead of dismissing her he said, "Come in." Uneasily, she followed and closed the door at his order.

The five Travs stood in formation, the patriarch at the center with the younger men on either side and the two guns standing behind. Maybe Vi was only here so that Sangster would also have muscle in the room, although Sal was usually his pick for that. She stood behind him and a little to the left, mirroring one of the guns. Kilo had said to do Junior a favor if she got a chance. If the favor was stepping back while the Trav guns had a go at Sangster, she could do that without a twitch of regret.

Sangster addressed Robert Senior. "Citizen Palumbo, I must say again what an honor it is to receive you at my home. We have had a long and profitable cooperation these last few years. I hope that we may continue to do so for many years to come. Of course, this is not possible until the misunderstanding that arose the night of the card game has been resolved, and I have worked tirelessly since then to uncover the truth. I have not forgotten, as many in Lower Eastport have, who the real head of the Travs is. I asked you here in person so that you may hear and decide whether our cooperation can continue to thrive or must be dissolved entirely."

When he said *the real head of the Travs,* Robert Senior's eyes darted sharply to Junior at his right. Junior continued to look forward, not at Sangster but at the wall somewhere behind his shoulder, expression unchanged.

"Come in," said Sangster. There had been no knock, but the door opened at once, and Vaughan Riley stepped in. Her gaze met Vi's for half a second and then flicked away. Her expression was as blank and remote as it had been the day they visited the bar.

"I believe you all know Miss Riley," said Sangster. "You may not have recognized Miss Ferreira, who was also present that night."

She wasn't prepared for the *Miss,* and it struck in a wave of humiliation. In his eyes he already owned her. Her hands balled into fists; she fought to keep them at her sides and looked again at Vaughan, who did not look back.

Sangster was still talking. "...has finally given a full account of what happened, and it is one you should hear as well." He looked to Vaughan.

Vaughan said, quietly but clearly, "On the night of the card game, Citizen Ferreira approached me. We had met before, and she knew I was an admirer of hers. We spoke a little while, and then she asked me to do her a favor. She asked me to find a pretext to wear Citizen Sangster's coat downstairs."

Vi should have been ready for the betrayal, just like she should have been ready for Sangster's familiar address. She wasn't. Cold panic flooded her. What had Tempe said to Vaughan? How many of her secrets could Vaughan give away?

Junior spoke. "Why would she do that?"

"At first she claimed she just wanted to get a look at it, that she'd heard it was something special. Naturally I didn't believe that. Finally she admitted the truth: the Travs were pressuring her, and her bar and family were both at risk. They had said all she needed to do was get me to bring the coat downstairs. I shouldn't have agreed, no matter how much I felt for her, but I did. I'm sorry." She turned her gaze to Sangster, and then just for a second let it slide to meet Vi's. "It was the only way I could find to help her."

Fifteen years ago, Vi had stood in a different office and given the authorities everything they asked for. This betrayal was tiny compared to that one, so what call did she have to be angry? She was angry anyway. *We can both be brave,* Vaughan had said, her lips a whisper away from Vi's. In the end they were both the same kind of coward.

Vaughan continued, now looking directly at Robert Senior. "I didn't see what harm it could do. Even when your son's men grabbed me and pretended to find that token in the coat pocket, I didn't entirely understand until afterward. I apologize."

Robert Senior did not acknowledge the apology. Looking to Sangster, he said, "I am an old man; let me make this clear. You are claiming that my son persuaded Citizen Ferreira to persuade Citizen Riley to bring your coat downstairs, all so that our men could pretend to find the token on her?"

Sangster gave a single grave nod. "I have been aware for some time that the acting head of the Travs wished to sever our connection, despite the many benefits it has brought to your organization. He would have met with resistance if he could not claim treachery, as he has done now."

"Indeed. What do you say to that, Junior?"

Junior, a little tight in the jaw, said, "I did wish to sever the connection. The balance of cost and benefit had been shifting in Citizen Sangster's favor, and I feared it would continue until it was entirely our loss. I have said this to you."

"I remember. You remember my reply."

"Yes, father. I have not broken my word. I have not taken any rash action. This story is an invention."

No one had so much as looked at Vi since her name was

mentioned. They didn't seem to care whether or not she would corroborate Vaughan's story. Or maybe they all took it for granted she would, since she was here taking orders from Sangster. She looked across at Junior. *If you get the chance to do him a favor, take it,* Kilo had said. And on the other side, *I have eyes on your former home.* What would it be, if she defied him now? A cop rushing in to "discover" evidence of some other crime by Nana or Dusty or Roman? An accident striking as soon as one of them left the house? Kilo hadn't given any indication of when zer plan would come to fruition. No promise it'd be soon enough to protect her people from the consequences.

She squeezed her fists. If she waited until it felt safe to kick free of him, she never would. Feeling like she was stepping out over empty air, she said, "It's a lie."

Every head in the room turned toward her. Sangster, Junior, and Robert Senior all opened their mouths to speak, but Sangster got in first. "You mean he's lying that the story is an invention. He did pressure you to make that request of Miss Riley."

"No. He didn't ask me to do anything. I was getting pressure from the Travs, but it was for you. One of the benefits of that connection you're talking about, I guess."

Sangster's smile was paper-thin. "I think you must be confused. Understandably so. You've been very worried about your family. It must make it hard to be clear about who is threatening you and who is protecting you." His eyes said what he really meant: he would make sure she regretted this.

Vi felt shaky all through, but it was the good kind. She was a fighter, she was a *fucking* fighter, and she was done trying to be anything else. "Not really. All you fuckers are threatening me. I don't understand what went down at Burke's and I don't care. I'm just saying how it is. Junior didn't ask me to do anything. The only one who's tried giving me orders is you."

Vaughan was wearing the same berry-red lipstick she had that night on the fire escape at Burke's. She looked at Vi, lips pressed together, fear in her eyes. "Then why did you ask me to bring the coat downstairs?"

Vi got it. Not such a complete betrayal after all; Vaughan had kept Tempe entirely out of it, and Vi could just about forgive her on that basis alone. Now she was asking Vi to offer a different story, since she didn't like the one Vaughan and Sangster had cooked up. Vi shrugged. "Heard it was something special. Wanted to try it on myself."

A snort sounded, loudly, from the second suited Trav, who hadn't spoken yet. "You expect us to believe—"

He was cut off by a knock on the door. "Ritchie here, sir," called the man from the other side. "I have something you'll want to see."

Sangster had been looking at Vi with a blankness that was more menacing than a scowl. "Pardon me a moment," he said to Robert Senior.

Vi didn't see Ritchie when the door opened, because in front of him, arms twisted behind zer back, was Kilo. Ze wasn't in the depot clerk getup; it was zer own short hair, unstyled and falling a little into zer eyes, and a plain black server's uniform. Ze didn't look at Vi.

"Found that waiter you were looking for," said Ritchie. "He

was trying to sneak in with the hired staff. I thought, as you're dealing with the business, you'd want to know right away."

The front window of Sangster's office was higher than ground level because of the slope. Still not a full story up, not too bad a fall. The stupid ugly plaque on the desk was heavy enough to break the window. That would be the move: grab Kilo, grab and hurl the plaque, crash backward through the window, fall and roll and then hope one of them had a good idea for what came next.

"It's not needed at this time," said Sangster. "Take him downstairs and wait for instructions."

"Yes, boss," said Ritchie.

They hadn't even come through the door yet. She couldn't grab Kilo that way. Dive through the door instead, knock Ritchie down while she grabbed zem, then barrel on past. To where?

"Hold on." Junior's voice rang with the confidence of a man used to being obeyed. "That waiter was at Burke's the night of the card game. I believe we'd like to hear what they have to say."

"I have reason to believe this is a career criminal," Sangster answered. "Not exactly a reliable witness."

"We are not inexperienced in dealing with career criminals, Citizen Sangster."

Sangster looked at Robert Senior. "I would hope not to waste my honored guest's time."

Robert Senior gave a thin smile. "If I didn't trust in your good faith, I might think you were trying to prevent my learning something."

Sangster coughed. "Of course not. Come in then, Ritchie. We'll hear what the waiter has to say."

Ritchie pushed Kilo into the room in front of him, making sure ze had to stumble a little. Ze looked around the room, as if sizing them all up. Vi waited for her turn and then darted a glance toward the window when Kilo's eyes finally met hers. Kilo gave a slow, disdainful blink, then turned zer gaze toward Robert Senior.

"Appreciate the chance to be heard," ze said, in a voice a few shades rougher and deeper than the one Vi was familiar with. "But I actually think it's someone else who has something to say." Zer arms shifted slightly behind zer back, and as Ritchie tightened his grip a voice sounded.

"Then that's all we need. Once the old man realizes it's me with your support or Junior without it, he'll make the right choice."

The sound came from Sangster's wristband, but the voice was the one Vi had just heard from the third Trav man. All eyes turned to him while he paled.

"Andrew," said Robert Senior. "Explain."

He stammered, "I don't... it's a fake, it's a trick. Who did that?"

"I can explain," said Junior. "I became aware some time ago that there was someone working against me from fairly high in the organization. Plans fell through, secrets were leaked, always the ones that would do the most damage to me personally. The theft of the token was the most dire, and I could not let the situation stand. Not knowing who in the Travs I could trust, I sought outside help." He looked to Kilo, who straightened up and gave him a nod in return.

"I am, as blondie there says, a career criminal. I work

freelance, but I'm happy to lend a hand if an organization needs it, especially to someone as respected as Citizen Robert Palumbo Junior. We arranged to have me caught under suspicion of having the token and held in Trav hospitality for a day or so. Near the end of my stay, I was approached by Andrew there. He suggested if I didn't like the idea of admitting I'd stolen the token from the Travs, I could give it to him, and then when he was running things instead of Junior, he'd make sure no one held a grudge against me. He was very persuasive. If I'd really been who he thought, I'd have been tempted."

Andrew's jaw had dropped. He looked from Kilo to Junior, shocked and frantic. "I didn't... I never... you can't believe an outsider's word over mine."

"Andrew, little cousin, do you think you weren't already my first suspect? My only doubt was whether you could be as effective as you were without someone backing you."

Andrew went red. Kilo continued. "There are only a few thieves in Eastport capable of that token job, and I know them all. The one who'd done it was glad enough to hand it over to regain mutual goodwill." Ze looked directly at Junior, and he gave the faintest of nods.

"You had it?" Andrew cried. "Since when?"

"The actual token has been back in my possession for some time now," said Junior. "I kept it secret, in order to discover who else was working against me."

This made a stir among the Travs. The two guns exchanged a look of surprise, and one of them grinned admiringly at Junior. Andrew's jaw stayed hanging open. Robert Senior was watching his son's face closely.

Kilo continued, "He says discover like he didn't already have a pretty good guess who it was. But even if it was someone else, it was a good bet they were a big enough player to be at the card game. I reached out to Andrew, telling him I had the token and could hand it over that night. He couldn't take it home with him, not surrounded by Travs, so we figured he'd pass it on to his backer. And we all know whose pocket it ended up in."

"What?" Andrew cried out. "You did what? You never reached out to me! I never even touched it! That's true, uncle, I never saw it that night, I swear."

Junior continued, ignoring him. "It would have been ideal to find the token on Sangster himself in front of all the players of the card game. Instead, for whatever reason, Citizen Riley took the coat downstairs, and it happened to be found there, which muddied the waters. I was certain in my own mind what had really happened, but felt I should not come before you, father, without stronger evidence."

"It's not hard to find once you know where to look," said Kilo. "Let's hear some recent transactions: keyword gold rush."

From Sangster's wristband came the standard electronic reader voice. *"September 30, 349, Brett Sangster to Andrew Palumbo. Five million dollars. December 11, 349, Brett Sangster to Andrew Palumbo. Eight million four thousand dollars. February 25, 350, Brett Sangster to Andrew Palumbo. Six million dollars."*

"There's plenty more," said Kilo. "Just let us know when you're satisfied."

"Well?" Robert Senior turned to Andrew.

"They're lying," Andrew said. "I never touched the token. I never even knew where it was."

"And the money?"

Andrew was twisting his fingers, looking panicked. "That was... he gave lots of money to the Travs. We did lots of jobs for him."

"Has Andrew been placed in charge of handling commissions without my knowledge?" Robert Senior asked dryly.

"Certainly not, father. But give him a little time, maybe he'll be able to invent side jobs to match all those sums and dates."

Andrew looked to Sangster, fear and pleading obvious for everyone to read. Sangster gave him one unimpressed glance, then addressed the old man in the chair.

"We have strayed from the essential point. Regardless of who you choose to believe, no one can dispute that the good faith between myself and Junior is irrevocably broken. If he continues to lead the Travs, my association with the organization has come to an end."

"I value our association, Citizen Sangster, but I do not appreciate an attempt to force my hand on the question of leadership."

"Have I done so?" Sangster asked. "Junior's hostility to me predates any of the transactions you heard. I believe you have your own knowledge of that. When another Trav leader, also of your blood, showed me more friendliness and a forward-thinking interest in cooperation, I naturally came to prefer associating with him. But we would not have reached even this impasse today if not for your son's effort to push me out entirely. Who is forcing your hand?"

"If Andrew stole the token—" Junior began, but Sangster intercepted him.

"If Andrew stole the token, then for the dignity of your organization you could not possibly let him lead. But has that been proven? Are you compelled to accept that that is what happened? In the end, you must do what is best for the Travs. My money has been valuable to you, but in the future you will find that I have even more to offer in the area of friendship. Ritchie, had the secretary of trade arrived yet when you left?"

Ritchie grinned. "Yes, boss, and he's been enjoying the peach puffs."

"I'm glad to hear it. In a little while, I will be having a much more pleasant meeting with him and with the Eudoxian magnate, whose car you can see if you look out the window. The enemy of my friend is my enemy, and the secretary of trade and I are about to become very good friends."

Vi might buy most of her goods clear, but like every business owner in Eastport she knew that the department of trade strategically closed its eyes to a portion of the smuggling that made up every large gang's bread and butter. Vi didn't know how much damage it could do the Travs to have the secretary actively hostile to them, but judging from the three men's faces it was a lot.

"Junior," said the patriarch grimly. Junior's jaw clenched. Andrew started to grin again.

Kilo stretched, got a cuff from Ritchie, and laughed. "So

gloomy all of a sudden. Anyone can invite a bunch of fancy names to a party."

Junior met zer eyes. "Well said. Since Citizen Sangster is not trying to force my father's hand, I'm sure he won't object to showing his before I fold. I do not wish to undermine the Travs with an ugly fight. Let us return to the party showing a united front. If the secretary of trade is as good a friend as Citizen Sangster claims, I will pledge my resignation before we leave here."

"Who will make that determination?" said Sangster.

"I will," snapped Robert Senior. "Agreed?" He looked to his son first. Junior nodded.

"Very well," said Sangster. "Then let us rejoin the rest of my guests." He didn't look as if he was in any doubt of the final outcome. Vi looked to Kilo, trying to get a read on how badly the plan was ruined, but ze was staring at the floor as if nothing happening now was particularly interesting.

"What about this one, boss?" asked Ritchie, giving zem a rough shake.

"They have been working for the Travs," said Junior. "It is for the Travs to decide how to deal with them."

"They were caught snooping on my property."

"On business of the Travs."

"On *your* business," Sangster returned. "But I'll concede. At the end of the evening, I'll hand them over to the Travs, and trust that whoever is acting head by then will deal with them appropriately." He and Andrew exchanged a look. "In the meantime, I hope you won't object to my holding them for the duration of the party."

"As long as they are in the same condition then as now."

"Of course," Sangster smiled. He then turned to Vi. "You have disappointed me. I had hoped we could work well together, and I've shown you nothing but kindness in your time here. Of course I can no longer have you as one of my staff. You will also be held, and I'll decide afterward how to deal with you."

Vi and Kilo were taken down to the gym and cuffed to iron pipes, with Ritchie standing guard. He grinned unpleasantly at Vi. "I always said it was a mistake taking you on. Once the guests upstairs are gone, we're gonna find out how long it takes to make you wish you were back in jail."

It suited her fine to have him focused on her instead of Kilo. "If you keep me cuffed, maybe you can do it. Then you can brag what a big man you are, beating on someone who's chained to a pipe."

"I don't need to brag. I just need the fun of hearing you beg me to stop."

He wouldn't get that, no matter what happened. She just hoped things went the way Kilo wanted them to upstairs, so ze'd be out of here before Ritchie was unleashed. She didn't see a lot of hope for herself; no reason the Travs would protect her, or her family. Didn't matter. She was fighting now, and she'd go down fighting.

Chapter Fifteen

When the Eudoxians arrived at the gala, Brett Sangster was not there to greet them.

"I was under the impression that it was a grave discourtesy to be late," said Taillefer Quentin, ostensibly to no one in particular.

Tempe, who had spent the whole ride working to give that impression through displays of anxiety about the time, said apologetically, "I must have been mistaken. Customs are surely different here from the place where I was raised."

Sangster emerged several minutes later, preceded by three men whom Tempe recognized from photos as the Trav leaders. Judging by their expressions, things had gone to plan so far. There was no sign of Vi or Kilo, but she could not afford to worry about them now. Finishing off this play would take focus and finesse.

Clemence Dorsey was among the guests, playing the merry yapper. Vaughan Riley had also emerged with Sangster, and Dorsey dove on her like a falcon, wrapping an arm around her shoulders and emitting gushing invitations for a future performance. Tempe diverted her course through the party; she did not want to encounter Vaughan Riley at this stage. She saw out of the corner of her eye that Sangster saw Quentin's irritation and was doing his best to soothe it. The secretary of trade hovered nearby, pretending to be in discussion with the transit chief while clearly giving half his attention to Sangster and the Eudoxians. They were interrupted every few seconds by obligatory greetings from other guests. There was a distinct coolness between the transit chief and the secretary of justice when the latter made his rounds; that might be something she could make use of in future.

First to finish the current job. Vaughan Riley had detached from Clemence Dorsey, so Tempe drifted through the crowd and alighted as if by chance at Dorsey's side.

"A day of celebration for you," said Dorsey, tipping her glass to Vaughan. "Once this deal is settled, does your work get easier or harder?"

"Easier," said Tempe with a smile, "more details and less investigation."

"You must be relieved then."

"I will be once the deal is settled. Great men are temperamental, you know, and I'm a little worried about our host's approach. Eudoxians don't like presumption, and this gathering rather makes it look like Citizen Sangster considers us a sure thing."

"Aren't you?" Clemence Dorsey's eyes went very wide and innocent.

Tempe gave a prim smile, as of one who knew she was on the verge of saying too much. "I only wish the festivities had been saved until after the papers were signed."

Clemence Dorsey was too deft to push the topic further. She turned the conversation to clothes, recommended a few shops, and found an excuse to leave Tempe's side. A few minutes later, she was squeezing her way in between Sangster and Quentin.

"This is simply exquisite, Brett," she said warmly. "You must congratulate yourself on throwing a party worthy of the occasion and your honored guest."

Quentin's face became even more rigidly smooth. Sangster threw him an anxious glance and said, "I would not presume to congratulate myself on anything but the honor of Seigneur Quentin's friendship."

Dorsey gave him a knowing smile and murmured, "A strong friendship indeed. I heard a little rumor that you wear a token of it under your coat." She said it so quietly Tempe had to read her lips, but by Quentin's start, she knew he had heard.

Sangster paled. "I'm sure I don't know what you mean."

Dorsey tutted. "The only man in Eastport to wear nimbic silk, and you keep it hidden in the lining of your coat. Some of us might feel you're looking down on us, that you think we'd tear ourselves up with envy to know you've received such favor." She gave Quentin a sly glance. "Or maybe the givers asked you to keep it quiet. I admit I don't know all the fine points of Eudoxian discretion."

Quentin's eyes could have frozen metal. Sangster gave a smile even more toothy than usual. "Your gossip is not up to standard, Clemence. I don't know where you heard such a thing, but you've been led astray."

"Oh? I apologize if I've spoken out of turn. I blame your excellent wine, Brett. I'll go have some more and find somewhere else to get myself into trouble. Do please excuse me."

Clemence made her exit, but Quentin had not thawed. Sangster attempted a confidential attitude. "Some types of people are highly susceptible to rumors and fabrications, as I'm sure you've found. I was fortunate enough to purchase a few yards of nimbic silk at an international trade meeting, and I can only imagine that somebody, on learning that, leapt to unfounded conclusions..."

Tempe did not stay to listen to the rest of his excuse. The lie was all she needed. She drifted away, tapping a message to Jacob as she went: Any news?

As arranged, Jacob answered her with a video. She found a private corner to put up her screen and play it, though she had already watched it the previous night. It would not do to skip any of the motions. She watched to the end, and then, as if she'd just learned the alarming truth, looked around for any of her colleagues.

She hoped the first one she saw would be Octavia or Junyi, and it was Octavia. Tempe hurried to her side. "Have you seen the Seigneur? I have something to show him without delay."

Octavia, who had been in the middle of conversation with one of Eastport's preeminent bankers, at first tried to brush her off with a vague indication of direction. Then, probably remembering both that Tempe was rarely agitated and that a calamity for one of them was a calamity for all, she detached herself from the banker. "What is it?" she said, following.

"I have suspected for a little while that Sangster might be manufacturing—forging—nimbic silk. My assistant has just found what looks like proof."

Octavia stared. "Impossible."

Tempe shook her head. "He has a whole laboratory devoted to imitating Eudoxian conditions for fabrication. They have reverse-engineered many techniques. Not impossible."

"And the proof?"

"Several bolts of it in one of his warehouses. I've just received the video." She opened her screen. Octavia watched a few seconds of it, then stopped her.

"You're certain? It couldn't be anything else?"

"My assistant inspected them personally."

Octavia was the economic specialist. Tempe did not need to prompt her to grasp the most dire implication. "Where are they?" She took the lead, dragging Tempe in her wake to find Quentin and Sangster.

When they did, Marcel was between the two great men trying to ease the atmosphere. Octavia detached Quentin with a word of urgency, and Marcel naturally followed.

Tempe got the full measure of her status in Octavia's eyes by how comfortably she took ownership of the discovery. "We have found out something that might have dire implications for today's business. I could not let you continue with Citizen Sangster before knowing. Tempe, show him the video."

Tempe unfolded her screen. "You may remember, sir, that a few days ago you allowed me an agent to investigate certain suspicions about Citizen Sangster. This is what he found."

The video itself was enough for grave suspicion. Most of the nimbic silk on Earth had come from a rival Eudoxian magnate and his business partner in Beijing, where it was carefully rationed out to high-end couturiers. Already the chances of Sangster having bought enough to line his coat stretched belief; the idea that he had purchased and stored several bolts was unthinkable.

Quentin turned to Tempe. "You say he has the capability to forge manufacture?"

"He does, sir. I believe he has had engineers working in great secrecy to exactly that end."

Octavia, with her head bowed, said, "With a trade agreement in place, he could claim that these came from Eudoxia, and the terrestrials would not know enough to question it. The ramifications..."

"I am able to grasp the ramifications," said Quentin, his hands clenched. "Have him come here. And the secretary of trade — no. Just Sangster."

Sangster had been hovering nearby, plainly aware of trouble in the air. Tempe had volunteered to fetch him, and as she motioned him back to the secluded alcove where they huddled, she saw that the three Trav men were gathered not far off, and at least two of them seemed to be keeping a discreet eye on the brewing storm.

"Your coat," said Quentin. There was no courtesy in his tone, nor room for refusal. It plainly chafed Sangster to be spoken to as a subordinate, but he would never have gotten this far with the Eudoxians if he didn't know when to pretend to lay his ego aside. He carefully removed his coat and handed it to Quentin.

Tempe looked it over as if she hadn't already examined it at Burke's. The entire lining was nimbic silk. For all that her colleagues would insist on calling it a cheap mockery, by look and feel it was indistinguishable from the Eudoxian product.

"You claim that you purchased this silk?"

"Yes indeed, at an international conference," said Sangster. "To be perfectly candid, I suspect the provenances of the seller might not have entirely held up under scrutiny. It was a weakness to buy it, and having done so, I felt the only discreet thing I could do was to wear it privately, a reminder of my strong intention to someday forge legitimate connections with our celestial cousins."

It was a good play. If it had only been the coat in question, it might have worked.

"And how," said Quentin, his voice like ice, "do you account for the four bolts of silk lying in one of your warehouses?"

Tempe could almost see the calculations in Sangster's head. His first temptation was to deny it, but the specific number showed that they had firsthand confirmation. To claim that someone else had planted it would only show that he did not have control over his holdings. To claim that he had purchased it would be ludicrous. He closed his eyes and bowed low.

"I must beg your excellency's pardon for an extraordinary presumption," he said. "The bolts in the warehouse are of my own manufacture. In my eagerness to prove the efficacy of our simulation techniques, I humbly attempted to reverse-engineer some Eudoxian products. The success was beyond my expectation. I will gladly offer those bolts to you, your excellency, as a token of goodwill."

"And what use could we possibly have for some cheap terrestrial forgery of Eudoxian goods?"

"I think you will find, your excellency, that my silk is indistinguishable from the Eudoxian article to both eye and touch."

It was the worst thing he could have said. He continued with assurances that the engineering techniques were kept in the utmost secrecy, but only Tempe heard him. Quentin was in a towering rage.

"Leave me!" he roared.

"I beg your excellency will give me a chance to explain further—"

"Get out of my sight!"

Half the party must have heard the bellow. Sangster turned and left, his coat still in Quentin's hands. Quentin threw it to Octavia. "Burn this." He turned to Tempe.

"Is our agent in that warehouse now?"

"No, sir."

"Have him go back and remove every scrap of that travesty."

"Yes, sir."

"Where is the secretary of trade?"

Marcel cleared his throat. "Seigneur, I believe we should depart and discuss in private before taking any further action."

Quentin whirled on him. "You! You knew about this."

"On my honor, seigneur, I did not." He glanced uneasily at Tempe. "Professor Carroll mentioned a suspicion to me, but I could not bring myself to believe such an outrage. It is my fault; in your service I ought to have followed up even on the most wild of suspicions. I humbly beg your pardon."

"And do you have any counsel for me at this time?" Quentin sneered.

"I would not dare, seigneur."

Marcel was right, of course; it would have been wisest to leave and decide on their response with cooler heads. Quentin was too angry to be wise. Tempe trailed behind, last of his train, as Quentin strode out into the party in search of the trade secretary. He found him and Sangster at a far corner of the garden, in low earnest conversation. They broke apart hastily at his approach, giving bright, desperate smiles.

"I very much regret the recent misunderstanding," Sangster began, "and I have been discussing with the secretary some additional favorable terms that might compensate for—"

"Hear me well," said Quentin directly to the secretary, barely allowing Sangster a glance. "I will accept no terms whatsoever as long as this man is a party to the agreement."

The secretary blinked. "On behalf of the city of Eastport, I apologize most profoundly for whatever offense our citizen has given. I hope that you will not allow it to dissolve an agreement that has been many months in the making and is expected to bring much benefit to both parties."

"It is dissolved," said Quentin. "There will be no agreement, not with your Citizen Sangster nor with any of his business partners. If the city of Eastport wishes to establish a partnership with our house, it must be done with some other party. Someone who is in no way connected to him."

Whatever money had already passed from Sangster to the trade secretary, it could not compare to the amount that would flow through his hands in the course of an established trade agreement with a Eudoxian magnate. The secretary turned his shoulders away from Sangster and said, "I will naturally be more than pleased to help Seigneur Quentin seek out a suitable partner."

Tempe glanced around. Ann Bredon was standing not far off, as were a number of others. Already one listener was scurrying away to report to someone. Of Eastport's wealthy citizens present, more than a few would be eager to fill the sudden vacancy. If that meant cutting ties with Brett Sangster, they would be digging into their contracts and severing agreements with his wine still in their mouths. She looked further until she saw the three Travs. The youngest of the men was looking about him, seeming bewildered, but the one called Junior bent down and whispered something to his father, who gave a grim smile.

Kilo was pretending to be asleep. Or maybe actually sleeping; Vi wasn't ever going to bet on what was real and what was an act with zem. It was better for her either way. The last thing she wanted was for Ritchie to find out Kilo wasn't a stranger to her, and the best chance of avoiding that was for nobody to talk at all.

Time dragged. She thought about exits. Doubtful that Ritchie would let her out of the cuffs before starting in on her, but assuming she somehow got free she'd need a next step. Up the stairs into the house? Out the rear fire exit? Or through the tiny window that was in the corner of the shower room? The fire exit led out to the backyard; good odds Kurt would be there helping or supervising the after-party cleanup. He was the one she was most worried about if it came to a fight. He could slow her down, maybe even stop her if she was in bad enough shape by then. She hadn't ever tangled with Sal, who would probably be near Sangster as usual. He wasn't as big as Kurt, but there had to be a reason Sangster picked him for personal guard duty. Through the house she might have to face him.

The shower room window opened on an outside wing of the house, near the parking area. Good exit point, but the window was high up. She'd have to pull herself up and then get it open. She shut her eyes, trying to remember if there was anything to brace on in there. Risky. If she couldn't get the window open, she'd be cornered. Maybe getting past Kurt or Sal was a better bet.

It was so quiet that she heard it clearly when Kilo's wristband gave three short buzzes. Ze stirred and stretched zer legs out. "Hey, you. Ferreira or whatever. You ever try breaking out of mag cuffs? Those big muscles have to be good for something."

Vi knew she couldn't, certainly not at the angle her arms were pinned, but she didn't think Kilo was talking just to hear zemself. She straightened herself up and started making an effort. Ritchie pulled a stunner out of his belt and walked toward her.

"Sit tight and don't move, or I knock you out," he said. "I've been sitting here planning what I'm gonna do once I'm cleared to make noise down here, and I'm not—"

He crumpled to the ground. Kilo stood behind him, hand raised to where his neck had been.

"Time to go, barkeep." Ze kicked the heel of zer boot up toward Vi's cuffs, and they fell open. Vi shook her arms to get the feeling back. "I think house, not yard, yeah?"

"No. There's a window." With Kilo here, it was a no-brainer. She led zem into the shower room.

"Lovely," Kilo grinned up at the window. Hoisted on Vi's back, ze made quick work of the latch, slithered through, and then leaned in to give Vi a hand.

Vi shook her head. "Back up and give me room." She jumped to grab the frame and haul herself through. Kilo was already crouched looking through the arch that led to the front courtyard.

"Clear," ze whispered. "Get to the cars."

Vi's instinct was to crouch and scurry past the archway, but Kilo walked straight across, brisk and purposeful, so she followed suit. As soon as they were in the lot they stepped between cars to hide them from both house and road. Besides the shiny black Trav car, there were several other personal vehicles with their individual decor, and a few private street cars just sitting. Down in Lower Eastport, you'd never see that many private cars idle in one place; one or two minutes empty and then they'd be sliding off to answer a call from a nearby stop.

Kilo fished in the cuff of zer boot and held something out to Vi. It was a wristband. It looked like a kids' band, flat and cheap with a fastener, but sized for an adult. It was still a wristband: she put it on and instantly felt less exposed. She looked at Kilo, who was going from car to car, inspecting. It hadn't struck her until now that ze had come here for her. Whatever zer other goals were, ze had planned on getting her out. Had made preparations specifically for that.

"This one," ze said, standing by a car that wore a smooth powder-blue coat of paint.

"Not a street car?" Vi didn't recognize the insignia, but this car clearly belonged to someone.

The door opened with a hiss as Kilo shook zer head. "The street cars are here because someone's got them on reserve. They'll get a ping as soon as it leaves. No one's monitoring this one; why should they when it's got their name all over it?" Ze stepped inside.

Vi followed, reluctant but without any better ideas. The door slid shut. Kilo grinned up at her. "Relax, my dear respectable barkeep. They'll get it back. It's you I'm stealing, not the car."

Her heart lurched in time with the car as it pulled out onto the road. She sat down heavily on the padded bench. Kilo sprawled back on the one opposite, one leg crossed over the other.

"I've been in less comfortable hotel rooms," ze said. "Too bad we have to ditch it, I'd have some ideas for how you can pay me back."

Vi was still dealing with *it's you I'm stealing* and the easy way Kilo had handed her the wristband and the simple fact that she'd been rescued. Her problems had always been her own to solve, but this time someone had rescued her, and that someone was Kilo. It was a lot to take in, even without the idea of pressing zem down into the upholstered bench of a stolen car. She pulled her mind back to the immediate moment. "When do we have to ditch the car?"

"Just before we hit the border."

"And then what?"

"Then you get in a street car and go home."

Vi shut her eyes. The thought of home was also too big to take in right now. She gripped the seat and focused on unsolved problems. "What about Sangster?"

"Losing you is going to be the least of his worries. Your dance partner saw to that. I'll be surprised if he's still in Eastport this time next week."

"And you? Will the Travs still be after you?"

"Me? The person Junior relied on to help uncover the conspiracy against him?"

Vi could never be sure when Kilo was telling the truth, but sometimes ze made it very clear ze was lying. "You weren't really working with him."

Zer toe danced a cheerful pattern in the air. "Of course I was. The question you want to ask is how long I've been working with him."

Just this once she didn't mind playing along. "How long?"

"Would you believe three days?"

"I don't know what I should believe."

"No one ever does. You're one of the only people I know who admits it. Look at it like this: there's two ways the story could go. One is, I stole the token from the Travs last fall, and every month

Junior failed to find me is a bigger embarrassment to him. The other is that I helped him find the token months ago, and he's been executing a secret plan to weed out his enemies ever since. He likes the second story better, and so do I. Embarrassing a mob boss might be funny, but it's bad for your health."

They rode in silence while Vi tried to sort out all the pieces in her head. "You were at Burke's," she said at last, "and you put the thing in Sangster's coat pocket. You never handed it over to that Andrew guy, he was actually surprised by that."

"Barkeep can read," Kilo murmured. The patronizing tone should have been offensive, but there was something soft in the corner of zer smile.

"You wanted Sangster to be caught with it—why? What did you have against him?"

"Never met the man before today. But if you're a thief looking to get rid of something hot, one good way is to stick it on someone the owner will be happy to blame. Not that that has anything to do with me: like I said, I was working with Junior the whole time."

"And what about Tempe? Did she catch you at Burke's?" She'd spent much too much time thinking it over, and it was the only possible way she could imagine the two of them meeting.

Kilo snorted derisively. "I was eleven the last time I was caught during a job. We're old acquaintances, Tempe and I. Although not as old as you." Ze rolled to the side and propped zer head on zer elbow. "I figure it was at least twelve years ago that you knew each other."

"Why?"

"She's never been to Eastport before. You got here twelve years ago and never left."

She felt stupid for being disappointed. As if Kilo could give her more insight about Tempe. At least she knew better than to ask what Tempe had said about her. That would only prompt another tease.

Kilo lifted zemself from the bench and crossed over to Vi. "I've just had an idea. We'll ditch the car in about ten minutes and then we're going separate ways. You should get a start on paying me back." Ze knelt over Vi, straddling her legs, just in case she was in any doubt about what kinds of payment Kilo had in mind.

"In ten minutes?" She was irritated by the teasing over Tempe. She had always hated Kilo's easy presumption. Her hands were already around zer thighs.

"I'm on vacation, starting ten minutes from now. Absolutely no working for at least three weeks." Ze tilted zer head to show a long stretch of neck.

Early on, Kilo had laid down very firm rules about marking zer skin. Sometimes it was none anywhere, which Vi tried not to think more deeply about. Usually it was nothing above the collar. Once, somewhere shy of two years ago, ze had announced ze was taking a vacation and goaded Vi into leaving vivid bruised spots all over zer neck. The goading had involved a lot of hints about other hookups ze meant to indulge, and Vi had been overtaken by a territorial spirit.

She looked into zer dark, glittering eyes. "Just had this idea out of nowhere, did you?"

Kilo gave a languid blink. "Mhm." Zer fingers crept up the

base of Vi's skull. Vi's heart was suddenly a jackhammer. She did not believe Kilo and Tempe were fucking. Tempe was too wise and too focused to fall into Kilo's well the way Vi had. But she felt the implication and the prospect of it down to her bones.

They didn't have to be fucking. Kilo would want to carry a mark to her anyway, tease her the way ze was teasing Vi. Probably ze was trying and failing to seduce her. Maybe Tempe would see it and think that Vi had sunk lower than she'd ever imagined. Or maybe she'd understand, which was more than Vi did. Maybe she'd come around one more time, in concern, to explain Vi to herself.

Kilo's nails raked the back of her neck. "I feel like I don't have your full attention, barkeep. Someone else you're thinking of?"

"What's your game?" Vi growled.

"If you can't tell, then I'm already winning."

She wanted to ask. She desperately wanted to ask, and she knew what she'd get if she did. Laughter, delight, Kilo's vicious joy in holding back something she wanted. She pulled zem in and sucked at zer neck, nastily, methodically, biting down until ze writhed against her. She did another one on the other side, higher, just under the ear. When she broke away ze touched the first mark with lightly trembling fingers.

"That will do nicely," ze said.

Vi's blood was up now. "How long did you say we have?"

"Less than five minutes." Ze kissed her, holding her lip between zer teeth and pulling off slowly. "I'll take that for a down payment and come back later for the rest." Ze gave a short sharp laugh. "After you've had a shower at home. You smell like a flower shop."

Chapter Sixteen

Kilo left Vi at a stop near the Heights border. Here there were walking lanes beside the street, and ze strolled off with a wave. Following zer instructions, Vi boarded not the first public car that arrived at the stop, but the second. She felt more out of place than she looked; for the party she'd been given a crisp shirt, vest, and pants to wear. She probably looked like a servant on an errand. Nobody looked at her twice, and she tried to make herself unobtrusive, standing at one end of the car.

At the border stop her anxiety kicked up again. She didn't even know what name the temporary wristband bore. Why hadn't she looked before now? But the officer didn't even look at the passengers' faces as he ran his scanner over every wrist. He scanned hers just the same, stepped off, and the car started moving again.

She had to change cars once to get within a mile of home, but after that she walked. The closer she got the more tense she felt, as if something was going to spring out at the last minute and stop her. Nothing did. She passed by the shuttered front of the bar, went around to the alley, and realized she couldn't unlock the back door. Putting her fingers in her mouth, she gave a sharp whistle, and a minute later there was Dusty with his apron and his ginger beard.

He glanced down the alley on seeing her.

"It's just me," she said. "I'm back."

His smile started and then got broader and broader. "Then what are you standing there for? Come on up."

On the stairs she caught the smell of Nana's adafina, rich and spicy. Of course, it was Friday. Her throat closed up and she blinked hard.

Dusty flung open the apartment door. "Look what I found," he boomed. Nana turned from the stove and dropped her spoon.

"I'm back," said Vi again. That was as many words as she could get out without her voice shaking. Nana came to her and put both hands on her cheeks, searching her face. Vi blinked and blinked again because Nana's face kept blurring. She looked okay; anxious, but okay.

Behind her she heard the sound of Roman's cane. "Back for good?" he asked.

"Yeah," she said. Her voice cracked. Nana pulled her head down to rest on the small old shoulder. She had to bend nearly in half, but she didn't mind that. She buried her forehead in Nana's shoulder and let the tears leak, while Nana squeezed and squeezed the back of her neck.

THE CITIZEN OF EASTPORT

Kilo's prediction was off by a day. Eight days after Vi went home, there was a modest news bulletin saying that the Heights baron Brett Sangster had left Eastport after selling off most of his local ventures. He'd gone on a jet headed southwest, according to information Roman dug up. A popular destination for wealthy exiles.

Vi had been re-banded a couple of days earlier, just in time to keep her from going stir crazy. She still didn't know who she had to thank for the speed of the process, but the officer who handed her new band over said that the murderer of Joseph Melnick had been identified and all charges against her were thereby dropped. No mention was made of the fact that Vi was supposed to be in remedial custody at Brett Sangster's, and since the cop didn't bring it up neither did she. She did ask who the murderer had been.

"Identified," said the cop flatly, "and on the run."

That was the standard outcome for a mob hit that couldn't be entirely covered up. They'd send one of their low-rank guns out of town with plenty of cash to set up somewhere else, and the cops would be regretful that they'd been unable to pursue the culprit past the boundaries of Eastport. It was how things had always worked. Vi had never been angry about it before, but now she felt an urge to shake the officer, to ask if he realized or cared that one citizen had been murdered and another one framed or jailed and the mechanisms of the city had essentially shrugged it off. She was still fuming as she stalked down the street. When she got home, Nana took one look at her face and asked what was wrong. A torrent poured out of her. By the end of it she was yelling about Eliza Dalton's shop and Arthur's gang debt and a dozen other bitter, unfair things she'd thought she'd swallowed down. When she stopped, Nana was looking at her with a funny smile.

"What?" Vi asked, now self-conscious.

"It is good to see you like this again," Nana signed, and refused to elaborate further.

The next morning she awoke to a notification from the city: her back rent had been paid and the bar could re-open. She didn't believe it until she logged into her account and saw the record was clear. Dusty was the only person besides herself who could have submitted the payment, and Nana was the only person who could have given him the money. She tugged on a shirt and stormed out into the main room, where Dusty, Nana, and Roman were all sitting around the table waiting for her.

They let her shout her piece, but it was already done. The best she could do was insist on paying Nana back over time. She was slightly mollified when Roman pointed out that they'd waited until she was safely back and the pressure removed. Nana had wanted to pay it the day the bar closed, and Dusty had refused.

"So you three can just decide what's best and leave me out of it," she tried sulkily. That was a mistake. Nana had plenty to say on the subject of handling problems on one's own and leaving others out of it, and she said it so vehemently she rose out of her chair, hands moving sharp and ferocious.

"Okay, Nana," Vi said in the end, the same way she had done

when she was half her present height. "I'm sorry, Nana."

"If you say you must pay me back, then stop fussing here and go re-open your bar," Nana finished.

Vaughan Riley walked into the bar alone this time. Her clothes were less eye-catching than they'd been before, but you couldn't not stare at her. She looked around as she walked through the tables, meeting the gazes of the few present customers and giving quiet nods.

Vi was relieved to see her and said so. "I didn't know where you'd ended up with... everything." A few more news items had come out about Sangster's former holdings, but nothing at all about the singer.

"I've been keeping quiet. At first I kept thinking it couldn't be real, or that he'd find a way to drag me after him."

"I get that." Those news items hadn't been widely spread: she'd had Roman looking for every bit of information he could get, needing to know that Sangster was really gone.

"He cleaned out my account and cancelled all my upcoming tours; that part feels real," Vaughan said with a wry smile.

"I'm sorry."

"It could be worse. I'm still Vaughan Riley." She looked around the bar. "Can you spare a few minutes back in your office?"

The bar was nearly dead. It was early in the day, and business had been slow. That was how it went; close up for a little while and people found new places to go. Vi left Luce in charge and led Vaughan to the back.

"I need to control the news," Vaughan explained. "A little mystery and distance before I start making headlines again. I'm going to travel for a while, sing for my supper in different towns."

Even without Sangster behind her, she'd be able to afford some fine suppers on her name and her voice. "Good luck to you."

"I came to say thank you. And I'm sorry. I wasn't as brave as I said I'd be."

"You did alright."

"If I'd done better, I'd be asking for that reward we talked about."

Any anger she'd felt toward Vaughan that day was long gone. "You could still ask for it."

"I could have trapped you under his thumb for good. I thought that's what I was doing. I don't think you'd have ever forgiven me if I had, even though I thought it was for the best."

"Maybe I wouldn't have. Didn't happen that way, though. And I—I like the idea that something like that might be forgivable."

"All right, then." She stepped closer and laid soft hands on Vi's arms. "I'm asking." Her lips were full and shining, turned up toward Vi, enticing. Vi took gentle hold of the round tip of her chin.

"How long is it since you were kissed?"

"Four years."

"Then I'll make it a good one." Vi tipped her chin up and kissed her. Vaughan's mouth parted sweetly under hers, inviting and responsive. Vi wrapped an arm around her back and pulled her up onto her toes, cradling her head, kissing deep and thorough. When Vaughan started to tremble, she gently let her back down. Vaughan leaned against her for a minute, hand curled around her neck, then sighed and stepped back out of Vi's arms.

"I used to daydream about that."

"Hope it met expectations."

Vaughan answered that with a smile. "I have one more favor to ask you. I'm auctioning off some of my old wardrobe for a bit of pocket money. Selling different pieces a few different places, one in the Heights, one at Burke's. I hoped maybe you'd be willing to host one of them here. For a cut of the profits, of course."

Vaughan Riley's wardrobe would bring a lot more than pocket money. And it would bring in masses of customers. "That's a favor to you, is it?"

Her eyes danced under the curling lashes. "I don't want to show my face, and I hate managing things like that."

"So do I. My bartender Luce, though... she'd be over the moon."

"Then I'll leave it in her hands."

After Vaughan left, Vi sat in the office for a long time. Eventually she realized she was staring at that sketch in the corner, the one Vaughan had been looking at the first time in the office. "Who the fuck are you gonna be, then?" she said out loud to no one, and when no one answered, she stood up and grabbed a hammer.

She hung the picture opposite her desk, where she'd see it when she was sitting there doing the books. Then she tapped into her wristband and messaged Tempe.

```
Are you free to come by the bar sometime?
```

Tempe wasn't free that day, but she was the next. Vi waited for her in the alley, where she'd directed Tempe to come to avoid curious eyes. She paced the width of the alley, drummed against the side of the dumpster, and when Tempe finally appeared she jumped.

"You seem more surprised to see me now than when I walked into your bar after a decade and a half," Tempe said.

"This time I was hoping you'd come," Vi answered, as if that was any kind of explanation.

"Here I am."

Here she was. Vi had a lot to say, and she wouldn't get through any of it if she got stuck on the amazement that Tempe was actually here, willingly, again.. "First, thank you. I'd be fucked if it wasn't for you. I think you probably could have done what you had to do without helping me, and you helped me anyway. I don't deserve that. Thank you."

"I'm glad I was able to." She looked as if she was about to say something else, then stopped. "You said that was first. What's second?"

Vi cleared her throat. "I don't know exactly what you're doing here, I only picked up a few hints from Hannah. And I don't need to know. Don't tell me anything you shouldn't. But I know she thought she was doing something good, and I know you. I should have helped her when she asked me. I'm pissed off that I didn't. If there's anything I can do, now or sometime later, I'll do it. You don't have to trust me with anything and you don't have to tell me what it's for. Just tell me what you need, and I'll do it."

Tempe searched her face. "Are you sure?"

"Dead sure."

Tempe nodded and turned away. She walked to the dumpster and looked at its readouts, as if there was some deep wisdom to be found there. Then she returned to Vi.

"I have to tell you a little, and then I'll ask again if you're sure. There's someone that needs to be stopped. For things he's done and things he's preparing to do. It's my job to stop him. He's powerful, more than Brett Sangster was. I can try to keep you out of his sights, but I can't promise you won't end up there."

Vi curled her fists. "Turns out you can end up in a powerful asshole's sights even if you live like a coward for most of a decade. I got it. Answer's still yes." She took a deep breath. "Talking of things we can't promise. I want to say what happened fifteen years ago won't ever happen again, no matter what they threaten me with. I want to think it wouldn't. But I could promise every day and mean it, and when it comes right down to it I still don't know what I'd do."

Tempe touched her arm. The contact sent prickles shooting through her body. Her fingers slid softly down until they reached Vi's hand and curled around it. "Everybody has pressure points," Tempe said softly. "Hannah came to you in the first place because one of her other contacts cracked, and I don't know which one. So in truth I do need help quite badly, and I can do my best to keep you out of anything that might bring danger to your family, for both our sakes. But neither of us can make guarantees." She laughed a little. "I'm more reconciled to that now than I was at seventeen."

Vi squeezed her hand back. It was the only thing keeping her moored in a sea of hope and fear and relief so fierce it was almost sickening. "Then you've got me."

Kilo's favorite crash pad was the one above the alley that faced Vi's bar. It was the smallest, just a narrow hall closet that the residents on either side assumed belonged to the adjoining apartment. It held only two duffels of emergency supplies and a hammock strung by the window. It was the narrowness and lack of any comforts that made Kilo feel so secure there: a tiny space all Kilo's, not worth anybody taking away. And from the window ze could see the door to Vi's office.

Ze had had zer second and last private meeting with Junior. He was satisfied with the results of their play: his secret plan to expose Andrew had been whispered throughout the organization, and he was being hailed as a master strategist. Kilo was also satisfied. Even if Junior wanted to go back on their agreement, he couldn't order a hit on zem without undermining his own story. The only other people who knew ze had been the original thief were Arlo, now dead; Andrew, stripped of authority and awaiting further punishment; and Loren Caine. Kilo didn't see any profit in mentioning to Junior that Caine knew, or that he had been the one to tip him off about Arlo. Caine was a Pike man and no Travs would believe him over their own leader. He wasn't one to waste effort; the next time he came for Kilo he'd be using something new. That was a problem for another day.

Ze lay in zer hammock and watched as Vi and Tempe talked

in the alley. Couldn't hear what they were saying, but Vi, open as a book, was getting very emotional about it. Ze watched Tempe slowly take her hand, watched Vi hold on as if for dear life. The intensity between them made Kilo feel a little bit sore and a lot hungry. Ze wanted to know it, to touch it, to bathe in it. It felt like a gift, this thing that lay between zer favorite brawny barkeep and zer lovely sadist shipmate. Ze would unwrap it slowly—and delicately, since neither of them seemed to have much sense of humor about the other. That was fine; Kilo had enough sense of humor for all three of them. The last few weeks had been a lot of tense work for no payout. Ze was entitled to a little fun.

Vi, Kilo, and Tempe will return in Book 2 of The Eastport Ledgers. For news and announcements, as well as exclusive bonus scenes, subscribe to the author newsletter at http://vbruth.com/

Acknowledgements

First and foremost, to Beth. I was already thankful to you for supporting me, believing I could do it, and giving me quiet mornings to work. I didn't expect you to also give so many hours to the final draft, but I probably should have: you always have more opinions than planned, and they're always sound. Your sharp eye and careful attention made this book the best it can be. Thank you so much for that, and thank you even more for being my wife. I'm very lucky.

Thank you to the group chats that cheered me on and listened to me vent and flail. Especially to the hype squad, for the commiseration, cheerleading, and for making eyeball emojis at my teaser snippets. And to the problem children: you comfort and inspire me every day, and keep me grounded in my convictions about what kind of creator I want to be.

Thank you to Lee for the early draft comments that helped me hone in on the right direction. Thank you to my beta readers, Cass and Rache, for your feedback and enthusiasm.

I was lucky to work with two excellent editors: first May Peterson, whose insight and perspective on the first draft helped me shape the story, and then Kat Howard, whose thoughtful feedback helped me refine the final draft. Thank you so much to each of you.

Thank you to the others who gave their professional craft and expertise: Liv for the marketing advice and guidance, Sarah for the ebook formatting, and Eva for the spectacular cover design.

Thank you to the friends and family members who have encouraged me all my life. Especially to Mom and Dad, for nurturing my love of reading and stories, and for always affirming me when I said I wanted to be a writer. To Dan, Lane, and Peter, excellent brothers and partners in creativity from my earliest memories. To Meagan, who shared countless story ideas and character concepts with me when we were teens, and reached out with excitement the minute you heard I was actually publishing a book. And to Joy and Adam, for steady friendship and love that has held me up through the best and the hardest days.

And finally to the readers that will find and love this book. You're the reason I do this: thank you.

www.ingramcontent.com/pod-product-compliance
Lightning Source LLC
LaVergne TN
LVHW030318070526
838199LV00069B/6497